BOOK 2 OF THE EARTHBORN

BIOGENESIS

ADAIR HART

Editing done by Laura Petrella
Cover done by Tom Edwards
Interior design done by Colleen Sheehan
Proofread done by Alexa
Published by Quantum Edge Publishing

ISBN: 978-0-9967172-8-1
www.AdairHart.com

To get updates on new books and other notifications, sign up for my mailing list at:
www.AdairHart.com/MailingList.aspx

BIOGENESIS

ONE

Blake Brown eyed the Fredorian Defense Force personnel that he knew he was going to end up kicking the shit out of. He sighed as he eased back into his booth seat. Across from him was Seth Williams. They had decided to get a drink at a bar before the night was out, and Zane Gibbons was on his way out to meet them. It was 8:00 p.m. Earth time, about a month since their last mission, and Blake was getting anxious for the next one.

Waiting around was not too bad; they did have an ambassadorial compound to stay in, with all the resources and privileges that came with it. Although they could have had a drink at the compound, Blake enjoyed being out and seeing others. The bar was packed with FDF that night. A large FDF cruiser had come in, so the uptick in people was not too surprising. One unit in particular seemed to be eying them.

"Busy place," said Seth as his gaze swept over the crowd.

Blake poured himself a shot of cinnamon whiskey. "Sure is. Almost feels like we're back in the freelancing days."

"Yeah, except I'm actually not fearing being in a bar now. I forgot what it was like to not be beat down on a weekly basis."

Blake laughed. "You know you fucking loved it."

Seth shrugged.

Several men approached the booth.

The first man sneered. "You Blake Brown?"

Blake eyed the men. They wore FDF officer uniforms, white with gray segmented lines and a highlight of blue and silver. As they had been giving tough looks all night, their arrival was not unexpected. Blake raised his head toward the first man, who seemed the youngest of the bunch. "Yeah, who wants to know?"

"Tomas Flenders," he said. He crooked a thumb off to the left. "That's Chrisol." He nodded to the right. "And that's Kruschom."

"Okay . . . what do you want?" asked Blake.

Tomas drew his lips to the right. "You did something to my brother. He jumps at his own shadow now and has had a few nervous breakdowns. All he does is ask if you're around. I've been waiting for you to show up here." He raised his head a bit. "What'd you do to him?"

"I busted him trying to sexually assault my crew member," said Blake, smiling, baring his fangs. "You think I'm gonna let that slide? Let someone attack my crew? I don't think so. I let him live. He should be thankful, and you and your friends should be too."

Tomas clenched his jaw for a moment. "I heard you're a Daedrould, and you can do some . . . suggestion thing. You did that, didn't you?"

"No . . . and as hard as this might be to understand, your brother is just a *bitch*. He almost saw his life slip away. Glimpsing death can be scary . . . to the weak."

"Fuck you," said Tomas.

Blake narrowed his eyes. "You should leave. I don't want to . . . break . . . you too. Maybe being a bitch runs in the family."

"You gonna take that shit?" asked Chrisol, looking at Tomas while gesturing at Blake.

"Yeah, fuck 'im up," said Kruschom.

Blake smiled again, fangs exposed. "Just go back and drink your beer. I can see right through your . . . *toughness.*"

Tomas began to breathe harder.

A moment of awkward silence passed.

"Like your brother the bitch," said Blake.

Tomas's face reddened as he reached in to grab Blake.

Blake reared back and used his right arm to push Tomas's arms to the table and pin them.

Tomas struggled to pull away.

Blake used his other arm to hit Tomas in the face several times.

Seth jumped out of the booth and punched Chrisol. Kruschom kicked Seth in the stomach, causing him to fall over.

Blake pushed Tomas sprawling into several tables.

Chrisol squared his jaw and then swung at Blake as he slid out of the booth.

Blake ducked and threw an uppercut.

Chrisol flew into the ceiling and then fell down on Kruschom.

Blake grabbed Kruschom by the neck and lifted him off the ground. "I didn't start this . . . but I will end it."

As Chrisol and Tomas started to stand, they flew past Blake and into the bar counter.

Blake glanced over and saw Zane.

"All this fun and you didn't wait for me," said Zane. He strode over to Chrisol and Tomas, who were struggling to get up. "Should I wreck 'em? Break some bones?"

Blake tossed Kruschom to the ground and then stood in front of Tomas. "Nah . . . I think they learned their lesson." He focused on Tomas. "I bet you're wondering about now . . . Is Blake Brown going to drink me dry?"

Tomas and his friends looked at each other with confused expressions.

Seth laughed. "C'mon, Blake."

"All right, all right," said Blake, grinning and baring his fangs. "I thought I'd check. Here's the situation. You can walk out of here now and I'll forget this incident, or you can try for a second round and I'll use a . . . suggestion . . . to make sure this never happens again." He raised a finger. "I caution you, though . . . if you choose to go again, you and your friends will be laid up in recovery for the next few weeks. What's it gonna be?"

Tomas stood and licked his lips. "We'll go."

Zane laughed.

Blake pointed at Tomas. "I admire you trying to stick up for your family. You got more balls than your brother, but know this . . . Gary is a piece of shit, and I think you know that. Don't let his crap get on you. Now go."

Tomas and the others fled the scene.

Zane glanced at Seth. "You looked like you got hit."

"Kicked, actually," said Seth with a hand over his stomach. "I swear, bars are a curse to me now. I thought I was past all that."

Zane smiled and took a seat after Blake and Seth took theirs in the booth. He crooked a thumb back toward the entrance and faced Blake. "Jarvis was looking for you."

Blake sat up in his seat. "For what?"

"Not sure. I told him where you were, and he said for me to tell you 'moist biscuits,'" said Zane, laughing.

"Are you *sure* he said that?"

"Pretty damn sure. I thought maybe he was taking crazy pills or something," said Zane. "Maybe I don't want to know what that means . . ."

Seth laughed.

Blake sighed and motioned for Zane to scoot out. "I need to go then."

"What?" asked Seth.

"Ranger thing," said Blake. He slid out of the booth. "If I have time, I'll come back. If not, I'll see you tomorrow."

Zane popped back into the booth. "All right, enjoy your . . . moist biscuits."

Seth and Zane burst out laughing.

Zane glanced at Seth. "Just me and you then."

"Works for me," said Seth.

Blake nodded at them both, then headed out. Jarvis's code phrase was meant to be used whenever he wanted to speak in private at the nearest safe point, which in this case was the basement of a nearby building. Blake activated his chameleon shield. After a brisk ten-minute walk, he entered the dark basement. His vampiric vision showed Jarvis leaning against the wall a bit away. "You can't hide from me."

Jarvis smiled as he approached. "Wish I had night vision like you without having to wear goggles." He looked around. "We're secure." He closed the basement door and activated a light on his shoulder, illuminating the surrounding area.

"So what's going on?" asked Blake.

Jarvis sighed. "The FDF has knowledge of your last mission, and I mean intimate-detail-level knowledge."

"How do you know this?"

"I still have my sources in the FDF. I consider them trustworthy," said Jarvis.

Blake grimaced. "How intimate are we talking?"

"Supposedly they have a video feed of your debriefing, in addition to some of your . . . ship briefings."

"Hmm. That means we have a leak . . . or we've been hacked."

Jarvis nodded. "I hope it's a hack, for your sake. That's much easier to clean up."

Blake sighed. "Me too."

"Nonetheless, I'd suggest you watch for any unusual behavior. Ada can probably scan the ship for signs of tampering . . . assuming you trust her. She does have the means to hack you."

"Yeah, but no motive, at least not one I'm aware of. She's happy to be where she is . . . although she did find out everything about our first meeting with relative ease."

Jarvis raised a finger. "True, but if she was malicious, she could have ended this on Zakara Prime with no problems."

"This is going to be tough," said Blake.

Jarvis smiled. "Well, you'll get to deal with it tomorrow morning at nine. Rakar wants a meeting, same place as the debriefing."

"Why would he want to have it in a potentially vulnerable spot?"

Jarvis looked away for a moment. "Because you're the only person I've told about this situation."

Blake raised his head a bit. "Oh . . . well . . . then I owe you one."

"No, you don't. We're brothers for life, man. I can't count how many times you've saved my ass, even when everything was against me."

Blake swallowed hard. "All right, all right, don't go getting all sentimental on me."

"I'll keep my eyes and ears open. The next code phrase is dust rocks," said Jarvis with a grin.

Blake laughed. "That's a lot better than moist biscuits. Zane thinks there's something crazy going on between us now."

"I bet he does," said Jarvis, sharing in the laughter.

"All right, I'll take caution in the coming mission then," said Blake. He extended his arm and did a forearm shake with Jarvis. "Until next time."

/////////

Blake exhaled as he sat in the debriefing room that he had been in during their last mission. It was 9:00 a.m., and Rakar was late. The thought that someone was betraying his crew had kept Blake's mind tumbling all night long. He went through all the scenarios where information could have been leaked, and there were several opportunities, but if it was someone in his crew, that was another level of betrayal. It seemed even Jarvis did not know whom to trust.

Blake ran a hand over his mouth. He would get to the bottom of it. Letting enemies know your game plan was a surefire way to end up in a bad situation. His attention focused on Rakar entering the room. He wore a green-and-black two-piece outfit and looked like he could jump into a mission if he needed to.

"A little late today, aren't we?" asked Blake, wagging a finger at Rakar.

"I'm sorry about that. I was helping Andia with something."

"*Helping* . . . Is that what you kids are calling it these days?"

Rakar laughed. "Nothing like that." He took a seat next to Blake. "However, we do have your second mission."

Blake sat up in his chair. "Where we headed?"

Rakar interacted with the table console, causing the large screen ahead of them to turn on.

Satellite images appeared showing a facility nestled in a jungle.

"We picked these up a few days ago," said Rakar. "It's an FDF facility called Hadrassus, on a planet called Markus II in the Zolidack system."

Blake narrowed his eyes. "I heard the FDF took over that area."

"Yes, and all records of that event have disappeared. However . . . I received some images from a probe. It was destroyed, but not before transmitting what it saw."

"Looks like Hadrassus is a secret facility then," said Blake. "That wouldn't be uncommon with the FDF."

The screen changed to show a spaceport. Large white cylindrical capsules were being moved off ships.

"Look familiar?" asked Rakar.

Blake remembered fighting creatures during the previous mission that came from capsules like those on the screen. The creatures were experiments of Delkis, a criminal who was being controlled by a black slime. "Yeah . . . they do. I bet those capsules have more experiments in them, and our slime friend or its friends are involved, just like on our last mission on Zakara Prime. I also bet that what we're seeing is just the top of the facility."

"You're right on both counts. I suspect we'll learn more about the slime by investigating those capsules," said Rakar.

The screen changed to show the crosscut view of a massive underground structure.

"It's quite extensive," said Rakar.

Blake sighed. "And I take it that it's heavily defended. Does the FDF know you've got images of the capsules?"

"No, they don't, and it needs to stay that way. Although Hadrassus is registered with the FDF, it's classified at the highest level."

The screen changed to show a Fredorian in a dark-gray one-piece suit segmented with silver lines. The bald man was fair skinned and stood around six foot one.

"Hadrassus is operated by the Dorostatic Initiatives Corporation in conjunction with the FDF. They have Administrator Cadris Zoldan running operations there."

"Dorostatic Initiatives . . . weren't they busted a while back for their involvement in illegal genetic engineering?" asked Blake.

"They were. Their presence at Hadrassus is concerning, especially when it comes to our slime friend. Nonetheless, the Zolidack system is controlled by the FDF, but the presidential guard has clearance, so they can enter both the system and Hadrassus. That doesn't mean the FDF and Dorostatic Initiatives would like for that to happen. Another thing, entering the system requires checking in with the *Storetz*, an FDF cruiser guarding that system. Furthermore . . . ," said Rakar.

The screen changed to show circular flat ships with a large rectangular section in the middle.

"Rogundans," said Blake, grimacing. He had never liked the Rogundans. They reminded him of what a beetle with the head of an ant would look like if it was human sized and humanoid in overall shape. They had a large black-and-red shell on their backs, multiple arms, and two stout legs. While not the fastest, their sheer strength, ferocious disposition, and desire for violence made them popular in merc circles, in particular the slave trade. He knew from personal experience they had no qualms about killing others, even their own. They also had a bad habit of eating humans and other aliens.

Rakar nodded. "There seems to be quite a few of them. I suspect whatever is happening in those facilities includes slaves."

"Sounds pleasant," said Blake. "I have a bounty on me from a Rogundan crew. Let one live . . . and see how I'm repaid?"

"You gave them a choice, and it sounds like they didn't want to take advantage of it."

Blake shrugged. "It is what it is. So I guess then our mission is to visit the facility and find out what's going on. That's going to require Ada to get in and hack their system."

"Yes, and sadly, I can't tell you more than what these images show. Although you can get in . . . finding anything, especially when they don't want you there, could be dangerous," said Rakar. "What I can tell you is that there have been some scientists from the Skorith research space station who have been reassigned there, but their status has since . . . *disappeared* . . . from the official records."

"You think something bad happened. We can look into it. Before we check in with the *Storetz*, there's a system outside Zolidack I want to stop in at. It has a colony on a jungle moon."

"What's there?" asked Rakar.

"The colony is called Lono Hara, and I have some old friends there. I haven't seen them in a while. If something is going on in the Zolidack system, they'll have an idea. If anything, maybe it will give us an advantage."

"I knew you were the right person for this group."

Blake tossed his hands out to the side. "Of course, I'm Blake Brown."

Rakar laughed.

Although Blake was sure it was not Rakar that leaked information, it was unusual to not trust him with the information Jarvis had provided.

"On another topic, how's the crew doing? It's been a month since your last mission."

Blake tilted his head. "Seth's been doing good. He's been training hard with Sarah. I suspect he's tired of getting his ass kicked, although last night, it was his stomach that got kicked."

Rakar shook his head. "I heard about that. Sarah doing all right?"

"Yeah, she's a tough cookie, really proved herself on the last mission," said Blake.

"And . . . you had a blood bond with her?"

Blake cleared his throat. "Well, I didn't do it to out of lust, but yeah, we had a bond for a few days. I kept my distance other than a few times. A human experiencing a blood bond for the first time can give in to their raw desires, especially if that bond is with an ancient vampire of my status. I didn't want to mess up the team dynamic with that."

"Understood. See? You're thinking like a leader now," said Rakar, poking his finger in the air at Blake.

"Yeah . . . I guess, but you know the blood bond works both ways."

Rakar grinned. "I'm sure it was rough. How is Zane holding up?"

"He's doing okay. Most of the time he's out and about. He doesn't hang around the compound much."

Rakar rubbed his chin. "Interesting."

"Luke has spent most of his time working on the *Exceltion*. That man loves that ship."

"Yes, he was a good choice. I'm still a bit surprised he hung around maintaining it all those years. It was . . . an unusual decision."

Blake shrugged. "That's his thing. As for Kane, he seems to spend a lot of time at various clubs. He's also been studying the *Exceltion*'s systems in more detail. We've had a few meetings where he's proposed ideas."

"Another excellent choice," said Rakar. "I wish we would have done something like this in the rangers long ago."

"An Earthborn unit or specialized groups?"

"Both."

Blake smiled. "I'm with you there. As for Ada, she's with Seth whenever he has free time."

"You think they have something going on, don't you?"

"Of course. I know Seth. She's right up his alley."

Rakar eyed Blake. "You know personal relationships can compromise missions . . ."

"Yeah, but given that we don't know if we're walking away from any given mission, I'm allowing it. Sometimes it's better to get a taste than to have none at all. Mental health and all that. Besides . . . are you sure you're the one to be giving that advice?" asked Blake with a big grin.

"Fair enough," said Rakar. "I didn't know you were a psychologist now."

"Whatever works," said Blake. "I'd rather the crew be happy however they find it." He tilted his head. "I've been around for over four centuries. Happiness is fleeting. If you see an opportunity for it, you grab it, and hold on to it, because it *will* go away in time. Enjoy the moment for what it is."

Rakar drew his head back. "You're four times older than me. It's . . . hard for me to believe you're so old, but you speak wisdom that can only be borne of multiple lifetimes of experience."

"Don't I know it," said Blake, grinning, his fangs bared.

"Speaking of happiness and health, how has your medical AI been performing?"

Blake exhaled from his mouth. "Good. He wants to be called Doc, and the crew seems to have embraced him. Ada said they sometimes talk in cyberspace."

Rakar rubbed his chin. "Very interesting. You have a solid crew and ship, and I hope this mission turns out as well as the last one."

"Same," said Blake. "I'll get the crew together tomorrow morning."

Rakar stood and motioned toward the door. "Breakfast?"

"Sure, assuming the mission doesn't need to start right now," said Blake with a smile.

Rakar slapped Blake on the back. "Let's go."

TWO

S eth yawned as he surveyed the briefing room on the *Exceltion*. It was 9:00 a.m. two days after the bar fight. Although he had slept well, a majority of the previous night was spent showing Ada some movies from Earth. He smiled as he recalled how matter-of-fact Ada was about things. When he had tried to put his arm around her, she stopped him and asked what position she should sit in to maximize contact efficiency while maintaining comfort. Add in a bowl of popcorn, and it was a good night. Although there was nothing official between them, he hoped it would lead to something. She sat next to him and wore a formfitting white suit with blue lines on it that he did not mind at all.

Zane looked refreshed in his jeans, black boots, and white shirt. Kane had on his usual black outfit, while Luke donned jeans and a flannel. Kal wore some baggy beige pants along with a brown shirt. It seemed he always had some type of chest strap and belt with gadgets. Sarah's suit was similar to Ada's. It was easy to spot who was not Earthborn.

Seth enjoyed being around the crew, and he assumed everyone else had also received a message from Blake to meet for the next mission. The first mission was successful, but it was not as easy as Seth had thought it would be. Although he appreciated being where he was, he missed Earth. Things were simpler there, but he knew he would not have the opportunities there that he had here. His attention focused on Blake entering the room. He wore his usual black light-armor outfit with a full complement of weapons. Seth shook his head. Even in a meeting, Blake was ready to fight.

Blake nodded at everyone. "Welcome back. It's time for business."

"Bring it on," said Zane.

"I figured you'd be ready," said Blake with a grin. He tapped at the table console.

A projection shot up from the center of the table, showing satellite images of Markus II.

"This is a secret facility called Hadrassus on the planet Markus II in the Zolidack system," said Blake.

One image zoomed in showing the large white cylindrical capsules.

"Look familiar?" asked Blake.

Sarah gulped while rubbing her arm. "Those things again?"

"Yes, and it seems that there are a variety of sizes there, some much larger than what we saw. I suspect that whatever's in those, like the mutants we saw on Zakara Prime, is not out for galactic peace."

Seth laughed. "Yeah, probably not. Where'd the images come from?"

"Rakar's trusted source," said Blake.

"Do we know the source?" asked Ada.

"Doubtful, and he wouldn't give them up. That's just ranger protocol," said Blake.

Seth's eyes roamed the room for a moment. Something was off. Blake was concealing information. Seth knew Blake only did that when he did not fully trust whom he was speaking with. Given that it was the rest of the crew, that seemed odd.

The screen changed to show Administrator Cadris Zoldan with his name and other stats under his picture.

Blake motioned at the screen. "He runs the show at Hadrassus and works for the Dorostatic Initiatives Corporation."

"The genetic engineering fiasco," said Sarah. "I remember reading about that. Their experiments were . . . unsettling."

"Yep," said Blake. "Secret facility, slime friend's experimental capsules spotted, FDF, and genetic engineering criminals. What could go wrong?"

The screen changed to show a research facility in deep space.

"Nonetheless, before we head out there, we will stop by the Skorith research space station, the closest FDF research facility to the Zolidack system. Some scientists were reassigned, yet their status just . . . disappeared. It's assumed they went to Hadrassus, so we're going to find out what they did and anything related to their reassignment. That means we're going snooping. Our contact there is Director Charles Duton."

"By snooping, you are referring to me hacking their systems," said Ada.

Blake grinned. "That's one aspect."

The screen changed to show a large gas giant planet with a moon and a colony highlighted on it.

"After that, we'll hit Lono Hara, a jungle moon colony in a system near Zolidack. I have some friends there, and we can check the underground to see what's being said about anything going on in the Zolidack system."

The screen changed to show the *Storetz*.

"Before we enter the Zolidack system, though, we'll need to check in with the *Storetz*, an FDF cruiser, one of many, defending Zolidack, and then we'll head in to Hadrassus with everything we know. We can figure out our plan of attack once we have all the information we need."

Sarah wrinkled her eyebrows. "I've never even heard of those places before."

Kal tossed a hand out. "I've been to Lono Hara. Definitely a jungle environment, and also a merc hot spot. I've done a few bounties there."

"Same here," said Zane. "I can't say I've been to the Zolidack system, though, or this . . . Skorith place."

Kane smiled. "I've seen Lono Hara mentioned in the system logs of some of the ships I've worked on. Judging by who owned the ships, Lono Hara is probably a rough place."

Blake nodded. "Lono Hara would be known to those who dabble in merc work. Skorith is Fredorian controlled, but is a classified facility. The Zolidack system is not new to me, though." He gestured at Seth. "It's in the same system that Alcarez came from."

"Oh, great," said Seth. "I'm sure it's lovely then."

Luke raised a hand. "If we're going in after an inspection by the FDF, won't Hadrassus be informed of our approach?"

Blake nodded. "I'm sure they would be, but they won't know *why* we're coming. We have the right to visit it as the presidential guard. The FDF has Hadrassus listed as a research facility . . . but doesn't specify what's being researched. We're going to find out either way, and it could possibly be a trap."

"I'm thinking then the *Exceltion* will need to be ready to go at a moment's notice," said Seth. He grinned at Luke. "We can test out the *Exceltion*'s stealth capabilities if we need to get out."

"Aye," said Luke. "My thoughts exactly. The *Exceltion* is ready to go whenever we're ready. She can handle this."

"That's good to hear," said Blake.

Kane motioned at Ada. "We've been working on updating the *Exceltion*'s defense robots. Ada's made them into metal tigers."

"Correction. We made them into efficient defenders, not tigers," said Ada.

The group shared a laugh.

Ada tilted her head.

Seth lightly squeezed her arm. "He meant you made them tough and resilient, *like* a tiger."

"I see," said Ada.

Seth had been teaching Ada the various slang and idioms of English. Over the last month, it had been a rich source of misunderstanding, but he was patient with her and explained what they meant. She had complained that there was not a central source for them, and the ones she did find had different meanings based on different contexts and sources. It was inefficient, she had said. What she probably did not know was that such language was one of many covert signals among Earthborn to identify themselves.

Blake tapped at the table console.

The projection changed to show a side view of Hadrassus.

"Although we don't know where in the facility we need to go, or even how it's laid out other than this high-level summary, it probably has a data storage center of some type. Our goal is simple. Get in, get all the information we can, then get out."

"Smash and grab, just the way I like it," said Zane.

"Hopefully less smash and more grab," said Blake.

The projection changed to show Rogundan ships.

"We get to deal with the Rogundans as well," said Blake.

Sarah grimaced. "They're that . . . bug-like race."

Zane laughed. "That means smash to me. Rogundans aren't the most friendly."

"Yes," said Blake. "We'll deal with them if we have to. Hopefully not, since it is FDF-controlled space, and if the Rogundans are doing contract work, they shouldn't be involved with what we're doing. Anyways, we leave in a few days, so starting now, we have some things to do. Luke, I'm forwarding you Markus II's information. Work with Seth to determine the best places to utilize the planet's natural heat signature to help our stealth in case we need to get out undetected. I'm sure you have the *Exceltion* ready to go, but make sure anything you need to do for it is handled."

"Aye, you got it," said Luke.

"Kane, make sure our weapon systems are good to go and that all our gear is ready," said Blake. "Also, Doc has expressed an interest in interacting more with organics. When you were poking around in the systems, you activated him. He contacted Ada and now wants to be awake more often."

"No problem," said Kane.

"Ada, I need you to run a diagnostic on the *Exceltion*. Make sure we're secure and everything's good to go."

"I will do my best," said Ada.

"As you always do," said Blake. "Sarah, I'll need you to coordinate with the others. Make sure we're clear to meet with the FDF in that system and that Luke, Kane, and Ada have everything they need. Also, prepare an informational docket on the places and races and send it out to everyone."

"You got it," said Sarah with a smile.

Zane waved a finger between himself and Kal. "What about us?"

"You two sit and look pretty," said Blake.

The group shared a laugh.

Blake pointed at Zane and Kal. "I'll need help in configuring battle tactics and strategies against the Rogundans . . . and potentially FDF and whatever security forces Hadrassus has in that facility."

A silence spread over the group.

Blake narrowed his eyes. "I'm hoping . . . that this facility is not what I think it is, but if it is, we may be fighting FDF enforcers, specialized units that do . . . off-the-record missions, like us. Maybe we won't see them. Either way, I want a plan for fighting them if need be."

Zane and Kal nodded at each other.

"All right, here's to our next mission!" said Blake.

The group cheered and began to exit the room.

Blake laid a hand on Seth's shoulder. "We need to talk . . . in private."

Seth nodded. He followed Blake out of the briefing room and off the *Exceltion*. When they were a bit away, Seth asked, "What's up?"

"We've been compromised," said Blake.

Seth's eyes widened. "By who?"

"I don't know yet. I don't know if we've been hacked or . . . if there's a leak."

"A leak? I'd find that hard to believe."

"Yeah, me too," said Blake.

Seth licked his lips. "Am I the only one who knows?"

Blake shook his head. "Jarvis let me know, and now it's just us three that know."

"It could be me," said Seth, eying Blake.

Blake laughed. "Yeah, right. Giving information to the enemy would just lead to you getting beat on more."

Seth chuckled. "Of course. Still, I'm glad you trust me."

"You're my abductee brother," said Blake. "I don't trust easily, as you know, but I trust you with my life. You *know* that."

A lump formed in Seth's throat. "Always, man." He could now see that Blake was in a difficult spot. It added a new wrinkle to the mission. Not only would they have to deal with external threats, but now there was an internal one. "How we gonna handle this?"

"I don't know yet," said Blake. "For now, keep your eyes and ears open. Let's see what happens."

"All right, man," said Seth. It seemed this new mission was already off to a bad start.

Blake's eyes roamed the Skorith docking bay as he walked alongside Zane, Ada, and Kal. It had been about three days since the briefing, and two days since they had entered into condensed space. It was 1:00 p.m. Earth time, and everyone had had their lunch. Skorith was remote, out past most of the Fredorian rim colonies, but Zolidack, their ultimate destination, was out even farther. Blake had been out this far before on several retrieval missions.

Skorith was new to him, but he had always been aware of it and its function. The docking bay was brightly lit, and the metallic paneled walls and floor were relatively clean, indicating there was not much traffic coming and going. The near-empty docking bay also helped illustrate that point.

Humanoid robot guards escorted them toward a booth in front of a hallway.

Blake knew the robots were a bit more advanced than what he had seen in other facilities. These were bulkier, and although humanoid in form, the robotic aspects made sure there was no mistaking them for a human. Their metallic exteriors were on prominent display, along with their hexagonal faces with a bright-blue light in the middle. Their armor was made up of plates covering various fiber-like threads. He knew that they had better-than-average shielding and were meant to be guards.

A Fredorian man in a crisp formfitting white suit looked up at the group when they arrived. He tossed a hand out while sneering. "The *Exceltion*, crewed by the presidential guard."

"That's us," said Blake.

"Purpose of visit?"

"Confidential."

"Uh-huh," said the man. He tapped at the console in front of him for a moment. He sighed while shaking his head. "You're cleared."

Blake tilted his head. "Am I sensing a problem?"

The man narrowed his eyes. "Of course not. We love Earthborn and their filthy ways coming here and stinking up the place."

"I get the feeling . . . you don't like Earthborn."

The man shrugged. "All worthless to me."

"You know your ancestors were Earthborn, right?"

"That was then. This is now."

Blake shook his head. "Well, you should be thankful that there weren't *assholes* like you around when your ancestors came along."

The man's eyes flared. "You talk a lot of shit, but you're Earthborn, so that's to be expected."

Blake grinned, baring his fangs. "I'm also a Daedrould. I have an ability that makes people do things, without realizing it. All I need . . . is one bite."

The man retracted a bit.

"I could make it so that you think you're a dog and you try to hump every robot you see."

Zane and Kal laughed.

The man grimaced and motioned for them to continue on.

As the group proceeded into the hallway, Blake turned toward Ada. "You have the location of this Charles Duton?"

"Yes."

"What do we know of him?"

Ada went silent for a moment as they walked. "He directs one of the six divisions here."

Zane shook his head. "Sounds boring as hell."

Kal flapped a hand out, hitting Zane's arm. "Yeah, but it's these advancements in science and technology that make it out into our field."

"I guess," said Zane with a shrug.

After an hour of traversing hallways and rooms and taking several rectangular transportation units that could travel vertically and horizontally, they reached a large office.

Blake noticed that the office was defended by two robot guards and that the doorway was shielded. The security seemed a bit heavier than he had expected for a research facility, but he suspected that there were topics being researched that were not legal. That would bring in power players who would most likely not be afraid of doing whatever they needed to do to get an edge. The missing scientists were probably involved in that.

The doorway's shielding dissipated.

One of the robot guards spoke in a deep digital voice. "Director Charles Duton is waiting for you. Please enter."

Blake nodded at the robot and then entered the room, followed by the others. Once inside, he took a deep inhale. He could smell Charles, whose scent stood out among the sterile smell of the office. There was more sweat than normal, and his increased heartbeat suggested he was nervous. Blake noted that Charles was an older man, in the typical Fredorian outfit befitting a science director. It was crisp, formfitting, and mostly blue, with highlights of silver. A well-trimmed gray beard covered his fair-skinned face, and a gray crop of hair crowned his head.

"Welcome," said Charles. He motioned at the row of chairs before his desk. "Please, sit."

The group complied.

Charles interacted with his desk's surface for a moment, causing the room's lights to dim a bit and the shielding in the doorway to turn dark. "I've invoked a security protocol meant for private discussion. Nothing is recorded here."

"Sounds good," said Blake. "I suspect you know why we're here."

"The missing scientists, yes. I know they went to Hadrassus, but . . . how they went and their status concerns me. One of them was a close friend, Renee Swerning. I hope you have more success investigating this than the last group."

Kal wrinkled his eyebrows. "There was another?"

"Was . . . but they disappeared. It's been a few months, and their ship was reported destroyed by the Rogundans in the Zolidack system."

Blake noted the picture on Charles's desk, showing him standing proud with his arm around a young redheaded woman. He cleared his throat. "So these missing scientists, what did they do?"

"They were gene tailors and worked in our nanotech division."

Zane chuckled. "What's a gene tailor?"

Ada tilted her head. "Those who transform genes to alter the body."

"And what type of alterations would that be?" asked Zane.

"There are many options. Enhanced strength and better vision, to name a few."

"Huh," said Zane.

Blake ran his tongue over his fangs. "What were they researching specifically prior to their reassignment?"

"Something odd. There was a material that exhibited . . . *unusual* . . . characteristics."

"A black slime of some sort?" asked Blake.

Charles shook a finger at Blake. "Yeah! Except it wasn't black, it was blue. You know about that?"

"Blue slime . . . not really. I have an idea about black slime, though," said Blake. He sighed. So the black slime was not the only one around. He wondered if it behaved like the black slime that had controlled Delkis in the last mission. He glanced at Charles. "We're going to poke around a bit here. Where do you suggest we look?"

"The lab where Renee worked would be a good start," said Charles. "The team lead that replaced Renee there is . . . a bit rough around the edges socially."

Ada tilted her head. "It may also be helpful to talk with the workers in the docking bay where the scientists left from, assuming there are records there."

"There should be," said Charles. "Everything is audited here. I don't have the clearance except for my division and a few other places, but your group does. I did check the docking-bay logs, and the video feeds were missing from Renee's departure. Something weird is going on."

Blake rubbed his chin. "All right, then let's do that. Zane, Kal, you two hit the docking bay. Ada and I will hit the lab. Charles, can you give us the locations of both places?"

"Of course."

Blake nodded. "Good. We'll do what we can."

Charles licked his lips. "I meant it when I said I was glad it was your group. I may not know the details of what you do, but I do know," said Charles, pointing at Blake, "what you're capable of. Your exploits as a ranger extend even out here."

"I'm sure that pisses off the Fredorians working here."

"Not all. Sure, there are some Fredorian supremacists here, but mostly among the maintenance workers, not so much the scientists."

Zane cracked a grin as he glanced at Kal. "Ready to get shit on by Fredorians some more?"

"I don't think they'll give *you* shit," said Kal with a chuckle.

Ada glanced at Zane. "I hope they do not give you excrement either."

Charles chuckled. "Humor. Something sorely lacking around here." He sighed as his eyes misted. "I wish you all the best, and . . . if you find out anything about Renee, please let me know. She was a bright star . . . and I fear the worst. Five years under me and now . . . this."

Blake nodded at the others as he stood. "Let's see what we can find." He extended a hand toward Charles. "Thank you for the help. We'll be in contact."

"May the great selector guide you," said Charles, shaking Blake's hand.

Blake did not believe in the great selectors, cosmic beings that allegedly directed the evolution of all life, but he knew that Kreagans, and in particular Fredorians, worshiped them as gods. He pointed at Zane and Kal. "Keep communication silence and meet back at the ship as soon as you can."

They both nodded before heading out.

THREE

B lake looked around the large room that served as hallway central for the nanotech division. It had been forty minutes since their meeting. Like most Fredorian facilities, everything was clean and ordered. The sterile smell was nauseating. The floors shined, and the walls looked like they had just been waxed. Humanoid robots were cleaning, and personnel moved between hallways.

In the center of the room was an oblong kiosk that stood about six feet tall. It had several touch interfaces that were packed with various lights. Although he knew which hallway they needed to go to, he had another idea. "Ada, can you soft connect to that kiosk?"

"I should be able to. It's most likely a virtual intelligence," said Ada.

Blake nodded while looking around. "Let's do that then." Although he knew a hard connect involved a physical connection, soft connects only required a medium that allowed for transmission of electromagnetic waves. On Earth, he knew this as wireless. He motioned at a bench nearby. "Let's go there."

They took a seat on a bench alongside the wall.

"Accessing," said Ada.

Blake noticed people narrowing their eyes as they looked at Ada. His blood boiled. It angered him that due to a few rogue androids, sweeping legislation made them second-class citizens. Public perception was skewed by antiandroid political groups, and there was now a concerted effort to replace all specialized system AIs with virtual intelligences. That would create an imbalance in power against other species that did use AIs. An android resistance group had also sprung up in relation to the legislation. He noted that he was getting looks as well. Glancing down at his suit, he could see why. They saw an android sitting next to a lightly armored person. They probably thought he was a random merc.

"I have downloaded all the public information on the five scientists that went missing, along with their division information," said Ada.

"Find anything of interest?" asked Blake.

Ada shook her head. "I'm running a mining algorithm to detect any patterns. Please hold."

"Holding," said Blake with a serious look.

Ada tilted her head at Blake.

"Do your thing."

Ada grinned. "You were teasing me."

Blake laughed. "Sorry. This place seems uptight. I just wanted to relax a little."

"It's okay. Seth likes to tease me too."

"I bet he does," said Blake.

Ada raised a finger. "I've found something interesting. All five of the scientists were given the same reassignment."

"We figured as much already."

"Yes, but they left as one group, not as individuals, and were given a strict schedule to adhere to with a one-day notice. There is also a gag order in effect."

Blake rubbed his chin. "All of that is public?"

"No, but their systems are vulnerable. There is no security AI, and the virtual intelligence is no match for my abilities."

"Damn you're good," said Blake.

"Thank you. However, there was mention of some disconnected databases in each division. How shall we proceed?"

Blake stood and gestured at the hallway to the nanotech division. "Same plan. We go and talk with the team leader that replaced Renee, but maybe we can now access that division's disconnected database system while we're there."

Ada nodded and then stood and followed Blake.

They arrived at the nanotech division twenty minutes later.

Blake noted that it looked like a warehouse attached to the facility. Inside it were large shielded containers with workstations ringing them. Large mobile screens sat next to most of the containers, and the place bustled with activity as the scientists moved around. Thin metallic sections divided up the place, giving him the impression that this division was somewhat new; otherwise there would be proper walls. He checked his forearm device, then motioned in the distance. "Back there."

They reached one of the divided sections after a few minutes. Three Fredorian men bustled around inside the area while a robot guard stood outside.

Blake entered the section. "Who runs this area?"

One of the men approached Blake. "I do, Avery Collins. Who are you?"

Blake showed his presidential guard credentials. "Blake Brown, presidential guard, Earthborn Unit. We have some questions."

"A bit far from home, aren't we?" asked Avery.

"Yes, we are. That should give you an idea of how important it is for me to be here."

Avery leaned back a bit. "What do you want?"

"Information. Did you know a Renee Swerning?"

Avery nodded. "She was the former team leader for this section, but she got reassigned."

"To where?"

Avery shrugged. "How would I know? I was brought in to continue her research, not track her professional career."

"What was her research?"

"Gene tailoring with exotic matter. That information is public."

Ada raised a finger. "It is not. This facility is classified, and that information is private to this facility."

"I meant, public to someone with your credentials."

"Also incorrect," said Ada. "This is a secure FDF facility, and they do not share information with the presidential guard, although they are legally bound to do so."

Avery tossed a hand out. "Oh, great. So now you have me involved in some political struggle."

"Not at all," said Blake.

"Well, I'm not sure what else I can tell you. I'm not even sure I understand the point of coming here if you could have gotten this information before arriving here."

Blake looked around. "Is there . . . somewhere private that we can speak?"

Avery sighed. "Why?"

Blake narrowed his eyes. "You seem eager to get rid of me . . ."

"You're wasting my time with frivolous matters. I have more important things to do than . . . whatever this is."

"If we can speak somewhere privately, I can tell you why I'm asking these questions," said Blake. He looked around. "This area is a bit public."

Avery drew his lips flat. "Fine. Whatever will get you out of here. Follow me." He led them to a side office with a workstation in it and entered. Once everyone was inside, he sat and tapped at the workstation console, causing the door to seal shut. "Okay, here we are."

Blake rushed around the table and held Avery with one arm. With the other, he pulled Avery's head to the side and then sunk his fangs into Avery's neck. If Avery was going to be unhelpful, then he would become helpful in a hypnotic state.

Avery shouted in surprise, but then stopped struggling.

"I don't have time for your bullshit," said Blake. "Now, do you know where Renee went?"

"No."

"Have you ever met her?"

"Yes."

"Was she what you expected?"

"No."

"Why?" asked Blake.

"Her profile said she was outgoing. When I met her, she was short with me and seemed confused on the protocols in place for transitioning work matters."

"Confused . . . like she wasn't herself?"

"Yes."

Blake glanced at Ada, then back at Avery. "All right. Use your credentials to log in to the secure network here."

Avery interacted with the table interface.

Blake nodded at Ada. "Do your thing."

Ada knelt next to Avery and extended a hand under the table. After a moment, she said, "Accessing." Five minutes later, she stood. "I have downloaded all secure files related to the five scientists, and also deleted my audit trail. The video feed for this room was also deleted, and I have disabled the cameras."

"Good. I think we have enough information," said Blake. He laid a hand on Avery's shoulder. "Here's what you're going to do. You're going to take a nap and not remember what happened in this room. You'll remember it as an enjoyable experience if anyone asks, and unfortunately, you weren't able to help us with anything. What you will remember was how great Ada and I were. When you wake up thirty minutes from now, this hypnotic state will end and you'll leave this room. Do you understand?"

"Yes, I do."

"Good, take a nap."

Avery nodded and then leaned back. A moment later, and he was breathing slower with his hands clasped.

Blake glanced at Ada while gesturing at the door. "Let's go."

/////////

Zane surveyed the large docking bay that he and Kal were in. It had only one ship in it, and several cargo containers sat stacked neatly on the right side. The bay was brighter than Zane had expected, and it looked like activity was in short supply. Several humanoid robots were attending to cleaning duties and moving containers. His gaze fell on four Fredorian men lounging around and laughing near one of the shipping containers. If anyone knew about the missing scientists, they probably did, or at least had an idea of where to start. Zane nodded toward the men. "Let's check it out."

"All right," said Kal. "They don't look like they're too busy."

"Yeah, they're goofing off. With a robot crew to handle everything, those guys are probably only active when a ship comes in," said Zane, looking around, "which doesn't seem too often."

"Supply ships maybe," said Kal.

"Yeah, but those are on schedules, and usually spread out. Even if it's for replication element storage, those hook up outside the docking bays. These guys got it pretty easy."

"They could do that on Fredoria, no need to come out here for that."

Zane grinned. "Yeah, but they're racking time and experience this way, at least according to FDF records."

Kal nodded.

They approached the men, causing them to assemble.

"Hey, guys, you got a moment?" asked Zane.

One of the men stepped forward. "Who're you?"

"I'm Zane Gibbons, and next to me is Kal Modan. We're with the presidential guard, Earthborn Unit."

The man smiled. "Presidential guard? Earthborn?"

The men laughed.

Zane and Kal showed him their credentials via forearm device.

The men scrutinized the credentials for a moment.

"All right, so you got clearance to be here," said the man. "I'm Harry Clives, and I run this place." He shook a finger. "What makes you think we want to help some dirty Earthborn?"

Zane licked his lips. "Because we're with the presidential guard. Five scientists left here recently. The video feeds were mysteriously missing from their departure time, so we figured maybe someone saw something."

"And you want us . . . to help you? Just like that?"

Zane nodded. "Just like that."

"Too bad for you then. We didn't see shit," said Harry, raising his head a bit.

Zane sighed. "Facility records showed they left from here. I guess they were wrong. I'll notify the proper authorities that there is a discrepancy. C'mon, Kal, these assholes don't know shit."

"Wait!" said Harry. "No need for all of that."

"We're listening," said Zane.

Harry sighed as he looked at the others in his group. He faced Zane and Kal. "They left in a ship. That's all I know."

The men sneered.

Kal waved a finger at the other men. "What about them?"

"They don't know shit," said Harry.

Zane narrowed his eyes and pointed at Harry. "You know . . . I'm getting real tired of your crap. I could kick the ever-living *shit* out of you, and it would be the highlight of my day. This matter is of great importance to Fredoria, enough to send us here. Instead of helping us, and Fredoria by extension, you're being a *bitch*. What's up with that?"

"You may be with the presidential guard, but I'll be damned if you think I'm going to help some Earthborn trash," said Harry.

Zane reached in and grabbed Harry by the neck, lifting him off the ground.

The other men stepped back as Kal waved dual pistols at them.

"Now . . . little man, you gonna talk?" asked Zane. "I'm used to kicking the crap out of people to get what I want to know. I'm trying to be polite, but you seem intent on pissing me off. That's a really, *really* bad idea."

Harry struggled to remove Zane's grasp. "All right, all right, all right."

Zane dropped Harry to the ground.

While on his knees, Harry checked his neck as his breathing staggered. "It was . . . a Rogundan ship."

"And what happened to the video feeds?"

"Erased by FDF command. We have no control of that here."

"That happen a lot?" asked Zane.

"No . . . but when it does, we don't ask questions . . . like you're doing."

Kal smiled. "It's times like this I wish we could put them into a hypnotic state like Blake does."

"Yeah," said Zane. He glanced at the men. "Anything else any of you want to say before we go? If we find out later that you had information and you didn't tell us, that's obstruction of justice, and that'll go on your record. I'll also be back to *beat* that ass."

"There's a visual feed backup," said one of the men.

Zane eyed Harry. "Is that right?"

"Yeah," said Harry, glaring at Zane.

Kal motioned at the man who had spoken earlier. "Care to show us these videos . . ."

"Daren Crawsley," he said. His eyes darted over to Harry, then back at Zane and Kal. "I'll show you."

Zane smiled. "Finally, someone with sense. You should be thanking Daren, Harry. Otherwise . . . this could have gotten really ugly."

"Get your feed and get the hell out of here," said Harry.

Zane nodded at Daren, who headed off to a back office.

As they walked, Kal glanced at Daren. "What's with all the Earthborn hate?"

Daren sighed. "Not all of us are like that. I know we get painted like that because we aren't scientists, but it's only a vocal minority."

"Like Harry."

"Yeah."

"Well, we appreciate you helping us. This matter is important, and we'll make sure to note that you helped us," said Kal.

"I appreciate it," said Daren.

They arrived at the back office and assembled around a workstation with a series of consoles embedded in it.

Daren interacted with a console for a moment.

One of the screens began to show an isometric view of the docking bay.

Zane studied the five scientists as they headed toward the Rogundan ship. They had no gear or equipment and looked like they had just up and left their jobs, wearing their work suits. It was like they did not have a care in the world.

Kal wrinkled his eyebrows. "Scientists usually leave from this docking bay?"

"No, we usually handle supplies."

"So seeing a Rogundan ship must have been unusual then."

"Yeah. In addition to that, the scientists seemed . . . weird, like they were in a trance. As for the Rogundans . . . I just don't like being around them," said Daren.

"Neither do we," said Zane. "They kill Fredorian and Earthborn with equal prejudice. Unfortunately for them, Earthborn don't roll over." He motioned at the video. "Seems Fredorians are more than willing to, though."

Daren looked down. "The Rogundans didn't need to hold us at gunpoint, since it was a legal order, but they did anyhow."

"Figures," said Zane. "They were probably hoping one of you tried something. I suspect they might've taken one of you for a snack if you had."

"Maybe, I dunno. Harry said for us to keep our mouths shut, but . . ."

"Fredorian duty," said Kal. "That works for us in our favor for once."

Daren nodded.

Zane swatted Kal's chest with the back of his hand. "You two keep checking this out. I'ma have a quick chat with Harry."

Kal nodded.

Zane headed back to where Harry and the other two men were.

"You got what you wanted, why're you still here?" asked Harry.

Zane bobbed his head. "This is an official Fredorian investigation. Daren seemed to be the only one with a Fredorian-duty bone in his body. That will be noted when we leave. If you decide to hassle him over this . . . I'll be back to feed you your balls." He grinned. "I already spent several years in prison for doing that once."

Harry recoiled.

"I don't mind doing it again if I have to. I'll also make sure your official record showed you were a bitch. We have an understanding?"

Harry nodded vigorously.

Zane harrumphed and headed back to Daren and Kal.

FOUR

Blake glanced around the briefing table on the *Excel-tion*. It was 5:00 p.m., and he wanted to get in a quick meeting. Everyone had gathered and taken their seats. Blake had updated Charles on their way out, but made no mention of the event in the secured room. There was no reason for him to know, and if he did, it could be used against him. Blake cleared his throat. "We gained quite a bit of knowledge from Skorith. Ada downloaded all their previous research, and we had access to all their internal documents."

"Wow," said Zane. "Musta been a friendly person to give you all that."

Seth chuckled. "I'm betting that person will have a hard-on for Blake for the next few days."

Kal looked around. "Am I missing something?"

"He used a hypnotic gaze, which creates a blood bond," said Sarah. She glanced at Blake. "Right?"

Blake grinned, baring his fangs. "Yes, and he was kind enough to use his credentials to get us access."

Kal narrowed his eyes. "I've heard of the hypnotic gaze, but what's a blood bond?"

"It makes me more . . . *appealing* to whoever receives my blood. Their desire for me depends on how much blood I inject them with and what their personal view of me was before," said Blake.

Kal's eyes widened. "Sounds wild, man."

Blake grinned. "It can be." He cleared his throat. "Getting back to the topic at hand, there were some encrypted files, but Ada is working with Doc on them."

"Doc?" asked Kane.

"I take it you haven't started interacting with him more yet. He expressed an interest in expanding his routines, so why not?" asked Blake. "He's another AI, and between him and Ada, they should be able to crack it in time."

"No worries there," said Kane, nodding at Ada. "She'll smash it."

"The intent is to recover the data, not smash it," said Ada.

Kane shook his head while laughing.

"Oh, Earthborn slang again, I presume."

"Yeah. I meant that you'll recover it with no problems."

Ada nodded. "I'll add that to my natural-language database."

Kane grinned.

Blake glanced at Zane. "That covers how our trip went. How'd yours go?"

"The scientists left as a group on a Rogundan ship," said Zane.

"Figures," said Blake. "When you say left as a group, you mean they all left at the same time?"

"Yep, and we have a video feed," said Zane. He interacted with the table console, projecting the video feed over the table.

Kal shook a finger. "Funny thing . . . they didn't even take any personal items. Just what they wore on their backs. Daren, one of the guys who helped us, said they seemed to act weird."

Blake ran a hand over his mouth as he studied the projection. "Sounds like our mysterious black-slime friend from Zakara Prime may be involved, although the scientists were working on a blue slime."

"Black and blue slime," said Kal. "Lovely."

"All right," said Blake. "Our next step is to hit Lono Hara. I have some friends there, and we can check out what's being said. If there is anything going on in the Zolidack system, Lono Hara will know. It'll take the rest of the night to get there, so rest up."

Everyone acknowledged Blake and left the room, except for Ada, whom Blake flagged down.

Blake focused on her. "What are our auditing retention policies?"

"All ship systems data is purged after one month."

"One month?" asked Blake. "That seems a bit short. Is that standard?"

Ada shook her head. "FDF policy is standard six months, with central command sync after every mission."

Blake rubbed his chin. "Do you think it's unusual for the *Exceltion* to have one month?"

"Yes. However, that's what it was when we got the *Exceltion*."

"All right . . . go ahead and make the change so we're complying with standards."

"I will. Is there a problem?"

Blake raised his eyebrows. "Not at all. I was just curious."

Ada studied Blake for a moment. "It will be done."

"Good. Also, just a clarification, our personal offices and living spaces are secured from our internal systems, right?"

"They are," said Ada. "They don't show up when I'm in the system, at least not as accessible."

"Okay, that's all I had," said Blake. He nodded at her as she spun around and took off. Next on his list was to visit Kane, whom Blake found in the engineering lab.

Kane looked up from his terminal. "What's up, Blake?"

"Not much," said Blake. He tilted his head. "I had a request."

"Sure, anything, man."

"I'd like a full technical analysis of the ship. Not just the systems, but the actual physical items not connected to the system."

"I can do that. It may take a while to scan anything not in the system."

Blake nodded. "I understand. I just want to make sure that nothing is hackable."

"You got it, man," said Kane. "Last thing you want is something working for the enemy."

Blake chuckled. "Yeah . . . definitely don't want that."

"A'ight, I got you."

Blake nodded and exited. He hunted down Seth, who was in the command area along with Sarah. Blake tapped Seth's shoulder. "Got a moment?"

Seth nodded. "Sure thing."

They headed to Blake's office.

"These offices are secured per Ada," said Blake, closing the office door after taking a seat.

"Cool. So what's going on?" asked Seth, sitting in front of Blake's desk.

Blake shook a finger. "When you're going over Luke's ship inspection, check to see if there's anything unusual. He trusts you, and you've seen the initial report. Check for any anomalies in the reporting."

Seth wrinkled his eyebrows. "Got it."

"I have Ada doing something for me with the auditing logs. If she was the leaker, I thought she would object, but she didn't. If anyone is monitoring that change, they'd probably say something to her. For Kane, I have him doing a technical analysis of everything on the ship, to make sure nothing is hackable. I'll have Ada check his work, and I'll get Zane and Kal here in a few."

Seth smiled. "You're laying traps that will expose a leaker if we have one and securing everything down in case of a hacker."

ADAIR HART

"Am I that obvious," said Blake, grinning and baring his fangs.

"Okay, I can do that. What are you going to do with Zane and Kal?"

"I'll need your help there too. When we get to Lono Hara, they have a bar there called Orbitals that is frequented by FDF. I want you, Zane, and Sarah to go there, and I'll have Kal sneak behind and follow."

Seth dipped his head. "So if it's Zane, he would probably try to make contact, or Sarah, for that matter . . . What about Kal?"

"I'll have him relay a constant visual feed for me."

Seth nodded. "So if he was approached, you would know. You're covering every angle."

"I hate having to do this," said Blake, sighing. "If I had history with everyone, I wouldn't need to. It's a new crew, though. I was expecting some issues, but *not* this."

"We'll figure it out. I just hope we do before it bites us in the ass."

"That we will, my abductee brother."

Seth stood. "Anything else?"

"We're good. Enjoy the rest of the night."

Seth left the office.

Blake eased back into his chair. His gut instinct told him if there was a leaker, it was probably Kal or maybe Zane. Blake figured Ada would not be involved. He hoped it was not Sarah, but Kane and Luke were also on the possibility list. Maybe it was a hack. He would know soon enough from Kane's inspection, and if Ada detected any anomalies in it, unless she was involved somehow. Time would tell.

Blake ran his tongue over his fangs as the crew assembled in the briefing room. It was 10:00 a.m., and they had landed in a spaceport just outside Lono Hara. He noticed Seth eying the crew. Probably trying to figure out who was leaking, something fresh in Blake's mind. He cleared his throat once everyone was in. "All right, this will be brief. Ada and I are going to visit some of my old friends. Seth, Sarah, and Zane, there's a bar here called Orbitals with a lot of off-duty FDF and mercs of all stripes. See what you can scrounge up by any means necessary. Note that the bars here have dampening shields. Communication won't be possible once inside, so be careful."

"You can count on us," said Sarah.

Blake nodded. "Everyone else, you're free to do as you want. Just make sure the ship is secured before you leave."

Everyone acknowledged Blake.

"All right, let's do it," said Blake. He motioned for Kal to follow him and then headed to his office. He sealed the door after Kal had entered.

"What's up?" asked Kal.

"I need you to do a spy op and follow Zane, Seth, and Sarah to the bar, but stay out of sight. I also need a constant visual feed of who's coming and going out of the bar."

"Spying?"

"Yes. Given who we are, there could be trouble headed our way potentially. With you on lookout, hopefully we can head that off. If something does pop off, we'll have a visual feed of whoever entered and left."

"I could just go with them, but I guess that dampening shield would rule out relaying you a visual feed."

"Yep. Also, I don't want Zane and the others to know you're out there. If they get captured or something, it's best they not know you're around, and if they're escorted out, you can help them."

"I like it," said Kal, grinning. He tapped at a device on his chest. "I guess I should wait, then, until they leave."

Blake nodded. "Yep."

"This is more up my alley. All cloak-and-dagger and stuff," said Kal.

"I know, which is why I picked you."

"All right, man, they're as good as covered."

They slapped hands, and Kal headed out.

Blake took a deep breath and then joined Ada to meet with his contacts.

As they wound around the beaten-down dirt paths of Lono Hara, Ada glanced at Blake. "Why did you select me to come with you?"

Blake grinned, baring his fangs. "I didn't want to make my old friends hungry."

"I don't understand."

Blake tossed a hand out as they crested a hill populated by large trees covered in multicolored vines. "They're Ogeerians. Ten-foot-tall race that likes to eat humans."

Ada paused for a moment, then caught up with Blake. "A feline humanoid race. These are your friends?"

"*Friends* may be a strong word. I call them that because I know it antagonizes them."

"Is that wise?" she asked.

"When you hold all the cards in your hands, it can be whatever you want it to be."

Ada studied Blake for a moment. "I see."

"Don't worry, I also brought you along so you could try to soft connect to any exposed devices that they have."

"I will do my best," she said.

"I know you will."

They walked for forty minutes until they reached the outskirts of Lono Hara. In front of them was a junkyard surrounded by a steel mesh fence, with two Ogeerian guards in light armor outside. Both wielded massive guns, and the left one had a large ax on his back, whereas the other had a sword.

The left guard growled. "Where do you think you're going?"

Blake tossed his hands out to the side. "Fellas. I'm just here to see Dab Oshrin Keelrut. Oh, and tell him . . . Blake Brown has come calling."

One of the guards relayed the communication. After a moment, the other guard unlocked the gate and motioned in. "He says to come in."

"You boys keep on looking tough and scary," said Blake, grinning.

The guards growled.

Blake laughed as he motioned forward. "C'mon, Ada."

They entered into a ring of hastily made metallic shacks. Opposite them was a medium-sized compound, which they began to move toward.

Ada looked around. "They don't seem to prioritize cleanliness."

"They do lick themselves, but that doesn't extend to their environment," said Blake, shrugging.

Ada tilted her head. "I like that joke. It implies they don't find the environment worthy of their attention, while drawing focus to them licking themselves."

Blake chuckled. "Yeah, something like that."

They approached the large hut. The guards outside stepped back and waved them in.

When Blake walked in, he scrunched his nose. One thing the Ogeerians did not seem to mind was the smell of shit. That was something he never got used to.

They were led to a room in the back of the compound.

Blake eyed the black-and-yellow-furred Dab sitting on a large chair. His eye had a white halo around it, and he was surrounded by his crew lounging around the room. A thick haze filled the dimly lit air.

"Blake Brown," said Dab in a scruffy and bombastic voice. He wriggled his whiskers and peered forward. "And . . . looks like you brought me something quite lovely."

"I'm Ada, a member of Blake's crew."

Dab pulled back as the lounge erupted in laughter. "Well . . . are you now. Such a fine-looking thing, but . . . you're not edible."

"I'm not," said Ada.

Dab bobbed his head. "Maybe then you can *show* me what you're good at."

As Ada went to talk, Blake cleared his throat. "All right, keep it in your furry sheath. I'm here on business."

"All right. Then to what do I owe this visit?" asked Dab.

Blake raised a finger. "I've come to collect *one* of my favors."

Dab growled, causing the other Ogeerians to snap their heads toward him. "I *hate* owing you these favors. I could just . . . kill you now, and owe you none."

"One. You could try, but I guarantee that I would slice all of you up before you even knew what was happening. That's not even mentioning what Ada, with her superior strength, fast reflexes, and autoaiming, would do."

The Ogeerians' ears perked up.

"Two. I always have a backup plan. Something happens to me . . . you have a Covendrin party here, complete with ass kickings and beatdowns," said Blake. He knew they would believe that lie, at least he hoped they did.

Dab's eyes widened.

"You know . . . on the last favor I did for you . . . I could have just . . . left that evidence, instead of getting rid of it," said Blake. He arced a hand out. "Just imagine it. A world full of angry Covendrin mercs discovering who *really* killed one of their merc brothers."

"All right, all right!" said Dab. "You don't need to pull my tail. What do you want?"

"Information for a favor. If you don't have the information, then the favor is not tradable."

Dab extended a paw out. "Information . . . okay . . . about what?"

"Oh, you know . . . a little facility called Hadrassus on Markus II in the Zolidack system," said Blake.

Dab clacked his claws together for a moment. "What do you want to know about it?"

"Everything."

Dab tilted his head forward and peered at Blake. "You . . . planning on hitting it?"

"Nope. I just wanted to see if they wanted to buy a used spaceship."

The Ogeerians in the room laughed, but went silent with a look from Dab.

"Right . . . well, I don't know too much about that facility, no one does. What I do know . . . is there is something unnatural going on there. The Rogundans are involved, so that means the facility has some top-end mercs on the job."

Blake wrinkled his eyebrows. "Rogundans being top-end mercs is debatable. Nonetheless, the FDF has it registered as a classified facility. What do you know about FDF involvement other than that?"

"They control the system. They determine who enters and who leaves. I don't hear much chatter about Hadrassus."

"I already know that. What else do you have?"

Dab smiled. "I do have two things that you *wouldn't* know." He gestured at one of the Ogeerians near him. "Get the holo projector."

The Ogeerian scrambled out of the room, then came back with a cylinder that stood about two feet. On its base were supports, and a console sat on the side. The Ogeerian set it down and configured the projector.

Dab tapped at a device.

A projection shot up showing a regional galactic map. On the outskirts of the Zolidack system were multiple lines that spread to other systems. "We still monitor the Zolidack system. Although most ships go into condensed space, we sometimes confirm where they went. What you're seeing is the last two years of where ships came from and where they went to, at least for the ones we could verify. Also on this map is the location of several other facilities like Hadrassus in other systems."

Blake wagged a finger. "Now *that's* useful. Can you get a scan, Ada?"

"Processing," said Ada. She nodded. "It has been scanned."

Dab purred while his eyes roamed Ada's body. "I think I need an android in my life."

"I'm not for hire," said Ada.

The Ogeerians laughed.

"And the second?" asked Blake.

Dab formed a toothy grin. "We hijacked one of the ships leaving the system, but all the cargo was containers of slimes in various colors."

"Colors . . . like black and blue?"

Dab uttered a low growl. "Yeah, and green, red, and a bunch of other colors."

"Interesting. What'd you do with the ship and its containers?"

"Blew the ship up. I don't need that type of heat or scrutiny on me. There wasn't much to steal on it anyways."

"And the crew?"

"Fredorians . . ." Dab rubbed his stomach. "They made a good dinner."

Blake shook his head. "You need to stop eating Fredorians. You know they give you indigestion."

The room erupted in laughter.

Blake pointed at Dab. "I'm guessing you found out something before you did eat them."

"Yes. Yes, we did," said Dab. "Hadrassus is a research-and-development facility. However . . . what I think you want to know is that the captain said the black slime was . . . connected."

"To . . ."

"He didn't know, other than to say that wherever *it* is, *it* knows."

"And he didn't know what *it* was?"

Dab shook his head. "He didn't have a name for it, but he said he saw what it could do to others, and it terrified him. Speaking of which . . . he tasted . . . odd."

Blake narrowed his eyes. "That's why you really blew up the ship. That man's fear must have been genuine to convince you. If the black slime was on the ship, it might have known you hijacked it. You were a scaredy-cat."

Dab stood and growled.

"Relax . . . ," said Blake with a hand out. "No need to get your fur up. That too is useful information. I'll consider this favor . . . paid."

Dab nodded and waved a paw out. "Good. Now get the hell out of here."

Blake raised three fingers. "You still owe me *three* favors."

"Go!"

Blake grinned and then nodded toward the exit. "Let's get out of here, Ada."

FIVE

Sarah wrinkled her nose as the smell of the bar wafted around her. She could see that Orbitals was definitely a hangout for visiting FDF personnel. It had taken her, Zane, and Seth twenty minutes to get there, and she was no stranger to these types of bars, having visited similar ones with her *Arcturus* crewmates long ago. There was a mix of officers, enforcers, visiting mercs, and regulars all milling about. Although only a month removed from serving in the FDF, she could still recognize who was who.

There were more enforcers in the bar than she expected. That may be due to the proximity to the Zolidack system, and also being on the border of Fredorian space. Enforcers always made her skin crawl. They had military-sanctioned augments, giving users superior speed, strength, and cognitive abilities. The downside was the attitude that seemed to come with it, one she did not care for.

"Bringing back some old memories?" asked Seth.

She glanced at Seth and Zane, who sat across from her. "Yeah . . . sorta. I sometimes think I miss FDF life, then I remember all the bad times."

Zane grinned. "Then it's time to form some new memories."

She nodded. The *Exceltion* crew had been good to her, and she felt like she was bonding with them. Earthborn were nothing like how the FDF portrayed them to be in general. The informal nature of the crew was growing on her. She only had one mission under her belt, and although she was not happy with her performance, the mission had still been completed. The one thing that surprised her was how much she enjoyed taking command when decisions had immediate impacts, one of the benefits of a small team. Where this new mission would go, she did not know, but she was looking forward to putting another one under her belt.

Zane pointed out around the bar. "Lot of enforcers here. I can tell by their gear. Why would you need all that if you're trying to relax?"

"Probably on call," said Sarah. "They've been known to get called right from a bar or someplace where they're relaxing to go do something."

Seth shook his head. "No breaks between missions?"

"Less like missions, and more like actions. Sometimes they don't even know what they're doing until they check in."

Zane tilted his head. "Huh. So they compartmentalize. I guess that makes sense. If you need to hit something but don't want to share details, just order them up and go."

"Yeah. For the mission planner, it would be nice to have all those resources to use," said Seth.

Sarah smiled. "Some of the missions I was a part of on the *Arcturus* would involve multiple departments, and each only knew a specific part of the mission. It's why I like Blake's approach. Lay it all out, big picture, then dive into the details."

"Funny thing, he used to keep it all to himself when we were freelancing, and then clue me in as we went," said Seth. "After a few missions, he switched to the high-level view, then the details. It works better, and I'm glad we're doing that on these types of missions." He took a shot of cinnamon whiskey.

Zane poured Seth another shot. "So . . . what do we do here exactly?"

Sarah nodded at a drunk group. "Isolate someone who wants to drink and keep them coming. Slip in some questions and get them talking."

"You'll probably be much better at that than me," said Zane before downing a shot.

"Because I'm a woman?"

Zane laughed. "No, because they'd probably crap their pants if I sat next to them."

Sarah and Seth chuckled.

"Yeah, probably right," said Sarah. "Just watch our backs, I guess then, and listen around. I've been out with these types of crews before, and information can flow freely. Blake made a good choice in having us come here. Even bar regulars may have heard things. Speaking of which . . . ," she said, standing and nodding off to the side, "I think I see an opportunity. I'll be right back." She took off toward the booth with a lone red-skinned humanoid. The hairlessness stood out to her. Although she could not tell what species it was, she knew it was not human. It was probably male, based on the build. She stood in front of the booth. "Hello."

The humanoid eyed Sarah for a moment.

"Mind if I buy you a drink?"

"I'm not drinking, just watching, and no, I don't want company," said the humanoid.

"Oh . . . okay. If you don't mind me asking, what species are you?"

"Mazdarian."

She puckered her lips and bobbed her head. "Okay, well, I'll let you be. Sorry to bother you."

The Mazdarian nodded.

Sarah headed back to her booth and sat next to Seth. "Well, that one is not interested in company or talking. I thought him being alone would have been a good opportunity, but looks like he's just observing or something."

Zane grinned. "What'd he say?"

"Only that he wasn't drinking. Oh, and I asked him what species he was, well, I think it was a he. I've never seen his species before. He said he was a Mazdarian."

Zane sat up in his seat. "You sure he said that? Specifically?"

She drew her head back. "Umm . . . yeah. Is there a problem?"

"Not at all, but . . . maybe an opportunity," said Zane. He stood. "I'll be right back."

Sarah shrugged. "Good luck."

Zane took off.

Seth glanced at Zane walking away. "I've heard of the Mazdarians. That's the race that inhabits the planet that sent Zane to jail. Lander or Lancas or something."

"Ahh . . . I don't think I've heard why he went to jail," said Sarah.

Seth smiled. "He took a prince's privates and fed them to him, and then uhh . . . stuck something up the rear."

Sarah's eyes widened. "Wow . . . why'd he do all that?"

"Over a woman," he said, tossing his hands out to the side.

"Must have been some woman."

Seth laughed. "I guess so."

"Well, it's still early. We can keep looking."

"Sounds good to me."

//////////

Zane searched out the Mazdarian that Sarah had spoken to. He was easy to pick out. A flood of memories swept through Zane's mind. Merum Walz, the woman he thought he might spend the rest of his life with, was no more due to Prince Lessissot and his desire for her. Zane gritted his teeth. He had no remorse for killing Lessissot and would do it again.

Tillian Walz, Merum's daughter, was now on Zane's mind. He did not know where she went after the incident, but if anyone knew, it would be someone involved in the Mazdarian criminal element, which could often be found at bars throughout the region. Fredorians generally frowned on interspecies relationships, but he did not care. He stood before the table with the Mazdarian. "Got a moment?"

The Mazdarian eyed Zane. "I'd rather be alone. I seem to be popular today."

"Yeah, the woman from before was part of my group. She said she talked to you, and . . . I have some experience with Mazdarians."

"You do, do you?" asked the Mazdarian, eying Zane. "All right." He motioned at the empty booth seat across from him.

Zane slid into the booth. "I'm Zane Gibbons."

The Mazdarian drew his head back. "That name . . . Oh . . . Prince Lessissot's killer. I remember now. You did a great service for us that day. I'm Terisor. What brings you to me?"

Zane bobbed his head. "I was wondering since you're out here . . . and Mazdarians usually don't go someplace where there's no business . . . if you know of the Lortinian Cartel."

Terisor tilted his head as he studied Zane. "And why would a fine, upstanding Fredorian like yourself, excuse me, Earthborn, if I recall, want to know that?"

"I'm looking for Tillian Walz, the daughter of the woman who was killed by Lessissot. After that incident . . . I don't know where she went. I'm now out of prison, and I'd like to find her, maybe give her a better life than what she would expect on Lancas Prime."

"A noble goal. I like the . . . sound of that," said Terisor. "Yes, I know of the Lortinian Cartel. They trade in all sorts of things."

"If anyone knows where she went, it would be them."

Terisor smiled. "Such high praise." He paused for a moment, then said, "We do pride ourselves in our work."

Zane's eyes lit up. From his past dealing with the Lortinian Cartel, he knew them to be fair, if not brutal, but they always honored their word. It was odd to have an honorable criminal element, but that was more due to the Mazdarian cultural influence. "I'd like to buy information on where she is."

Terisor stood. "Sure, but not here. We have a spot nearby. There is a secret back entrance to this place . . . Watch where I go, then head there in five minutes."

Zane stood as well. "All right. I'll update my crew that I'll be gone for . . ."

"At least two hours."

Zane nodded and watched Terisor take off. The secret entrance apparently was a small door off to the side of the counter. The bartender did not even flinch when Terisor used it. Zane hustled back to his booth. "I have something that came up with the Mazdarian. It'll be about two hours. You two be okay during that time?"

Seth nodded. "Should be. This is probably the safest spot here, other than our ship."

"I agree with Seth. What'll you be doing?" asked Sarah.

Zane licked his lips. "It's . . . personal."

"Oh," said Sarah. "Well, I think we should be okay. Like Seth said, this is a safe place, for the most part."

Zane grinned. "All right. Appreciate it."

"No problem, man," said Seth. "Handle your business."

"Good luck," said Sarah.

Zane nodded at them, then headed out the secret entrance.

Terisor was waiting, and when Zane arrived, they headed out.

"Our spot is about a good forty-five minutes from here," said Terisor.

"All right," said Zane. "Were you just sitting in there hoping to find some buyers?"

"Actually, no. I'm doing some field work, observing, if you will. I also wanted to relax a bit. It's nice to be around others sometimes."

"I hear ya on that," said Zane. He shut off his communicator, so if someone tried to reach him, it would seem as if he were still at the bar.

After forty-five minutes and some light discussion, they reached a small shack.

Zane surveyed the interior. It had another Mazdarian at a table with a console of some type. His hands were flying around it.

"That's Juttio. He handles requests . . . and is also our pilot."

Zane nodded at Juttio.

"Business . . . or pleasure?" asked Juttio, eying Zane up and down.

Zane grinned. One thing he had learned about the Mazdarians was that although they had males and females, both sexes could carry a baby. It was an evolutionary advantage that had served their species well in their harsh past. Although the female often was the carrier, the male could in rough situations. The sex organ in both sexes was the same, but unusual, relative to a human, and consisted of a tentacle-like appendage, something he found out was quite versatile. The males were differentiated by their multiple scrotums. Mazdarians in general had no qualms about which sex they had pleasure with. He cleared his throat. "Business."

"That's too bad," said Juttio.

Terisor nodded at Zane. "He's Zane Gibbons. Prince Lessissot's killer, and now he wants to know the whereabouts of a Tillian Walz."

"Zane Gibbons!" said Juttio with wide eyes. "It's an honor. You took down someone that the Lortinian Cartel had been gunning for for a long time."

Zane looked down. "Well, I did it because that asshole took my woman."

"A Mazdarian woman . . . very unusual . . . for a human. Not unheard of, mind you, just . . . interesting," said Juttio. He eyed Zane. "Is it the red skin . . . or the lack of hair . . . or something else?"

"Juttio . . . business," said Terisor.

Juttio nodded. "I was just curious. It'll be two hundred credits. Standard access fee to the network." He tapped at the console, causing a deposit account number to appear.

Zane tapped at his forearm console and, after a moment, said, "Done."

"Now we're in business," said Juttio. His fingers were a hurricane moving across the console interface.

The screen flashed with various possibilities, then stopped on one.

"There we go. Tillian Walz. Several of them, but this is the only one with a mother of Merum. Looks like . . . Tillian was taken in by Mortikki Sans," said Juttio.

Zane squinted and shook his head. "Never heard of him."

"He's a pimp . . . and involved in the slave trade," said Terisor. He nudged Juttio. "Find out where Mortikki is now." He glanced at Zane. "Consider it on the house."

Zane nodded. His heartbeat had jumped up.

Juttio accessed the console again and, a moment later, pulled up an advertisement. He shook his head. "He's set up shop on Jirwana III. Nasty place."

"Do you mind if I copy that information?" asked Zane.

"It's yours to keep," said Terisor. "What are you going to do?"

Zane gritted his teeth. "I think I need to feed someone their balls."

Juttio and Terisor laughed.

"We would pay very, *very* well for the video feed of that. Mortikki is no friend of the Lortinian Cartel," said Terisor.

Zane got the information onto his forearm device and then sighed. "I'll deal with this later, but appreciate the help."

Juttio grinned. "Keep in touch, and we're serious about the video feed."

"Yes, we are," said Terisor.

Juttio licked his lips. "And if you want to . . . relax . . . later, you know where I am."

"I'll keep it in mind," said Zane. He cleared his throat. "I better get back to my crew."

"All right. Good luck," said Terisor.

Seth sighed as he eased back into the booth. It had been about forty minutes since Zane had left. Sarah had returned from another trip out. He had spent most of his time watching her, to make sure no one messed with her, but for the most part, it was uneventful. This time, she looked flustered. He narrowed his eyes. "What's up?"

"Enforcers," said Sarah.

"What about them?" asked Seth.

"They took exception to me approaching one of their members who was sitting by himself."

Seth chuckled. "Why would they do that?"

Sarah sighed. "They knew me. Apparently, we're well-known in the FDF enforcer circles. There was an official notice when our group was created, and it was sent out to all enforcers. Odd thing too . . . there was also an update on our last mission."

"Really?" asked Seth. "How detailed was it?"

"I don't know, but they knew Blake had bit me. They called me a vampire whore," she said, scrunching up her face.

Seth clenched his jaw. "Fuck them then."

"And now it looks like they're coming over here."

Seth observed the group of six men approaching. He could see that they were larger than a regular human, and they still had on their battle suits.

The lead man stopped in front of their table. He pointed at Sarah, then Seth. "So . . . looks like you're now doing another Earthborn."

Seth snorted. "Why don't you crawl back to your table."

"No . . . I don't think so. I'm Johan Crusche, leader of the Fourth Squad of the Twenty-Second Company in the Fredorian Defense Force Enforcer Division."

"Good for you," said Seth.

Johan raised a finger. "I wanted you to know my name, and the others as well." He went around and named the other five men. "This is important, because when it's asked who wrecked your shit, you'll know who. I *want* anyone who asks . . . to know."

Seth laid his hand on his pistol. "Are you going to be a problem?"

Johan grinned. "Earthborn. So quick to draw a weapon. Is it *any* wonder Fredorians have a bad reputation among other civilizations? They don't know the difference between a Fredorian and an Earthborn. To them, we're all human." He raised a finger. "But there is a distinction. One betters Fredorian society. The other tarnishes it."

"How so?"

"We give you refuge, food, drink, and opportunities, and you *spit* in our faces. You cling to your own communities, fail to integrate, and cause trouble wherever you go. You're *filth*," said Johan with spittle flying.

Seth shrugged. "Well, that's your opinion."

Johan grinned. "Yes, it is, and it's widely shared by many Fredorians."

"You do know Blake Brown runs our unit, right? And that we're officially here as the presidential guard?" asked Seth.

"Of course I do. The legendary ranger. And the presidential guard? What a joke. You know . . . Lono Hara is just outside official Fredorian space."

"And?"

"That means anything that goes down here isn't officially recorded."

Seth shook his head. "If I were you, I'd leave."

"Or what?"

"You don't want to find out."

Johan reached in and grabbed Seth. With a yank, Seth went flying out and hit the counter.

Sarah jumped up and punched Johan, sending him falling back.

Another enforcer grabbed Sarah from the back while a third punched her hard. They then threw her into the wall on the opposite side of the booth.

She kicked and connected with one of the members, sending him crashing to the ground.

Seth shook his head as he stood. He went to grab his pistol and saw that his belt had been yanked off.

Johan and two others approached Seth.

Seth kicked the legs out from under the right one but was grabbed from behind by the left one.

Johan pummeled Seth.

Seth could barely see after a minute, and his last sight was Sarah unconscious on the table.

CHAPTER
SIX

As Blake walked back to the *Exceltion* with Ada, his forcarm console lit up. After opening it, he checked the visual feed that Kal was relaying. It showed Seth and Sarah unconscious, lying just outside the front of the bar. Blake's stomach churned.

Kal's image appeared in a separate window. "Not sure what happened in there, but going to help them out."

"Are they alive?" asked Ada.

"I dunno. I just saw 'em get tossed out."

"Where's Zane?" asked Blake.

Kal shrugged. "I can't reach him."

"All right. Go to them and guard them until we get there. We're on our way," said Blake.

"You got it," said Kal.

The screen shut down.

Blake closed his forearm device and then glanced at Ada. "Let's go, we need to hurry."

They hustled through the winding streets and reached Kal after a twenty-minute run.

Ada knelt next to Seth and Sarah and, after a moment, said, "They're alive. It appears they have nonfatal internal damage." She took off her backpack and pulled out two syringes, handing one to Blake. "Inject her with these microbots. They should help stabilize so we can move them."

Blake grabbed the syringe and injected Sarah, while Ada got Seth.

"Want me to go inside and find out what happened?" asked Kal.

"No. You and Ada carry them to Doc. I'm going to get some answers."

Kal nodded. "All right."

"You good, Ada?" asked Blake.

"I'm good," said Ada.

Blake raised his lips, exposing his fangs, and, in a deep voice, said, "I'll be back." He entered the bar and looked around. There was no sign of a brawl, but given that the material of the tables and booths were resilient, they probably held up. He went to the bar and waved over the bartender. "You see a fight in here?"

"Nope."

Blake sighed. "Show me your deposit account number."

"One hundred credits."

Blake shook his head. When he saw the deposit account number, he transferred the funds. "There. You happy?"

The bartender nodded. "Two Earthborn got beat to a pulp by some FDF enforcers."

"Yeah, those Earthborn were my crew. Where are the enforcers?"

The bartender pointed over at a corner booth with six males. "There, but no fighting in here. I broke up the last one, and you should be glad I did. I don't think your crew members woulda survived."

Blake growled, exposing his fangs.

The bartender stepped back with wide eyes.

"Fine. Do you have their IDs."

"Yeah, they were quite vocal about it, actually."

"How much?"

"Free. I'll include it in the transaction we just did," said the bartender.

Blake showed the bartender his CID.

The bartender accessed his console and then said, "It's done. Good luck. Those guys are scary."

"They'll truly find out what scary is . . . later."

The bartender exhaled from his nose.

Blake left the bar and saw that two service robots from the *Exceltion* were there with transportable hovering slabs.

"I'll take care of them," said one of the robots.

"Doc?"

"That's me," said the robot.

"And me," said the other robot.

Blake nodded. "Be careful with them."

"Of course."

"Kal, Ada, escort them back. Make sure they get to the ship okay," said Blake.

"What are you gonna do?" asked Kal. "Need help?"

Blake shook his head. "I'm gonna take over your scouting spot."

Ada tilted her head. "To watch for Zane."

"That and . . . I know who did this. I want to have a chat with them when they leave later."

"I can help, man," said Kal.

Blake shook his head. "This may not be all there is, and if there's trouble at the ship, I'll need you to handle that shit."

"You got it."

Blake watched Kal and Ada leave and then scouted out a nearby rooftop. He activated his chameleon shield when he was in position and then waited.

Twenty minutes later, Zane exited the bar.

Blake jumped down from his perch and hustled toward Zane. When Zane crossed into a small side street, Blake deactivated his chameleon shield and slammed Zane into a building wall. "Where were you?"

Zane's eyes widened. "What's going on?"

"Seth and Sarah got beat to within an inch of their lives. You weren't there to help them," said Blake. His eyes glowed a dim blue as he growled. "Where were you?"

"I . . . had something personal."

Blake pressed Zane into the wall hard again. "You let something personal . . . take precedence over the *team*?"

"I . . . I didn't know they were in danger."

Blake let off Zane and stepped back. He sighed. "That's because your communicator must have been off, or you were somewhere with a dampening shield. If the bartender hadn't stepped in, we would be planning their funerals."

Zane licked his lips. "I take it someone attacked them. Who was it?"

"FDF enforcers."

Zane clenched his jaw. "Damn." He looked down. "I fucked up."

"Damn right, you did," said Blake. He ran a hand through the top crop of hair on his head while sighing. "What am I to do now?"

Zane exhaled from his mouth. He swallowed hard. "I understand . . . if you want me to leave the team."

Blake shook his head. "No. That's not the answer, but I need to know what was *so* damn important that you would abandon them."

"I found out where Tillian, the daughter of the woman I was with from Lancas Prime, is at."

Blake paused as he studied Zane. "Hmm. I would probably have done the same if I was searching for Seth and in your position, but now I'm on the other side of that." He ran a hand over his mouth. "So you know where she is?"

"Yeah. She's with a pimp on Jirwana III."

"How old would she be?"

"Thirteen."

Blake clenched his jaw. "After this mission is over, we'll pay the pimp a visit."

Zane looked up. "You serious?"

"Yeah. I'm still pissed about you leaving, but . . . I understand. Shit happens. We'll deal with it. Next time . . . let me know if you want to fucking do something personal during a mission. I can then at least plan around it."

Zane cleared his throat. "You got it, man, and . . . I'm sorry to put you in this spot."

"Just . . . head back to the ship for now. I'm gonna continue monitoring the bar. You're going to help me exact retribution on these FDF fuckers in a bit. Be ready to fight, nonlethal. I'll let you know when and where I need you. While you're at the ship, you may want to check in on Sarah and Seth. They're in the med bay."

"All right," said Zane. He stepped away from the wall and went to say something, but then turned and headed out.

Although Blake wanted to be angry with Zane, Blake could see himself doing the same thing in that situation. He went back to his perch and continued to monitor the bar.

Several hours later, Johan and his crew exited the bar.

Blake trailed them for a bit and then contacted Zane to head out. The enforcers were headed toward the spaceport, so Blake figured maybe they were going to take off. Although he smelled alcohol on them, even from a distance, he knew that they were not intoxicated. Probably just hung out at the bar to relax. At least for Zane, it would be a short trip. Blake relayed the coordinates to a small side street that Johan and crew would be passing through. When they entered it, Blake silently jumped down behind them and waited for them to run into Zane.

Zane had received Blake's message about where to be. Seth and Sarah were healing, but the beating they had taken indicated that the assault had continued even after they were unconscious. Zane figured that was probably when the bartender stepped in. At least they were alive and could be healed. Ada was a constant in the med bay, and Zane found it curious that she was not angry with him like Blake was. She was disappointed, which hurt even more.

Zane focused on the side street exit that the enforcers would be approaching. Blake was camouflage shielded on the other end of it, so they would have the enforcers trapped between them. Zane stepped in front of the group and cracked his neck. "What's up?"

They stopped.

Johan tilted his head. "And . . . who are you?"

"The big Earthborn guy that would have stomped your shit had I been there when you assaulted my friends," said Zane. He pointed a finger at Johan. "I'm here to fuck you up."

"You think so?" asked Johan. He circled a finger around his group. "Your math is lacking, as I would expect from an Earthborn. It's six on one, and we're enforcers. We're also outside the bar now. There won't be a bartender to stop us this time."

Blake appeared behind the group and then cleared his throat. "Make that two on six."

Johan and part of the group swiveled around.

"Blake Brown," said Johan. "Well, I guess we'll get to see just how tough you really are. I'm so tired of hearing how legendary you are. Two more Earthborn for our final night. I wouldn't have it any other way."

Zane growled. "I'm gonna wreck that ass."

Three of Johan's crew charged forward toward Zane.

Johan and two others attacked Blake.

Zane bulldozed into the three enforcers, causing them to spill back.

The first one kicked Zane's leg, which did not move.

Zane reached down and grabbed the first guy's foot and twisted.

Crack!

The first enforcer cried out as another jumped to help.

Zane came down hard and smashed the knee of the first enforcer he still had in his grip. With a backhand, he sent the second one flying into the wall.

The third guy punched Zane in the face, causing Zane to stagger back briefly.

Zane smiled as he licked the blood on his lips. "That all you got, pussy?"

The third enforcer engaged Zane, and the second had gotten back up and was trying to flank.

Zane caught the third man's fist and squeezed. Zane pulled the enforcer in close and head butted. The man fell to the ground and went limp. The second enforcer pushed Zane into the wall.

Zane gritted his teeth, grabbed the guy by the throat, and took a step forward while lifting, then slammed him into the ground.

The second enforcer writhed in pain and was slow to move.

"Who's the bitch now?" asked Zane. He looked over and saw that Blake had taken down two members and was facing off with Johan. Zane crossed his arms as he came up behind Johan. "Guess it's just you."

Johan pivoted and saw the enforcers downed by Zane.

"Yeah, it was me that wrecked them," said Zane.

Johan shook his head. "You might win this fight . . . but there's a lot of us. You won't win them all."

"Actually . . . they won't know about this," said Blake.

"Oh, so you're planning on killing us?" asked Johan, turning back around. "How presidential of you."

"No, I'm not a piece of shit like you. However . . . ," said Blake, nodding at Zane, "I have another idea."

Zane rushed forward and embraced Johan in a bear hug from the back.

Blake bared his fangs while grabbing Johan by the hair. "You're going to have a change in attitude." He pulled Johan's head to the side and sank his fangs into Johan's neck.

Johan cried out, and after a moment, his eyes went blank.

Zane released his grip on Johan and stepped back.

Blake raised a finger. "First things first. Whenever you see an Earthborn, you will talk like they are the greatest thing ever. If anyone shit talks them, you will defend them."

"I will do as you say," said Johan.

Zane laughed.

Blake grinned. "Then you're going to send an official apology to Seth Williams and Sarah Olson of my crew. In that letter, for all to see, you will let it be known that you used poor judgment and that the presidential guard deserves better treatment."

"I will obey."

"Good. Furthermore . . . you'll have a burning desire to wipe your own shit on your face, whenever you can. Your unit . . . will be known as the shit-face unit."

"Understood."

Zane guffawed.

Blake smiled. "You won't recall this incident. What you will remember is that you went back to the ship and got into a fight among yourselves about who was the biggest bitch. You all knocked yourselves out."

Johan nodded.

"Now . . . go to sleep."

Johan lay down and closed his eyes.

"Damn," said Zane. "That hypnotic shit is crazy. How long does it last?"

"Depends on how much blood I give them. They will have this for about a month. They won't remember this actual hypnotic event, though. It will be a blur to them," said Blake. He pointed at one of the men trying to crawl out of the alley.

Zane saw it was the one with the busted ankle and knee. He ran up to the member and grabbed him by the back of the suit and then dragged him back. "What do we do with these others?"

"They get the same treatment as our friend Johan. For the ones knocked out, my blood will wake them."

Zane nodded.

It took them another ten minutes, but they replicated the hypnotic commands with the rest of Johan's crew. They placed Johan's sleeping crew against the walls and then headed out.

Zane licked his lips. "I'm glad you asked me to help."

"Well, I want to be angry with you, but . . . we all make mistakes. How you act afterward will determine to me how sincere you are."

"It won't happen again. You have my word."

Blake nodded. "I'll take you at it. Just keep me in the loop next time."

"No problem, man. I'll be there when Seth and Sarah wake up, and I'll understand if they're pissed at me."

Blake chuckled.

"What?"

"They won't be pissed at you, especially if they know why you took off. Seth will be pissed off he got his ass kicked again, and for Sarah, it will be over not being able to handle the fight. I'm gonna check with Luke and Kane and see if there isn't something that will give them a nonlethal advantage. I'll also step up their combat training."

"Cool," said Zane. "If I can help in any way, let me know."

"I'll hold you to that. No bitching if it's early morning shit."

Zane nodded. "No bitching."

"All right. As far as I'm concerned, we're past this."

"Appreciate it," said Zane. As they walked in silence, he realized how close he had come to being booted from an opportunity that he knew was rare. Thinking back, he could have scheduled the visit with Terisor for a time after everyone was sleeping back on the ship; then he would have been there to help Seth and Sarah.

Zane smiled as he thought about being able to get revenge on the crew that harmed them. Blake's reaction was surprising, but Zane could see that this team was different. Blake was a fair leader and could be downright brutal when needed, the type of leadership Zane respected. Although he was upset about Seth and Sarah, it stung that he had lost some respect from Blake and Ada. Zane raised his head a bit and drew his lips tight as he continued to the ship. He would earn it back.

CHAPTER
SEVEN

Blake glanced at his forearm device as he approached the med bay. It was 6:00 p.m., and Seth and Sarah had regained consciousness. Ada had alerted Blake, and he wasted no time in hustling over. Although he had initially been angry with Zane, it had been tempered since the beatdown of Johan's crew. Blake understood why Zane did what he did and did not think he would do it again. Unfortunately, the damage had been done.

Blake was still unsure if Zane actually went to find out information on Tillian. He could have visited an FDF contact. Going to Jirwana III later would confirm whether or not Zane was lying, or maybe he knew where she was and was using it for cover. Blake sighed. He hated not being able to trust everyone fully. With his lips pulled in, he entered the med bay and stood between Seth's slab on the right side of the room and Sarah's on the left. He noticed Ada sat to the right of Seth.

"Hey, man," said Seth.

Blake glanced at Seth and Sarah. "I'm glad you both are awake."

Sarah grinned. "It'll take more than a few FDF losers to take us out."

"I'm sure. Are you both healing all right?"

"They are," said Doc, shuffling in from the side of Sarah's bed.

"Good. What's the recovery time looking like?"

"Only a day or so. There were a few broken bones and some bruising, nothing that can't be healed quickly."

Blake grinned, baring his fangs. "The wonders of Fredorian medical technology."

Doc nodded, then hustled back over to Sarah's side.

"We'll be up and at 'em in no time," said Seth.

Blake clenched his jaw. "It shouldn't have happened in the first place. I know we joke that you and bars don't get along, but this . . ." He shook his head.

"We'll heal. I don't think they meant to kill," said Seth.

Sarah sighed. "Well, at least we hope they didn't mean to."

"The bartender stepped in when you went unconscious," said Blake. He puckered his lips for a moment. "Then the asshole had you tossed out, like garbage. Thankfully Kal was there monitoring the bar."

Seth wrinkled his eyebrows. "You had Kal covering us?"

"Well, the bar, actually. I wanted to see who went and came. He notified me when he saw you two tossed out."

"Ahh. Well, I'm glad he did. Who knows what woulda happened with us just laying around outside. Maybe those assholes woulda come outside," said Seth.

Blake grinned. "They could have, but . . . we won't need to worry about them anymore."

Seth's eyes widened. "You didn't kill them, did you?"

"Nah," said Blake. "Zane and I . . . had a chat with them when they left the bar. They now have a furious itch to smear shit on their faces. They will be known as the shit-faced unit."

Seth and Sarah laughed.

"You didn't," said Sarah.

"I did," said Blake.

Ada tilted her head. "And they'll do that for how long?"

"A month. That should be enough time. Oh, and expect an apology from them sometime in the near future."

Sarah shook her head. "It'll probably make them more pissed when they find out why they've been acting weird and that they sent a letter."

Blake shrugged. "Maybe, but they won't remember the actual hypnotic event. It will always be a mystery to them, although, I guess they could figure it out, but they would never have any hard proof outside of us saying anything."

"I like it," said Sarah.

Seth furrowed his eyebrows. "I know you're probably pissed at Zane . . . but don't be. This is on us."

Blake sighed. "We'll cover that as a group later." He eyed them both. "You know . . . I could speed up this healing even more with a few bites."

Seth tossed a hand out, then grimaced. "No way, man, and my pants are staying on."

Sarah drew her head back a bit. "I miss something?"

"It's a long story," said Seth.

"Sounds like it."

Blake could see that the mere suggestion of biting had accelerated Sarah's heartbeat. The blood-bond memory still must have been fresh in her memory. "Well, I just wanted to stop in and make sure you were recovering. Get some rest, and," said Blake, grinning and baring his fangs, "take the rest of the day off."

Seth chuckled. "All right, man."

Blake glanced at Doc. "Will they be able to move around tomorrow?"

"Around 11:00 a.m. if my model is correct," said Doc.

"All right," said Blake. He shot a look at Seth and Sarah. "We'll have a meeting tomorrow in the afternoon around 1:00 p.m. then. I want to clear the air around this event prior to going to the *Storetz*."

"Works for me," said Sarah.

"Same," said Seth.

Doc looked around. "Same for me."

Everyone looked at Doc.

Doc smiled.

Blake chuckled. "Doc, if you want to attend the meetings, you're more than welcome to."

"Maybe I will," said Doc.

Blake nodded as he turned to leave. "All right, see everyone tomorrow."

Kal relaxed as he checked his console in his living quarters. It was about 6:30 p.m., and he had just had a solid meal. He was used to rationing out his food, even with replicators, and had gotten used to it, but on the *Exceltion*, rationing was not a concern.

His thoughts turned toward Seth and Sarah. They were in good hands with Doc. Kal wondered if Johan and his crew would have killed Seth and Sarah. Death would have swooped in and changed everything. That was the world as Kal knew it. He wished he could have helped, but at least he saw them when they were tossed out. It pissed him off that the bouncers treated them like they were sacks of garbage to be strewn on the street.

Knock! Knock!

He jumped a bit. Being so deep in his own thoughts sometimes took him to another place. "Who is it?"

"Zane."

"Come on in."

The door slid back, and Zane entered the room. "Not bothering you, am I?"

Kal shook his head and gestured at a nearby seat. "Not at all, man. What's up?"

Zane sat his massive frame down and heaved a few times. He glanced at Kal. "I guess you know what happened."

"Up to when we got Seth and Sarah back to the ship. I've been in here for the most part since then."

Zane sighed. "Well, I fucked up."

"What happened?"

"I saw an opportunity to find Tillian, the daughter of the woman I was with on Lancas Prime," said Zane. He ran a hand over his bald head. "It's so rare to find Mazdarians anywhere, and usually it's the Lortinian Cartel . . . so when I found one in the bar, I took advantage of it."

"Ahh," said Kal, waving a finger. "So that's where you were. Silenced your comms."

"Yeah. I got the location for a few hundred credits and came back. Blake jumped me outside the bar."

"Oh, shit," said Kal with wide eyes.

"Yeah. He gave me a second chance, and then we got the enforcer dirtbags who attacked Seth and Sarah."

Kal shook his head. "I asked if Blake needed help with anything, and he said no."

"Figures. I think he wanted to see how I would react."

"So you fucked them FDF dudes up, huh?"

Zane eased back and grinned. "Blake used that hypnotic thing, made them have a burning desire to smear shit on their faces for the next month so they'll be known as the shit-face unit."

Kal laughed. "No shit? Damn, man, I wish I had that hypnotic thing. It would make things so much easier. Man . . . I'd hate to be on Blake's bad side."

"Yeah."

"So . . . everything good now?"

Zane sighed. "Well, I need to talk with Seth and Sarah in a bit. I figured I'll wait till a little later tonight. I did talk with Ada some, and she was disappointed, and I gotta be honest, that shit stings. I wanted to explain myself to you so that you didn't get it twisted."

"I feel ya, man. If you had to do it all over again, what would you have done different?"

"I would have waited until I had free time, then checked it out. I didn't have to do it right then and there. It coulda been scheduled. I just got . . . excited, you know? First time I saw an opportunity to find Tillian since I came out of prison. I should have also told Blake. You know, trusted him."

Kal nodded. "We all make mistakes. Hell, as justice hunters, we know that better than anyone else."

"Yeah."

"Well, damn, man. I appreciate you giving me a heads-up."

Zane licked his lips. "I forgot to ask Blake, but . . . do you know how Seth and Sarah were found? After the fight?"

Kal grinned. "Yeah. Blake had me monitor the bar and relay a constant visual feed. When they got tossed out, I called him."

"Ahh. Figures. Blake probably didn't tell us you were scoping the joint in case we got captured and questioned."

Kal wagged a finger. "Yep."

"Smart. Of course, I don't think anyone expected such a brutal fight to happen either."

"Yeah. Supposedly safest spot on Lono Hara. I think, though . . . given that we're Earthborn, any place with FDF is going to be rough. Makes me on edge that we have to visit that FDF cruiser before going into the Zolidack system."

Zane nodded. "I'm with you there. We were already treating the FDF as unfriendly, but they can be downright hostile."

Knock! Knock!

"Who is it?" asked Kal.

"Kane."

Zane stood and nodded at Kal. "All right, I just wanted to keep you in the loop."

"You don't have to go."

"I . . . have some things to do."

Kal slapped hands with Zane. "Cool."

Zane opened the door, acknowledged Kane as he entered, and then left.

"What's up, Crazy K?" said Kane.

Kal laughed. "That's my other nickname. You been looking around, haven't you?"

"It's all good, man. I had some time, and since I'm in the systems all the time, figured it would be a good way to read up on everyone."

"Cool, cool. So what's up?"

Kane motioned at the workstation console on Kal's desk. He tapped at the side of his head, causing small screens to extend out in front of him. While moving his fingers around, an image appeared on the console screen. "When I was looking at your records, and that awesome video feed with the Selva Tong death squad, I saw that you liked gadgets." He tapped his chest. "I love gadgets. With that in mind . . . I created some based on what I saw in the video feed."

Kal studied the screen. It had a small object with flat faces on the sides, bottom, and top, with triangular faces connecting all of them. The lines were black, but the faces were green. Underneath it were the words "rhombicuboctahedron acid mine." It reminded him of a twenty-four-sided die.

"I saw the acid mines you used. These are an upgrade. These babies are compact, fit in your hand, and you can throw them at a surface and they'll stick," said Kane.

"My other ones could do that," said Kal.

Kane grinned. "Yeah, but yours exploded. Watch."

The screen showed the acid mine splitting in half while still connected by a metallic rod. Slightly under the top half, small tubes converged in the center. The top half began to spin, flinging acid everywhere.

"Whoa," said Kal.

"And here's the best part," said Kane.

The screen showed the tubes bending to a forty-five-degree angle.

Kal's eyes widened. "It can fling that shit everywhere."

"Yep," said Kane. "It has a small interface on the top face. You can configure the angle, timer, and other things."

"Damn, I coulda used these before."

Kane raised a finger. "But wait . . . there's more!" He wriggled his fingers.

The screen showed the same structure, but the faces were red.

Kal noticed that the faces had a circle in the middle.

"When this one goes off, it shoots off all the top faces, then explodes," said Kane.

"It have all the configuration stuff too?" asked Kal.

Kane nodded. "Yeah. Different configuration options, obviously, but if you want a lot of damage in a small space, this is your go-to mine. You can configure it for proximity or other factors, or you can manually trigger it."

"Sweet, man," said Kal.

The screen changed to show a lineup of other mines.

Kane pointed to the one with blue faces. "That's your holographic illusion one. You can program it with different holograms." He pointed at one with silver faces. "That's a slicer. It extends small graphene lines and spins them at high speeds. It'll shred kinetic shielding and any living matter in seconds." He motioned at the mine with purple faces. "That one will emit a spray and then light it on fire. I call it the fireball special."

Kal laughed. "That's great, man." He pointed at the last one, which was larger, with yellow faces. "What's that one?"

"I call it the electric octopus," said Kane. "It shoots out a lot of wires and then discharges a shock through them. Anything touched by it will get lit up. Works great on mechanical systems. Obviously, once used, the mines are useless, but with the *Exceltion* . . ."

"Man, it's like Christmas all up in here."

"That's what I'm talking about!" said Kane, tossing a finger in the air. "Oh, before I forget . . . Your sniper rifle can shoot these as well. It can also shoot some small sensor gadgets, which will give you remote vision and help you line up shots."

Kal exhaled. "I . . . I mean . . . holy shit. You did your research."

Kane smiled. "Yep, and they can all be activated remotely. They still have an activation delay timer if you want, but remote is the way to go to be safe. I'm also working on a belt like what Gobe Rallz had. I have it in a bulky turret for the moment. I'm not sure how he got his working, but I'm working with Ada on it. I have some test simulations you can play with on your console workstation. I already sent it to your workspace. Oh . . . and each mine has limited chameleon shielding. With a low thermal signature, they're effectively invisible."

"Damn," said Kal.

They slapped hands.

"All right, man, I'm gonna visit Seth and Sarah," said Kane.

Kal nodded. "I'm gonna play with the test simulations you set up."

"Cool," said Kane with a laugh. "Let me know if you want any tweaks or anything." He exited the room.

Kal sat back in his chair. He thought about Zane coming in and updating him on what went down. It probably seemed to Blake that Zane had abandoned Seth and Sarah. Being on Blake's bad side was not somewhere Kal ever wanted to be. He did not know what the long-term impacts would be with Blake and Zane, but it seemed the healing process had already begun.

Kal smiled as he eyed the console screen. There was a lot of effort put into the design of the gadgetry he was seeing. Having someone like Kane on the ship was smart, and Kal liked Kane's unique personality. Kal exhaled from his mouth as he dove into the test simulations.

EIGHT

Kane peeked into the med bay. It had been an hour since he had visited with Kal, and Kane wanted to check in on Seth and Sarah. Looking around, he saw that Doc was in his stick robot form with a hologram over it, while Ada sat to the right of Seth. Ada was holding Seth's hand, and they all appeared to be chatting.

Kane studied Seth. His face was mashed up, and bruises were everywhere. Parts of his body were wrapped, while various patches and gels were on other parts. Sarah was about the same. Both had a gauzelike pad over an eye. Kane entered the room and stood before them.

"Hey, Kane," said Seth.

Kane grinned. "Damn, S-man, I would ask what's good, but shiiit, it sure don't look that way."

Seth chuckled, then winced. "Yeah. It's all good. We got Doc, and he's doing a great job at patching us up."

Kane nodded and glanced at Sarah. "How are you both feeling?"

"Doing okay," said Sarah. "It hurts to move . . . but I can definitely feel the healing going on. Thankfully it was only a few broken bones at the worst."

"Whew. That's nuts. It still amazes me how advanced Fredorian medicinal technology is. If this was on Earth, you would have months, if not years, of recovery ahead of you," said Kane.

Seth nodded. "Yep. Doc says we should be fully healed in a day or so."

"Just amazing," said Kane. He made some boxing motions and danced around. "You both know if I was there, I'd have tossed some heads."

Sarah and Seth both laughed and then grabbed their sides while grimacing.

Ada tilted her head. "I don't believe you would have been successful."

"I was kidding," said Kane. "They would have probably used me as a bat to beat the others down."

Sarah and Seth laughed and grimaced again.

"Man, laughing hurts," said Seth.

Kane nodded. "I just wanted to see how you two were coming along. However . . . I had a second purpose in coming here. Since there will be situations where lethal force can't be used, I figured maybe nonlethal means could be used in a gadget, you know, help even the odds."

Sarah smiled. "A stun gun would have worked wonders."

Kane shook a finger at her. "I thought about that initially, but I realized that sometimes you won't be able to get to your gun fast enough."

"Yeah, that's what happened to me. Hell, I had my belt stripped," said Seth.

Kane tapped at the side of his head and then wriggled his fingers in front him as if typing away in the air. After a moment, he dunked a finger toward Ada.

Ada paused for a moment, then said, "An interesting proposal."

Seth glanced between them. "You two playing footsies in cyberspace?"

"Nah, man, it ain't like that. Check it," said Kane. He dunked another finger at a large screen on the wall off to the side.

The screen showed a forearm wrap with a part of it that extended into the palm.

Sarah furrowed her eyebrows. "A stun gun built into a forearm support."

"Yep, but here's the kicker," said Kane, wriggling his fingers.

The screen showed the discharge shooting forward first and then perpendicular from underneath second.

"You can toggle it so it shoots forward or," said Kane, raising his hands, "shoot it if your hands are raised or you have your hands on your head for whatever reason."

"I like it," said Sarah. "That would have definitely evened the odds a bit. How many discharges does it have?"

"Well, it has finite storage, so you can discharge until the meter says the storage is drained. So if you want a longer shock, you can, or a smaller one if it will deal with the situation," said Kane.

"Awesome," said Seth. "I assume you already replicated them?"

Kane nodded. "Whenever you're ready to use them." He raised a finger. "And . . . I'm also working on a lightning aura belt, similar to what that bounty hunter used that you and Ada ran into on Zakara Prime."

Seth pursed his lips. "Thankfully I didn't have to run into it, but Blake said it packed a punch."

"That would have been useful in the bar too," said Sarah. She grinned. "The only problem is it probably can't tell friend from asshole."

Kane laughed. "Yeah, that would definitely be an issue. If you're alone, though, it would be a good deterrent. I'm working on the form factor of it so that it could work with your under-armor suits."

"Where do I sign up?" asked Sarah.

Kane wagged a finger at her. "As soon as I get it working, we'll be good." He glanced at Ada. "I could definitely use your help there, whenever you're free, of course."

Ada tilted her head. "Send me what you have. I can process in parallel."

"All right," said Kane. He ran a hand over his mouth. "Don't know if I'm stepping on toes here, but . . . I heard Zane wasn't there to help . . ."

Seth shook his head. "Nope, he had some personal thing to deal with, so he took off, but he isn't to blame for all of this. Those guys woulda still probably come over."

"Yeah, but the fight mighta been more even."

Sarah glanced at Seth, then at Kane. "Maybe, but they were enforcers. Even with six on three, it still woulda been rough. I'm sure it will spread around what happened."

Kane sighed. "Well, I hope these new gadgets will help you out the next time around." Although he was trying not to show it, it pissed him off that Zane had left Seth and Sarah over a personal matter. Kane realized he could be reading their obituary now instead of talking to them. He cracked his neck. "A'ight, I'ma roll out. You two keep healing, and Ada, I'll shoot you over what I got."

Seth nodded. "Cool, man, appreciate you stopping by."

Sarah smiled. "And thanks for putting in time for those gadgets."

"It's all good," said Kane. "*I* got your back." He nodded at the both of them and then left the room. As he headed back down to the armory, his mind focused on Zane. It was hard for Kane to keep down the disappointment he felt toward Zane, but maybe the personal reason justified it. Kane figured he would play it cool toward Zane until Blake said something. Kane's eyes flared. For now, he would just do everything in his power to make sure Seth and Sarah had a fighting chance if there was another situation.

////////

An hour after Kane left, Seth sighed as he adjusted himself on the med bay slab. It was comfortable, but lying still was not in his nature. He wanted to get up and move around, but with a broken finger, dislocated shoulder, and other injuries, it would take a day or so to fully heal. It made him thankful that Fredoria had such advanced medical technology. He shuddered to think what his recovery on Earth would have been like.

Ada was on his side, faithfully looking over him. He enjoyed having her around, and it made recovery a little less boring. Looking to his left, he saw that Sarah had a device on her head. Kane had come back and brought her a headset that allowed her to tap into the ship's cyberspace environment. From what Seth understood, she could view entertainment, news, and the like and control it with her hand, which appeared inside the cyber environment. Seth added it on his list of things to check out at some point. It was 8:30 p.m., and he was beginning to feel like his old self again. His attention focused on Zane entering the room.

Zane licked his lips and looked around. "Mind if I . . . stop in?"

Seth gestured at a chair between the ends of his and Sarah's slabs. "Not at all, man. C'mon in."

Zane took his seat, facing both of them.

Sarah took off her headset and nodded at Zane.

Zane looked down for a moment and then addressed them. "I wanted to let you both know . . . I fucked up. I'm . . . so sorry this shit fell on you. I put something personal over the team, and this happened. I put you both at risk."

"It's okay," said Sarah. "I'm disappointed in my performance, but Kane has a few utilities that should help even the score if there's a next time."

Seth crooked a thumb at Sarah. "What she said. Getting tossed is just par for the course. Unfortunately, my curse extended to Sarah this time."

"I wish it was okay, but I could have scheduled that visit with the Mazdarian later, *after* we had finished the team's goals," said Zane. He sighed. "Anyways, I wanted to tell you both the reason I left. The Mazdarian was a member of the Lortinian Cartel, from the planet Lancas Prime, where I was sentenced for killing a prince. Although the woman I was with . . . died, her daughter and I were close. I didn't know where she went. When I saw the opportunity to find out, my emotions got the best of me."

"Did you get the information?" asked Sarah.

"Yeah. She's with a pimp on Jirwana III."

Sarah's eyes widened. "Uhh . . . how old is she?"

Zane clenched his jaw. "She'd be thirteen this year."

Sarah glanced at Seth, then back at Zane. "We should go get her, put her in the Fredorian system."

"Blake said he would help me after this mission," said Zane.

Seth grinned. "Hell, we all will. We're a team."

Zane nodded. "I . . . appreciate it. My . . . commitment to the team became secondary for a moment of weakness."

"Nah," said Seth. "I know if I were in your shoes and Blake was missing and I saw an opportunity to find out information on him, I'd probably do the same thing."

Zane smirked. "Blake said the same about you."

"Figures."

Ada tilted her head. "Would you do it again?"

Zane shook his head. "Not like the way it was done. I'd do it later, where the only risk was me."

"Would that not have compromised the team if you were injured?"

"Maybe," said Zane. He exhaled from his nose. "I get where you're going. I should have brought it up to Blake and gone from there."

Ada nodded. "That's the path I would have taken."

Seth shook a finger at Ada. "You're discounting emotional involvement, though. Sometimes emotions can be overpowering."

"I see," said Ada.

"If you were gone and missing, I'd be out there hunting for any tidbit I could find, regardless of where I was or what I was doing," said Seth.

"You would?"

"Of course," said Seth.

Ada's eyes lit up as she smiled.

Sarah motioned at Zane. "Don't feel bad because we couldn't defend ourselves. What's done is done. We should focus on what's next and how to mitigate the situation if it occurs again."

Zane raised his head a bit. "Well, if it makes you feel any better, Blake and I got those FDF fuckers."

"Yeah, we heard," said Sarah, chuckling. "I hope you have a video feed."

"Yeah. Blake wants to show it at a meeting tomorrow. He wants to clear the air on this situation and make sure everyone is on the same page going forward. I just wanted to stop in and . . . personally tell you what happened."

"Don't worry about it," said Seth. "The issue to me is not that you weren't there. It's that we couldn't handle the situation. What if we were deep in a facility and we ran into them again. If we can't handle them in a bar . . . we'd get wasted on the mission."

"A valid point," said Ada.

Zane stood. "All right. I'll let you heal up and rest in peace. If either of you want to chat, hit me up." He nodded at them both and then exited the room.

Seth sighed. "He feels guilty."

"He shouldn't," said Sarah.

"Well . . . Blake probably tore him a new one is my guess. He can be . . . persuasive at times."

"Huh. Okay, well, I'ma go back to this cyberspace environment that Kane set up. He has a cool simulation of the new devices that I can test on dummies."

Seth grinned. "Damn it, now I want one."

Ada stood. "I will get you one." She exited the room.

Seth extended a hand and then laughed. "Wow. I was just thinking out loud."

Sarah smiled. "I think she would do anything to make you happy."

"Huh?"

"I'm not blind."

"What do you mean?"

"Seriously?"

Seth laughed. "All right, I get the hint. The Fredorian attitude toward human and androids . . . is that being close is not so good."

"Well, who someone chooses to be with is their decision, no one else's. I know a lot of other Fredorians who think like me, and that view seems universal among Earthborn."

Seth nodded. "Yeah. On the other hand, I think Blake would do anything to make you happy."

"What?"

"I'm not blind."

They shared a laugh.

"All right . . . maybe that blood-bond thing was . . . interesting. I know how the FDF views it at least."

Seth shook his head. "Let them think whatever. What's important is what you think."

"You're right, of course. There's nothing going on. He's keeping it professional, which I appreciate."

Seth grinned. "All right. Then let's focus on this new stuff Kane got us. I'll see you in this environment." He watched as Sarah put her headset back on. Although she probably would never admit it, he had watched her eye Blake quite a few times. That was not unusual since he had that effect on women in general, and some men, but if there had been a blood bond, especially with someone as potent as Blake, that did not just go away.

The fact that it saved her life made it even more powerful. Sarah might not realize it, but if there was any desire for Blake in the first place, it would now be amplified. Seth suspected Blake knew that, which is why he was probably going out of his way to keep things professional. It was a topic that Seth knew Blake would avoid discussing, but Seth suspected he knew where it would end up. He tossed back his head and stared at the ceiling as he awaited Ada's return.

NINE

B lake surveyed the crew around the briefing table. It was 11:00 a.m., and they were on their way to meet with the *Storetz*. He took a deep breath as he went through what he was going to discuss. Although he had no problem with clearing the air about what had happened with Seth and Sarah, he wished he did not have to. The fact that he did not know who was leaking or if they had been hacked still ate at him.

He cleared his throat. "Our next stop is the *Storetz*, an FDF cruiser that handles ship and crew inspections. I'll go over that here in a second, but first . . . we need to talk about what happened on Lono Hara with Seth and Sarah. I want *everyone* to be on the same page, with the same information." He gestured at Seth and Sarah, who both wore a support exosuit. "They were attacked at the FDF bar, knocked unconscious, and then tossed out like garbage."

Seth grinned. "We gave them a fight, though. Sarah hit that asshole Johan right in the mouth."

"So I've heard," said Blake. He pointed at Kal. "I had Kal monitor the bar. I wanted to know who was coming and going, especially if it was known we were visiting. He saw Seth and Sarah being tossed out. Now . . . I know you're asking, Where was Zane? He had just found out where the daughter of his dead girlfriend was." He glanced at Zane. "Although I wanted to be angry with him, I know I woulda done the same thing had it been Seth I was looking for."

Zane looked down. "I fucked up, put personal before team. I could have scheduled that shit later."

"It's all good," said Seth. "Like Sarah said before, we shoulda been able to handle ourselves." He flicked a finger at Kane. "We'll have some new toys to help even the score if it happens again."

"It won't," said Zane. "You have my word . . . for what it's worth."

"Works for me," said Sarah.

Kane shook his head at Zane. "No offense, man, but that was a straight-up bitch move."

Zane sighed. "Yeah . . . I know."

Blake raised a finger. "Maybe it was, but it's done. I want to show you a video about what Zane and I did . . . from Zane's perspective." He interacted with the table console.

A projection shot up showing the video from the Johan fight.

After it was finished, Kane laughed. "You made them want to smear shit on their faces!"

Blake nodded. "Yep. Make sure to check up on them over the next month. It should be interesting to see how it plays out."

Luke rubbed his chin. "It looks like from that fight, even if Zane was in the bar, the outcome would probably have been the same."

"Most likely," said Blake. He waved a hand between Seth and Sarah. "Not to diminish their fighting capability, but they *were* fighting enforcers. They're not an easy fight, and outnumbered . . . you're lucky to be alive. However, it's been dealt with, and we can move on. Any issues?"

The group looked around at each other and acknowledged that they did not have any issues.

"Good. Now on to the *Storetz*. I had Ada go through the inspection protocol. Ada."

Ada nodded as she connected to the table access port.

The projection over the center of the table changed to show a list of protocols.

She pointed at the list. "There are sixty or so protocols. I'll go over the ones we should be aware of."

The projection changed to show five protocols.

"The first one deals with taking inventory. This is done by the docking-bay crew, under the supervision of a dock manager. All items are tagged in their local database." She raised a finger. "They do a full scan of each section. This allows them to do a comparison when the ship leaves, to see if anything has changed."

"We have to do this on the way out too?" asked Seth.

"Yes. It's unfortunate, but it is protocol," said Ada.

"We should probably do our own scan afterward to make sure they don't install anything," said Luke.

"Good point," said Blake. "Let's plan on doing that."

Luke nodded. "I'll handle it." He gestured at Ada. "I didn't mean to interrupt."

"It's okay," said Ada. She pointed at the second protocol. "After we dock, the crew is to line up outside. Each member will submit to a background check and meet with an inspector. Blake will meet with the lead inspector. The rest of us will be told where and when to appear."

Sarah shook her head. "This is usually only protocol with aliens. We're the presidential guard. I'm sure some of it will be skipped."

"Maybe," said Blake. "It depends on the dock manager and the lead inspector and what they want to do."

Seth sighed. "With our luck, they'll put us through the motions."

Ada nodded and then pointed at the third protocol. "All weapons are to be left on the ship. They're not to be carried on the *Storetz*."

"Self-explanatory," said Kal. "I'd probably end up shooting one of them."

Ada motioned at the fourth protocol. "While on board the *Storetz*, we will be given passes that track our location. This is to provide location information in case it's needed."

"Damn, why don't they just chip us," said Luke.

Ada tilted her head. "That would most likely be met with violence."

Luke grinned. "I was kidding."

"I see," said Ada. She pointed at the last protocol. "Inter-action with the ship's crew is to be kept to a minimum."

"Lovely," said Blake. "Those are just the highlights. There's a lot of detail for each one, and while the other protocols are minor, like you must wear clothing, we need to observe them. Ada, forward that list to everyone so they have a copy. Sarah, you've had experience on an FDF ship. If you can, shoot out something about the culture or customs we should look out for. I want everyone to read what Ada and Sarah send, and understand it. The goal is to avoid any possibility that they hold us for some bullshit reason."

Ada and Sarah acknowledged Blake.

"It's bullshit they have to do this," said Zane.

"Yeah, but . . . they control the system. Right or not, we have to abide by the rules. Once we're inside the system, though . . . all bets are off. How long do these things usually take, Ada?"

"Roughly half a day," she said.

Blake nodded. "All right. We'll be there tomorrow around 7:00 a.m. Get rested up, read what Ada and Sarah send you, and let's hope for a quick inspection."

The group acknowledged Blake and began to disperse.

////////////

Luke exhaled as he surveyed the *Storetz* docking bay. It was 7:20 a.m., the *Exceltion* crew was lined up, and he was the last one in the line. In front of them was the dock manager droning on about the protocols. Luke's stomach churned.

It was no surprise that he was the first one to undergo the inspector meeting. He had information that they were seeking. His attention focused on the crew dispersing. The dock manager and Blake headed off, while Luke nodded at the others before heading out to the inspector. He only knew where to go thanks to Ada having a layout of the ship. After thirty minutes, he arrived at the inspector's office.

The office was like any other FDF office he had been to. An advanced desk sat near the back of the room, with chairs in front of it. Screens dotted the walls, and the cleanliness of the room was apparent. The door slid open.

"Come in," said a voice inside the office.

Luke sighed as he entered the room.

A man rose from behind the desk and gestured at a chair. "I'm Inspector Rollos Gibbitz. Please, take a seat."

Luke complied.

"There is someone on their way here," said Gibbitz. "He should be here momentarily."

Luke nodded.

After ten minutes, a burly man entered the room.

Luke noted that it was FDF Special Agent Crimson Horoll. His tan-skinned head had shaved sides and a mop of black hair slicked back on top. The formfitting dark-blue one-piece suit had silver lines segmenting it, and various medals shined on the chest. Luke had worked with Crimson before, and it was no surprise that with the *Exceltion* docking, Crimson would be there.

Crimson pulled up a chair next to Gibbitz and then smiled at Luke. "So . . . we meet again."

Luke drew his lips to the right.

"That's no way to treat someone who's only looking out for your best interests," said Crimson.

"Whatever."

Crimson eased back into his chair. "So what is Blake and his merry crew up to out here?"

"You don't know already?" asked Luke.

"We have an idea," said Gibbitz. "We need you to confirm it."

Luke looked down. He hated the feeling of betrayal that racked him. With a heavy sigh, he looked back up. "We're going to check out Hadrassus."

"For what reason?" asked Crimson, leaning forward.

"To see what's going on there. The experimental pods from Zakara Prime were spotted there."

Crimson glanced at Gibbitz, then back at Luke. "Well, then I guess we can prepare for their arrival." He grinned. "I'd advise you to stay on the ship."

Luke tossed a hand out. "You're not going to kill them, are you?"

"No . . . of course not," said Crimson. "They're more valuable alive." He glanced at Gibbitz. "I'd like a moment alone with this traitor."

Gibbitz nodded and then left the room.

Crimson leered at Seth. "You don't like me, do you?"

"Piss off."

Crimson wagged a finger at Luke. "Remember our deal. You give us insider information on Blake and his wretched Earthborn crew, and your son can continue to have a prosperous career as an FDF officer."

Luke's eyes flared. "One day . . . your blackmail is going to come back on you, maggot."

"No . . . I don't think so. Your interest in your son not having an . . . *accident* . . . will ensure that."

Luke glared at Crimson. "You're an evil man to put my family at risk for the sake of advancing your career."

Crimson stood with a red face. "No! It's Fredorian duty, something I would *never* expect an Earthborn to understand. That presidential guard, Earthborn Unit, is a travesty, the last cry of a failing government."

Luke shook his head. "Bollocks. You saw the video feeds I obtained for you on Zakara Prime. You're telling me that doesn't mean anything? And now it's seen at this facility? Surely you know the two are linked."

"We handle things ourselves," said Crimson, adjusting his uniform as he sat back down. "We don't need the rangers or the presidential guard snooping around. As a matter of fact, the rangers were taken away from Andia Kiggs because there's no need for them, just like there's no need for this damn presidential guard unit."

"So what are you going to do about the facility then?"

"Like I said, we'll handle it, but now we have to deal with Blake poking his nose where it doesn't belong," said Crimson. He grinned. "We'll deal with that too. As I said earlier, you do what you agreed to. This will end soon, and then you won't have to see me again."

Luke looked down.

Crimson shook his head. "I would never do what you're doing, betraying a unit that trusts you, but I guess . . . that's Earthborn for you."

"You'd take principle over your child?"

"When it comes to Fredorian duty? Absolutely."

Luke grimaced. "You sicken me."

"It doesn't matter what my effect on you is. What matters is what you obtain and bring back."

Luke sighed. "So when we get there . . . I guess you're going to do something to the crew."

Crimson shrugged. "You may be flying back the ship with just whoever is on board."

"Fine."

"Good. Now run back to your ship like the traitor you are."

Luke stood and clenched his jaw. After glaring at Crimson, Luke left the room. It pissed him off that he had to deal with this, but he would do anything to keep his son safe. He headed back to the ship, and when he got there, he went to Zane's room. He knocked on the door.

"Who is it?" asked Zane.

"Luke."

The door slid open.

Zane waved Luke in. "I gotta admit, you're the last person I'd ever expect to stop in."

Luke nodded and entered the room, then took a seat.

"My damn inspection is in an hour," said Zane with a sigh. "How'd yours go?"

"It was all right."

Zane eyed Luke. "I'm guessing you're here to ask me about the bar incident."

Luke sighed. "Well . . . just one question. Would you have gone to Blake first before meeting with that Mazdarian?"

"Looking back . . . yeah. No question. I trust Blake and know he has my back. I'm . . . ashamed that I didn't hit him up first," said Zane. He drew his lips to the right. "I mean . . . he's done ranger work for twenty years, freelancing for two, and now heads a presidential guard unit, on top of being over four hundred years old. If you have something personal that needs attention, he's the most qualified person I know to go to for help. I'm not sure if that answers your question."

"Actually . . . it does," said Luke. His eyes misted for a moment.

Zane furrowed his eyebrows. "Everything all right, man?"

"Aye . . . it is now, I think." Luke grinned. "I guess sometimes . . . you just need to have trust." He stood and raised his head a bit. "I appreciate the chat."

"Anytime, man."

Luke headed out and went to his room. The FDF docking crew was already inventorying the ship, so with nothing to do, he lay on his bed. He had a decision to make, one that could ultimately harm his son. He began to relax as he deliberated his choices.

TEN

Blake stood on an observation deck, gazing out at the stars, while standing next to Captain Joshua Rusch. Looking out into space was always comforting to Blake, but the inspection left a bad taste in his mouth. He noted that Joshua, like all FDF officers, wore a crisp, formfitting white suit with gray segmenting lines and a highlight of blue and silver. A communication device sat on his left forearm, and he had an aura of confidence about him, with his hands clasped behind his back. Blake knew Joshua to be one of the more hardcore FDF officers when it came to Fredorian duty.

"So . . . Blake Brown. The presidential guard. Earthborn Unit. How interesting," said Joshua.

"Yep," said Blake.

"And now . . . you want to enter the Zolidack system. For what reason?"

"Confidential."

Joshua turned his head and eyed Blake for a moment, then continued to look out. "I see. You know . . . by law, your presence here is allowed." He raised a finger. "It's a shame that two groups, sworn to Fredoria, can't work together."

Blake grinned. "I suppose then that you've read about the Zakara Prime mission."

"The public statement, yes. It was . . . disturbing, yet you did what I don't think the FDF could have."

Blake drew his head back a bit. He knew that was a compliment, but it seemed odd coming from Joshua.

"Furthermore, I know of your history. I don't care that you're Earthborn, and I may not like that you're a Daedrould, but your actions show you are loyal to Fredoria, even more so than my . . . fellow FDF."

"Well, I just try to do what's right by any means necessary."

"I know that," said Joshua. "That's why I'm confused as to your presence here. What needs to be righted? The fact that you won't tell me means it has something to do with the FDF."

Blake licked his fangs. "Maybe, but to be fair, the FDF hasn't been supportive of the presidential guard, and if anything . . . they've been adversarial."

Joshua sighed. "That's because they fear you. You represent an upset to FDF norms. If the Fredorians are truly elite, then how is it that a unit of Earthborn can outperform them?"

"You get that with the Kreagans already."

"Yes . . . but they're aliens. Earthborn are humans, just like Fredorians."

Blake grinned. "That's true. We're all human, at least I was over four hundred years ago."

Joshua turned his head to the side for a moment, then faced back outside. "I believe in objectivity, and I've reviewed your record. You've proven yourself over and over to Fredoria, yet you're looked down upon because you're Earthborn and also a Daedrould. I know that sounds odd coming from me. Your unit is also hassled, and I'm sure you view this inspection to be just that."

Blake wrinkled his eyebrows. "I'll be honest . . . I wasn't expecting our talk to go *this* way . . ."

Joshua shrugged. "Whatever your reason is for being here, I suspect it has something to do with the FDF behaving . . . oddly . . . these last few years."

Blake narrowed his eyes. "What makes you say that?"

"I'm being objective now. There's a bar, a high bar, set for how the FDF is to perform. When it is lowered, for any reason, that is a cause for concern. Fredorian duty . . . becomes a punchline to a *joke*."

"So you've seen unusual behavior throughout the FDF then."

Joshua nodded. "Contrary to what you might believe, I liked the rangers. They did good work. I was opposed to the FDF absorbing them. That was a . . . bad . . . decision."

"Tell me about it. Rakar being forced out just makes it worse, in my opinion."

"I would agree. Rakar comes highly recommended by the Kreagan emperor, and we tell Rakar he isn't good enough? That doesn't make sense. On a more personal note . . . one of my close friends was kidnapped long ago. FDF wouldn't touch it, since it was outside Fredorian space. It was the rangers that went and got her back. As a matter of fact . . . you were the one who did it."

Blake's eyes widened. "I've helped many. Who was it?"

"Hollisa Curesch."

Blake grinned. "Oh . . . yeah, I remember her. I had to waste several Trags and the lone Grozadian merc that was with them, but I got her back."

Joshua nodded. "I never thanked you, because it would seem . . . improper, to thank a ranger, much less an Earth-born, or a Daedrould. I am thanking you now."

"It's all right. I was just doing my job."

"Yes, and you've remained steadfast. I can't say I know what's going on, but if you're here, at least I know there's someone competent involved."

Blake exhaled. He was unprepared for Joshua being this way. It could be a trick.

"Well, I'll let you get back to it," said Joshua. "This might help you." He extended a hand.

Blake shook his hand. As he did, he felt something press against his palm. From previous experience, he knew it was a data device, one used by rangers. He held it in place with his thumb as they pulled their hands apart.

"I hope you find what you're looking for," said Joshua.

Blake nodded and headed out. He had placed the device under his sleeve. What was on the device intrigued him to no end, but he knew to wait until they had cleared the ship. It was evident to him now that Joshua had the same view as Rakar: there was something going on with the FDF. It probably pained Joshua to help the presidential guard, but Blake knew that Joshua's main loyalty was to Fredoria. If the FDF was acting against that interest, it would spark a riot among those who viewed Fredorian duty not as something that must be observed, but as a way of life. He exhaled from his nose as he continued toward the *Exceltion*.

//////////

Blake twirled the device he had been given between his fingers as he sat in his office on the *Exceltion*. The day had gone by fast, and it was about 10:00 p.m. They had passed most of the inspection already, with finalization coming the next day. Ada had said it would be a half-day event, but he figured otherwise given who they were. Although he had his doubts initially, he suspected that their clearance rankled a few FDF officers based on what he had heard from the others.

Joshua was surprisingly upfront about some concerns. Blake understood now that the unusual behavior of some FDF had not gone unnoticed by even those in the FDF. It was not lost on Blake that Joshua trusted him more than the FDF at this point. A turn of events that Blake had not considered. He tilted his head as he smelled sweat. Not just any type of sweat; this was nervous sweat. He also picked up an increased heartbeat and shallow breathing. Whoever was coming to his office was on the verge of freaking out.

Luke peered into Blake's office. "I know it's late, but you got a minute?"

Blake drew his head back. "Sure . . . anytime."

Luke entered and took a seat in front of Blake's desk.

"How'd your inspection go?"

"That's . . . what I'm here to talk to you about," said Luke. He licked his lips. "Before I do, though, I wanted to let you know I talked with Zane."

Blake tossed a hand out. "About the bar incident?"

"Yeah . . . and well, I wanted to see his thoughts about going to you first for anything personal."

Blake sat up in his chair. "Obviously, that would be ideal. Do you . . . have something personal you want to discuss?" He could not imagine what Luke had to say.

Luke sighed. "Yeah, I do, actually." He swallowed hard and closed his eyes for a moment.

Blake narrowed his eyes. Whatever it was, it was tearing Luke up, at least physically.

Luke gestured at the door. "Can we close that?"

"Sure," said Blake. He swiped at his desk console interface, and the door slid shut. "So . . . what's on your mind?"

Luke bobbed his head. "Okay. Well . . . my inspection had an FDF special agent. One named Crimson Horoll. I've been . . . ," said Luke, gulping, "working with him."

"As in . . ."

"Collecting information on this team. Video feeds, locations traveled, who've we interacted with, everything," said Luke, looking down.

Blake clenched his jaw. Luke was the leaker. Although Blake had considered it, it seemed so far out of the realm of possibility he had never taken it seriously. Now here it was, right before him. Gift wrapped with a confession. "I see."

"Crimson was waiting on me to tell him about this mission. He knows where we're going and, more importantly, *why* we're going, and he intends to capture you and anyone who sets foot in that facility."

Blake nodded. "Interesting."

Luke looked back up and furrowed his eyebrows. "I . . . thought you would be a bit angrier."

"Well, I don't think you did what you did out of maliciousness," said Blake. "After Zane . . . it's best I hold any judgment until I hear *why* you did it."

"Right. Of course," said Luke, exhaling. "My son, Jimmy, is an FDF officer, serving aboard the *Galactus*. If I didn't cooperate with Crimson and his investigation into the presidential guard, Jimmy would have an . . . accident."

"So you're being blackmailed."

Luke looked down. "Aye, and I hate this feeling. I may have kept up the charade, but . . . I don't think Crimson is going to capture you alive. I think there will be an accident at the facility, and they have time to prepare."

Blake ran his tongue over his fangs. "You did the right thing in coming to me. I want you to know that. Yes, I'm a little pissed at what you did, but . . . your family was at stake."

"And Jimmy will still be in danger, even with me telling you this."

"Maybe . . . there could be a promotion for him, one which would see him transfer to a job under a trusted admiral."

Luke's eyes lit up. "Is that possible?"

Blake grinned. "We're the presidential guard, working for Rakar directly, and Andia indirectly. That's a lot of power that can be swayed around."

"I . . . whatever you can do, I'd appreciate it."

"I'll see what I can do," said Blake. "As for this, it's probably best we keep it between us. The crew doesn't need to know. Zane's issue was an error in judgment, but he wasn't being blackmailed. That's different. The less the crew knows of it, the better."

"Thank you."

"Now . . . when did you last see Crimson before this inspection?"

"It was after we got back from Zakara Prime. I visited him a few times."

Blake nodded. "All right. Here's what we're going to do then. You keep providing that information to him."

"Huh?"

"You're going to be my double agent. Come to think of it, Ada will need to be involved. We'll give you a misinformation packet that should keep Crimson happy. If anything, it will let us know what they think they know."

"I'd rather not see that maggot ever again, but . . . whatever you want me to do, I'll do it. I don't want to be kicked off this team. It's been a long time since I actually liked a crew and got along with everyone and . . . I don't want to let them down. Not only that, but I love this ship and would hate to see her used by a less worthy crew."

Blake rubbed his chin. "I agree."

"You don't seem too surprised that I was doing this."

"Well . . . remember, I was an intelligence operative for twenty years. I didn't think the crew would just gel after one mission. It takes time. I just hope there are no more surprises or incidents for the remainder of this mission."

"Yeah, me too," said Luke.

"All right. I appreciate you coming to me. Keep doing what you're doing, and after this mission, we'll get you that misinformation."

Luke stood and puckered his lips. His eyes misted, and in a cracked voice, he said, "Thank you."

Blake stood and shook Luke's hand, then watched him leave. With a sigh, Blake sat back down. His eyes searched the room for a moment, and then he called Seth and Ada to his office. When they arrived, Blake motioned for them to take a seat and then closed the door.

"What's up," said Seth. "I was just working on the Markus II layouts."

"I found our leaker."

"Really?" asked Seth.

"What leaker?" asked Ada.

Blake grinned. "Someone leaked confidential information to the FDF from our last mission. Ada, I'm bringing you into this because you'll be needed after the mission for this." He took a deep breath. "The leaker is Luke. The FDF was blackmailing him. Luke came to me just before this meeting and confessed."

"That was why you were interested in the audit retention policies," said Ada.

"Yep. When the mission is over, he will report back to the FDF . . . but with a bunch of misinformation. We're going to craft the narrative. This will require doctored documents, altered video feeds, and other things. Seth, you can trust Luke at this point. I don't think he's a bad person. On the contrary, he's a good person in a bad situation, and he's trusting me. However . . . Luke thinks that only Ada and I know, so Seth, you'll need to play clueless on this."

Seth ran a hand over his head. "Well, damn, man. I would have never guessed." He grinned. "Be easy for me to play clueless."

"We woulda found out sooner or later," said Blake.

Ada glanced at Seth, then Blake. "You didn't trust me."

"I wouldn't go that far," said Blake. "I didn't think it was you, but I wanted to see if it was anyone else first."

Ada nodded. "I would not betray the team. I enjoy it here."

"I'm glad you do," said Blake. He tossed her a device, which she snapped up in midair. "I love your reflexes. Sure Seth does too."

"Ahh, man . . . ," said Seth, shaking his head.

Ada scanned the device. "Information storage."

Blake nodded. "One with the detailed layout of Hadrassus, and more importantly, it's current."

"Whoa," said Seth. "How the hell you get that?"

"I'm not sure of its veracity, but it was given to me by the *Storetz* captain, Joshua Rusch. He thinks there's something going on in the FDF, and he doesn't trust them to investigate. He does trust us, so he says. Nonetheless, it's worth analyzing. Ada, I'd like you to pinpoint any vulnerabilities for Hadrassus; then we can figure out a plan on how to access it while we're there. Oh, and they now know we're coming and why."

"They do?" asked Seth.

"Yeah, Luke said that his FDF handler mentioned us being captured, but Luke felt that an accident is what would happen."

"Damn, man. All this subterfuge. Makes my head spin."

"Welcome to my world," said Blake, grinning and baring his fangs.

"I'm glad you're on top of all this."

Blake tossed his hands out to the side.

"Of course, he's Blake Brown," said Ada, smiling.

Blake laughed while pointing at Ada. "She gets it."

Seth shook his head. "I'm guessing tomorrow we'll formulate a plan."

Blake nodded. "Yep. You two get some rest. Or not . . ."

"Man . . . ," said Seth.

"I don't understand," said Ada.

Blake grinned. "I know, but Seth does. I'll see you two tomorrow."

ELEVEN

Seth grinned as he looked around the briefing-room table after a good night's rest. Per Blake's communication, this meeting was to go over the plan to hit Hadrassus. It was only 8:00 a.m., and Seth could see Zane and Kal were struggling to wake up, even with a cup of coffee. Sarah and Luke were alert and ready to go, and Kane looked wired like he always did. Seth could not remember the last time he saw Blake tired, and he didn't think Ada could look tired.

"Such an enthusiastic crew this morning," said Blake, with his lips pulled to the right.

"I could use a few more hours," said Zane.

"Me too," said Kal.

"Thankfully for the both of you, the plan is to leave in about three hours, when the inspection is officially over, so you can get some rest then," said Blake. "Luke, you do your inspection once we're gone."

"You got it," said Luke.

Blake interacted with the table console.

A projection shot up from the center of the table, showing several views of Hadrassus.

Seth studied the images. There was a small circular building with large bay doors. It sat on the surface and was surrounded by expansive landing pads. They reminded him of a miniature spaceport, minus the controller towers. A long shaft angled deep underground to a large square central structure. Four smaller tunnels perpendicular to each other extended out in each direction. They ended in smaller structures that were connected to each other in a circle, forming a giant ring around the central structure. Each of the smaller structures extended out farther into their own network of structures. Although the distances looked small in the images from the high-level view, he knew they were large based on the size dimensions.

Blake gestured at the projection. "As you can see, this facility is deep underground. What we saw up top was just the entry point."

"How'd you get this information?" asked Sarah. "It's much more detailed than what we had before."

"I got it from the *Storetz* captain, Joshua Rusch. He thinks there's something rotten going on in the FDF, and he supposedly trusts us more than the FDF to investigate," said Blake.

"Oh. I guess he would be in a position to know."

Blake nodded. "Although we have this information, it could still be a trap."

Kane rubbed his chin. "I can run an analysis on the data Joshua gave you."

"I did already," said Ada. "It appears to be recent information, and I detected no data anomalies."

"Well, there you go," said Kane, grinning at Ada.

"Yes, there I went."

Everyone chuckled.

Blake cleared his throat. "I want to get as much information as we can. I harbor no doubt that we'll run into a trap somewhere." He tapped at the table console.

The projection zoomed in to the large central structure.

Kal pursed his lips. "So . . . we gonna split up or something?"

"Not initially," said Blake. "Ada, Zane, Kal, and I will go to the main structure, or central hub as it's listed here. We'll meet Administrator Cadris Zoldan and then head to the north hub. We can split up once we get there. Ada and I will go to the research-and-development area. Zane, Kal, you two will hit up the genetic engineering division. Once we've cleared those, we'll hit the other divisions and hubs."

"Sounds like a plan," said Zane.

Blake sighed. "I know, and . . . I don't know what's waiting for us down there, or what we'll find. We'll at least be able to stay in secure group communications while we're down there, but we won't be able to contact the *Excelion*. When we're down there, we're on our own. The FDF hates us, and the Dorostatic Initiatives probably does too . . . and now we're getting all up in their business."

"Too bad for them then," said Luke, raising his head a bit. "They deserve whatever's coming to them."

Blake nodded. "I agree. For this mission, I want everyone to suit up with enclosed suits. Plan on fighting, and gear out accordingly."

Zane cracked his neck. "It's juggernaut suit time."

"Yes, it is," said Blake. He glanced at Seth. "You, Sarah, Kane, and Luke will have the *Exceltion* ready to fly away or fight. I don't expect any fighting near the *Exceltion* . . . but if there is, handle your business. It would probably help to launch some drones for surveillance."

"Aye, we'll keep her ready to go," said Luke.

Sarah nodded at Luke.

"Good. Now, we have three hours before we leave. Get some food, relax, and then be ready."

The group acknowledged Blake and began to disperse.

Seth watched as the group left. The FDF not knowing that their plan was exposed would work in the *Exceltion* crew's favor, but he knew that might not mean much if it got really bad. At least the leaker issue had been resolved prior to going to Hadrassus, and he was sure Blake's mind was more at ease. Seth did a final look around the room, then headed to the command area.

/////////

Sarah studied her console in the *Exceltion*'s command center. It had been about three hours since the meeting, and they were on their way to Hadrassus. Luke was performing a ship-wide scan with Ada's and Doc's help. Blake was in his command chair, Seth and Kane sat at their workstations, and Zane and Kal were somewhere else on the ship. The *Exceltion* was not using condensed space since they were inside the solar system and did not want to fly out of it. Flying at sub-light speeds was tedious, and it would be at least a day before they reached Hadrassus. What was on her console was troubling. She glanced at Seth. "You seeing what I think I'm seeing?"

"Yep. We're not alone out here," said Seth.

"Trouble?" asked Blake.

Seth sighed. "The ship profile indicates Rogundan."

Blake narrowed his eyes. "Hmm. Kane, get into the weapons control center. We may be in for a fight."

"I got you," said Kane. He stood and then headed into the nearby weapons control center. The front screen showed an image of him once connected, and a full tactical readout of weapon systems appeared on the wraparound screen to the left of center.

"Seth, what's the nearest planet with a breathable atmosphere?" asked Blake.

"Umm . . . looks like there's a habitable moon on one of the nearby outer planets. The planet it's orbiting is hostile to life, though. What are you thinking?"

"I just want to know the safest place to go if this doesn't go our way," said Blake.

"Good point," said Sarah. Her eyes widened. "Okay . . . now it looks like there are three Rogundan ships, and one of them is a heavy corvette."

Blake grinned. "It's almost like . . . they're hunting something."

"Yeah, us," said Seth. "Their firepower would eat us alive."

"Can the *Exceltion* outrun them?"

Seth glanced at Sarah, then at Blake. "The heavy corvette, yes. The two ships with it, no. Even if we did jump out via condensed space, or flew away, if they're still around, we'd need to deal with them somehow."

Blake ran his hand over his mouth. "I don't think we can expect help from the FDF. If we're detecting the Rogundans, then the FDF has already, and they're choosing not to do anything about it. I suspect that decision is out of Joshua's hands."

"Those fuckers," said Seth.

"If we went to that moon, they'd probably follow. We could find a hot spot to camouflage the *Exceltion*; then they wouldn't be able to see us and would be forced to land. We could even shoot some sensor decoys, make them think we're elsewhere, and when they land to investigate, we fly over and waste them," said Blake. He tilted his head. "Can we take out one of the smaller Rogundan ships before we go?"

Seth grinned. "Yep. We can launch an overwhelming amount of missiles at one. Most will be destroyed by the combined point-defense systems of the three ships, but some missiles will get through."

"Kane, be prepared to fire."

"All up in it," said Kane's face on the screen.

Blake nodded at Sarah. "Hail them."

Sarah interacted with her workstation. After a moment she said, "Communications established. Relaying."

A window popped up on the wraparound screen showing a large Rogundan.

Sarah grimaced. Although she had interacted with many species, the large insect-like ones always freaked her out. The red oblong head with large pincers and large beady black eyes made her skin crawl. As if that were not enough, the antennae waved around as if a wind was blowing on them. They had a large red-and-black shell on their backs, and their bodies seemed to be a mix of muscle and blackish-red chitin armor. Their beefy arms were large, and relative to a human, they were much stronger. They had a four-pronged claw for hands and stood on two burly legs. Their sheer size, at around seven feet and weighing close to four hundred pounds, made them formidable close-quarters combatants. She flicked a switch, then glanced at Blake. "Translator's active."

"Well, well," said Blake. "My favorite species. Rogundans. Are you in need of assistance?"

The Rogundan's antennae flailed around. "Blake Brown. I'm Commander Mozrah. Your translator probably doesn't do my name justice."

Blake shrugged.

"We've been waiting for you," said Mozrah. "Prepare to be boarded."

Blake shook his head. "Doesn't work that way, and you can forget trying to . . . *bug* . . . me about it."

Seth laughed.

Mozrah snapped his head toward Seth, then back at Blake. "You make jokes. We are serious."

"I figured as much. We're going to . . . bug out. See you around," said Blake, grinning and baring his fangs.

The communication window dissipated.

"Kane, light 'em up."

The Exceltion launched a barrage of missiles at the small ship to the right of Mozrah's ship, which showed up as ship number three on the screen. Mozrah's ship was number one, and the other ship to its left was number two.

"Seth, get us to that jungle moon!"

"On our way," said Seth.

The *Exceltion* pivoted and headed toward the moon.

Sarah's eyes were glued to the tactical screen as she saw the Rogundans perform evasive maneuvers.

The *Exceltion*'s missiles adjusted their trajectory as they flew.

The Rogundan ships shot their own missiles out, targeting the incoming ones, while another set flew at the *Exceltion*.

Sarah could see that although they had the same amount of missiles to match, the Exceltion's missiles were maneuvering around them. When the missiles got close to the Rogundan ships, their point-defense systems took over, shooting lasers and tossing out a small field of debris. Mozrah's ship's point defense was much greater than ships two and three and was able to destroy all but two of the remaining *Exceltion* missiles, which slammed into ship three and, after a brief explosion, disappeared from Sarah's screen. She looked at Blake. "Ship three has been destroyed."

"Yeah, but we have about eight missiles headed our way," said Seth.

Blake nodded. "I guess we'll get to see how good the *Exceltion*'s point-defense system is."

After twenty minutes of the missiles chasing them, Seth said, "Approaching the jungle moon and performing scans." He narrowed his eyes. "Brace for impact."

When the missiles were within a range where they could be targeted and hit with a high probability, Sarah watched as the *Exceltion*'s lasers began to fire. Several of the missiles were hit.

The *Exceltion*'s flak cannons had pivoted toward the missiles and fired. All but one of the missiles were destroyed.

"Shit!" said Seth.

The missile slammed into the rear of the *Exceltion*, causing it to shake.

Sarah thought her grip would break her workstation. She looked down at her white knuckles and gulped. When she was on the *Arcturus*, she rarely saw it engage in battle, and if it did, it had a small fleet that coordinated strikes. The flashing red light and muted alarm did not help the ambiance.

"Damage assessment," said Blake.

Sarah focused on her workstation console. "One of our main thrusters was hit. There is some hull damage, and I've sealed off a section. Minor damage to various other systems."

"Means we're in for a rough landing," said Seth.

Her eyes focused as the moon appeared on the screen. According to the temperature layout, they were headed to a central area. As the *Exceltion* entered the atmosphere, she examined the heat signatures. There were large swaths where the *Exceltion* could land. Seth had targeted a clearing amid the unusually colored purple and green trees.

"Fire the decoy sensors," said Blake.

Seth nodded. "Firing them now and scrambling our ion trail. The Rogundans should be able to detect the decoys."

"All right," said Blake. "Activate stealth."

"Activating stealth now," said Sarah. She watched as the two decoy sensor trails appeared on her screen. She understood that the trails would show up through the jungle's thermal signature since when it landed, the sensors would shoot up a bright light that would be hard to miss. Given where they were landing, it would be about a three-to-four-mile hike between each sensor and the *Exceltion*. The screen also showed the *Exceltion*'s trail scattering across the breadth of the jungle.

"Landing now," said Seth.

Blake cracked his neck and spun his chair around as Kane reentered. "Kane, be prepared to launch some drones if needed. Looks like we're going to ground to fight."

"Love to, but we're down one launcher, for a while anyway," said Kane.

Blake ran his hand over his mouth. "All right." He tapped at his chair. "Zane, Kal, Ada, come to the command center."

After five minutes, they arrived.

Blake gestured at the regional layout on the wraparound screen. He pointed at the first red dot, which showed Rogundan ship number two landing via a flickering transmission. "We're going hunting. Zane, Kal, get to that ship and neutralize their crew. I want the ship intact so we can analyze it." He motioned at a second red dot. "Ada and I will take Commander Mozrah's ship. This atmosphere is interfering with transmissions, so keep that in mind."

Zane and Kal acknowledged Blake.

"Seth, Sarah, Kane, do any repairs you need to. I'm not expecting a firefight around the *Exceltion*, but if it happens, be prepared to defend it."

"You got it, man," said Seth. "Good luck."

Sarah and Kane nodded at Blake.

Blake stood and grinned, baring his fangs. "Let's hunt."

TWELVE

K al tugged on his suit as he and Zane marched through the forest. Although Seth had said the moon was habitable, it was walking the line of what Kal considered tolerable. He was used to wearing a looser-fitting undersuit and then slipping on lightly armored pads where needed. It made carrying many gadgets easier. Now he had on a light suit that covered his whole body. While it was not uncomfortable, it was something he did not wear often.

He glanced at Zane, who also wore a light suit. The juggernaut suit would be a hindrance in this terrain. Over private comms, Kal said, "So how much farther away is the decoy sensor and, I guess by extension, one of the Rogundan ships, assuming it landed?"

"About four point eight miles per Ada. We've only gone a mile so far. You getting tired on me?" asked Zane.

"Nah, man. This suit is a bit tighter than I expected."

Zane tossed a hand out. "You'll get used to it."

As they continued on, Kal pointed ahead. "Check out that huge-ass tree. That'd be a great vantage point."

"It's on the way," said Zane. "You want to check it out?"

"Yeah. Maybe I can see if the Rogundans sent anyone out."

Zane nodded. "Those Rogundan ships are probably having the same communication issues we are." He absent-mindedly swatted at his arm. "Damn bugs. They keep jabbing at my armor."

"Hold up," said Kal. He was not sure if his eyes were playing tricks on him. "That bug had a humanoid face. Actually, they look like small humanoids with wings."

Zane laughed. "You think tiny humanoids are out here trying to piss me off?"

Kal pointed at the ground. "How many bugs you know use spears?"

Zane knelt and shot a scan out from his forearm device. "Holy shit." He stood and looked around. "So we got small flying humanoids with weapons. Great."

"They seem curious. Let's hope it doesn't go further than that," said Kal. A shiver ran through him. He had been on contracts on jungle worlds, and it was always the insects you had to watch out for. Now there was a small humanoid version the size of his fist flying around. They could be trouble.

After twenty minutes, they got to the large tree.

Kal pulled out his grappling gun. "All right. I'ma take a peek and see what we're dealing with."

"I'll hold the base down," said Zane.

Kal chuckled as he shot at the first branch. When it connected, he tugged on the line and verified it would hold him. His suit had small jump boosters that would help, and when they fired, he pressed a button on his gun and then shot up to the branch. He repeated this until he was about sixty feet off the ground. Once anchored, he took in the scene. The place was beautiful, and if the atmosphere were more pleasant, it would be a good getaway.

"Seeing anything?" asked Zane over comms.

"Not yet. I was just taking in the view."

"Don't fall asleep up there."

They shared a laugh.

"I'm checking now," said Kal. He picked out several areas of interest, and then used his advanced binoculars to zoom in. He chose the first spot due to some of the trees moving erratically, although there was no wind. Zooming in showed that it was two odd-looking boar-like creatures fighting and running into the trees. The second spot was the decoy sensor from the *Exceltion*. A thermal image profile matched the Rogundan ship that sat in a clearing. "Confirmed the Rogundans landed by the decoy."

"Huh. Can you see any movement?"

"None. Just fluctuations, and nothing showing up on the other visual modes."

"Then we do it the old-school way. Eyes and ears."

Kal grinned. He enjoyed working with Zane. Everything was just easier. Granted, Zane was a justice-hunter veteran, so that was to be expected. Kal had been working solo for a long time, but now seeing what could be done with a functional team, he wished he had done it earlier. The first crew he had ever worked with ended up disastrous, especially when he knew he could have done the contract solo. His attention focused on the branch moving a bit. His eyes widened. "Uhh . . . one of those little humanoids just landed on the branch."

Zane laughed. "Say what?"

"I'm serious, man," said Kal. He did a slow wave, and the humanoid reciprocated the movement, then flew away. "Well, that was weird. I waved at it, and it waved back, then took off."

"I'll be honest, man, those little shits freak me out."

"You?"

"Yeah," said Zane. He paused for a moment. "There's two of them in front of me, and they're hovering just ahead."

"I bet they want us to follow them," said Kal. He took a few minutes to get down to the ground.

Zane shrugged. "Maybe they don't understand why we're here."

"They're headed in the direction of the decoy. Doesn't hurt to check it out."

"All right," said Zane. He extended a hand forward, and the humanoids flew away.

Zane and Kal followed the two flying miniature humanoids for a while. The humanoids stopped after a mile, pointed ahead, and then scattered.

Kal understood the scattering to be the universal sign that something unpleasant was coming their way. "I think they found a Rogundan patrol."

Zane hustled over to a large tree and hunkered down.

Kal shot his grappling gun up a nearby tree. Once on the branch and anchored, he activated his chameleon shielding. While not as effective as Blake's, it would do well out in this environment.

After a few minutes, a patrol of eight Rogundans came into view a bit away.

"There's eight of them, and I have an idea" said Kal. "We can sandwich them. You head out to their left and handle things there, while I snipe to pull them to the right. When I down one, they'll come for me. It'll take two shots due to their heavy kinetic shielding, assuming they're using a standard Rogundan one. After that, I'll drop, and then they can play with my new gadgets. While that's happening, you hit them from your side. Just keep your firing arc at an angle away from me. I'll reposition, and continue stretching them out. They'll be drawn back and forth."

"Ping-pong," said Zane, laughing. "Okay, I'm moving then."

Kal laughed as well. "Yep. All right. I'll let you know when to stop." He watched as Zane headed out.

After several minutes, Zane was in position.

"Okay, you're good. I'm setting up now," said Kal. He grappled down and placed an acid mine on the ground near a tree. At another tree farther back, he laid an explosion mine. He examined some trees back even more and found one he liked. Once he had hustled over to it, he laid and covered a line mine. He grappled up the tree and perched himself on a branch that gave him a good view over the most of the jungle. A smile crept onto his face as he remembered he had fireball and stun mines that could be used if needed.

He anchored himself and pulled out his sniper rifle. After adjusting it, he peered through the scope. "Okay, reassessing their position."

"Cool. I'm ready to beat some Rogundan ass," said Zane.

Kal chuckled. It took him a moment, but he was able to find the patrol. They had come much closer and were in a spread-out group pattern. His heartbeat raced as his breathing intensified. This was the type of situation he lived for. He lined up the first Rogundan in his sights. They stuck out with their big shells and seemed to plod along. He fired two quick, successive shots which shredded the Rogundan farthest to the right.

The reaction was immediate.

Kal dropped down out of the tree on the side opposite the line mine as weapons fire erupted all around him. "Okay, one down!" he said over comms. He ran to another tree and grappled up on the side away from the incoming Rogundans.

"They're coming right to you," said Zane.

Kal peeped around the side and saw that Zane was almost on the Rogundan farthest to the left. He reloaded two more rounds. "Zane, hold off for just a second until the first one hits my acid mine."

Zane sighed over comms.

Kal watched through his sniper scope as the first Rogundan ran into the acid mine. "Two down!" His eyes shone as he watched it dissolve parts of the Rogundan. "Zane, now!" Focusing on Zane, Kal was amazed at Zane's sheer strength as he crunched a Rogundan's helmet. The Rogundan dropped to the ground.

"Three down!" said Zane.

Kal took aim and hit the Rogundan nearest him. It went down in two hits. "Four down!" He reloaded.

The other Rogundans opened fire in Kal's direction and hustled toward him.

Kal dropped from the tree. He hunkered down when his explosion mine went off.

"Five and six down!" said Zane. "I think."

Kal wanted to assess the situation, but the Rogundans were too close at this point. He reloaded his sniper rifle, then put it back and pulled out his dual pistols. Glancing to the side, he activated his illusion mine and tossed it out, then headed back a bit. He found a tree and ducked behind it. Looking around it, he could see a Rogundan enter the clearing and fire at the illusion device and demolish it with his weapon.

Kal clenched his jaw. Thankfully he could get another.

As the Rogundan went to inspect the destroyed illusion device, the line mine went off, shredding the Rogundan's kinetic shielding. The Rogundan stepped back in surprise.

Kal stepped out from behind the tree with both pistols aimed forward. "Night, bitch." He unloaded a volley that melted the Rogundan's remaining kinetic shielding and then the Rogundan. Kal cried out in surprise as a shot hit his kinetic shielding and sent him flying back.

The last Rogundan had appeared.

Kal found it hard to gauge Rogundan emotions, but its wildly flailing antenna, moving mandibles, and hurried pace made him think the Rogundan was pissed.

The Rogundan aimed at Kal.

Kal knew a close shot like that with an automatic weapon would shred him and his kinetic shielding.

Zane appeared behind the Rogundan and placed his shotgun on the kinetic shielding at it's head. "I don't think so." He fired point-blank at a slight angle, spreading parts of the Rogundan's head over Kal's kinetic shielding.

"Whew," said Kal. "Cutting that shit awfully close."

Zane grinned. "Yeah, but eight on two . . . and Rogundans . . . and we *still* won." He cocked his head back and then barked and howled. After a moment, he helped Kal up. "Let's get to that ship."

Kal laughed as he stood. He narrowed his eyes, watching the small flying humanoids buzzing around the Rogundan, sticking it with spears. He gestured at them. "I get the feeling those humanoids don't like the Rogundans."

Zane shrugged. "Maybe we'll find out why at the ship." He waved forward. "Let's check it out."

Kal had the Rogundan ship and decoy sensor mapped, but all he had to do was follow the small flying humanoids. They appeared to be interested in leading them. His heart was still pumping from the fight, and he enjoyed teaming with Zane. Taking down a Rogundan patrol was risky, but with Zane, the odds were evened. The thought crossed his mind how much easier it would have been with Blake and Ada present also.

Zane raised a hand. "I think these humanoids are trying to tell us something."

Kal studied the humanoids as they flew haphazardly over some coverings on the ground inside a small clearing. He noticed one of them drop a small rock on the covering.

A large spiderlike creature emerged, snapped at the air with its beak, then slid back into the hole.

"Whoa," said Kal. "We woulda walked right into that."

"Yeah," said Zane. He nodded at the humanoids, who took off on another route. "Guess it's official. We got some guides now."

"Works for me. Three miles or so to go."

They followed the humanoids around the opening, and after two and a half hours, they reached the marker.

Kal could now see the Rogundan ship, but it was the commotion nearby that caught his attention. Two Rogundans were using a machete-like weapon to slash at a tree with what looked like holes and miniature huts on the branches. He shook his head. "Looks like the Rogundans are trying to get a snack."

"Then let's introduce ourselves," said Zane.

"Sounds good to me," said Kal. He pulled out his sniper rifle. "I'll take out one, you get the other."

Zane cracked his neck. "Ass beating time."

Kal knelt and steadied his sniper rifle.

Two shots later and one of the Rogundans was on the ground. The small flying humanoids swarmed the body, tearing it to shreds with various weapons.

Zane charged with his mace out. When he reached the second Rogundan, he smashed its head. As its kinetic shielding faded, the humanoids ripped into the dead body.

"Let's check the ship!" said Kal. He put his rifle on his back, and then pulled out his dual pistols. He rushed toward the wide-open sliding door on the Rogundan ship.

"Wait!" said Zane as he ran toward the ship.

As they neared it, weapons fire shot out the door.

Kal rolled to the side and fired.

Zane crept around to the side.

"I think I got him," said Kal.

Zane pulled out his shotgun and then stepped into the ship, with Kal behind him.

Kal's eyes widened as he saw a console near the dead Rogundan, making increasingly louder noises. "Oh, shit! Get out! Get out!" He grabbed Zane and tried to pull him out as the ship exploded around them.

Everything went black.

////////

Blake was not expecting the moon's atmosphere to be as harsh as it was. His helmet was up as he surveyed the damage to the *Exceltion*'s exterior. The Rogundan missile had left a crater when it crashed into the left side. Thankfully the *Exceltion* had thicker-than-normal armor. Luke was outside scanning the area, while Kane was inside running ship diagnostics. At least Luke's scan for potential FDF modifications on the *Exceltion* had shown nothing so far, although Luke had said the scan was not fully complete. He said that he would finish it after primary systems were back up and running. The *Exceltion* was on emergency power, thanks to the missile.

Blake had already sent Zane and Kal off toward one of the decoy sensors, where Blake knew a Rogundan ship had landed. Ada was in her suit next to Blake. He accessed his group communication channel. "Ada and I are heading out."

"Good luck," said Seth. "Communication may be spotty, but your short-range communication between each other should be good. I already tried to contact Zane and Kal, but that's a no go."

"All right," said Blake. He nodded at Ada. "You ready?"

Ada nodded. "Always."

Blake grinned. He liked that Ada was loosening up. It made him think Seth was having an influence on her. He motioned in the air. "We might not be able to use the thermal scanners on your drone effectively, so we'll probably need to go visual, but even that'll be limited."

"Zane and Kal will be without a drone to help them," said Ada.

"Yeah, but they'll be okay. They're used to this type of work. Let's head out."

They moved into the jungle.

Blake wanted to lower his helmet and sniff around, but he knew that even with his resilient body, it would be rough. Relying on his helmet's information was acceptable, if not limiting. He kept an eye on the drone Ada had launched as it flew ahead. The connection was intermittent due to the unusual interference from the moon, but it at least gave some heads-up.

As they passed the first mile, Ada paused. "There is a Rogundan patrol off to our right, approximately two point four miles away."

Blake focused on the screen. He shook his head when he saw that the Rogundans had open face helmets. Apparently this was their type of atmosphere. The patrol had about six members, and they were heavily armed. Blake knew that after taking out one of their ships, they may not honor their commander's wish to capture. One thing Blake understood about Rogundans was their sense of camaraderie. Their merc groups were very close knit, and losing even one member was grounds for a brutal reprisal, and now here they were with a ship gone. "Let's head toward them. When we get there, we can use one of the drones as bait to lure them into a kill zone."

Ada nodded.

When they passed the second mile, they arrived next to a small brown river.

"This water is acidic," said Ada.

"Yeah . . . I'm not thirsty anyways."

Ada jumped back as a large snakelike creature with two massive front legs lurched forward out of the water.

Blake pulled out his dual blades. He lowered his helmet while facing the creature.

The creature turned toward Blake and roared.

Blake uttered a deep growl as his eyes glowed a dim blue. His blades swayed in the air.

The creature paused.

Blake took a step forward, and the creature backed away into the water.

"You scared it," said Ada.

"Of course, I'm Blake Brown," he said, putting his blades back. He raised his helmet again. "Actually, we had an understanding. It knew power when it saw it . . . and we didn't back down. My unusual behavior probably was the real reason it backed down."

"I see. Perhaps it thought it might hurt itself for the effort. From what I read of Earth's apex predators, this is not uncommon."

Blake nodded. "Probably. I like the idea that I scared it better."

Ada smiled. "While you were scaring the creature, I verified that Commander Mozrah's ship landed at the other decoy sensor. It is about three miles north. The patrol is only a mile away now. Also, there are three other patrols around. I have marked their positions."

"They don't know where the *Exceltion* is," said Blake, viewing the patrol locations. "They're executing a standard search pattern. I'm glad you can patch together what's out there. This spotty coverage is giving me a headache." He tilted his head and focused on a spot on the other side of the river. "I sense something. We're being watched."

Ada followed Blake's gaze. "My drone does not show anything, nor do my internal sensors."

"Something's . . . ," said Blake, pointing across the river, "there."

"Should we pursue it?"

"No. If it was malicious, it would have already attacked. It's just observing, whatever it is. Let's continue toward the ship," said Blake. "Back on topic about the other Rogundan patrols. Any that reach the *Exceltion* will have to deal with its defenses. If Zane and Kal get the Rogundan ship at the other decoy sensor, and we get this one, the Rogundans will be trapped; then we can mop up."

"Okay."

They headed up the river some until they found an area low enough to cross.

As they were about to step into the river, Blake grabbed Ada and pulled her back into the jungle. He pointed out. "Rogundan drone."

"I see it," said Ada. "They may have better visuals due to having dealt with this type of environment before."

"It still won't help them," said Blake. He studied the multiple dots scattered around his HUD. "There's two patrols ahead of us. I suspect if we take them down, it'll draw the other two."

"How do you wish to proceed?"

"I'll fight them in the jungle. With my chameleon shield, it'll be a slaughter, but I'll need to move fast. If you can keep the drone's visual feed and their locations up, I can use that."

"I will need to filter the drone's feed for you in order to have a stable overview. I can also use the assault drone to assist you."

"Works for me," said Blake. "Okay, let's hit that first patrol. They're still deep in the jungle. When we get to them, I'll get in position, and then you can use your assault drone to pull them to me. I'll go from there. Once that patrol is down, we'll repeat for the second one."

"We'll play it by ear."

Blake grinned. "Now you're understanding."

Ada nodded. "I'm ready."

"Good, let's move."

They waited until the Rogundan drone had passed and then crossed the river. After a few minutes, they reached the area just ahead of the Rogundan patrol.

Blake scouted around until he found a densely packed area with bushes and trees. Looking up, he could see many vantage points, with the benefit of the trees as cover, to break the line of sight. He grappled up to a branch on a massive tree. "Okay, stay hidden, and get your assault drone going."

Ada pulled out her assault drone and connected to it with tendrils in her finger. After a moment, it launched. "You should be able to see a view from its perspective now."

"I see it," said Blake. He pulled out his dual energy blades while activating his chameleon shield. Although he wanted to use his striker, he knew that it would take too long to go through the Rogundans' kinetic shielding. His FHP-10, while lethal and silent, could go through kinetic shielding, but with its limited shots, it was his last resort. He would rather have it available for an emergency than expend it when a blade could be used.

"The assault drone has weakened one of the Rogundans' shielding, and it has drawn the others to its location. They are following," said Ada.

"Time to kill," said Blake. He watched as the Rogundans approached. When they had gone past, he jumped down and landed with both blades going through the trailing Rogundan's head. Blake moved to another spot as the other Rogundans turned around and headed back.

Three Rogundans approached the dead body.

Blake burst forward and decapitated one. He caught the body and faced it toward the other Rogundans.

They opened fire on Blake.

Blake charged forward and when he was near the left Rogundan, he shoved the dead body ahead.

The left Rogundan fell back with the dead body on him.

Blake took fire as he leaped toward the right Rogundan and plunged both blades into its chest. He then jumped and landed on the left Rogundan, who was trying to get back up. With one quick swipe, the Rogundan was decapitated. Blake took a moment to catch his breath. A shot hit him, knocking him off the bodies. He focused as he rolled to the side. Another shot and his kinetic shielding would be gone. He crept to a nearby tree and paused. "Ada, you there?"

"One moment," said Ada.

Blake watched as the two red dots on the overhead map faded.

"I have disabled the two that were coming toward you."

Blake laughed. "You did?" He stepped out and headed over to where Ada was. When he got there, he noticed that one Rogundan looked like it was full of holes, while the other was missing a part of its face. "Whoa. What'd you do?"

"I used my FLP-40 to remove one of their shields, and then them. The other I punched."

Blake drew his head back. "I knew you were strong, but you punched half his face off."

"Yes, I did," said Ada with a smile. "They were coming in fast, and I decided to surprise them."

"Well, that worked great."

She tilted her head. "The second patrol is coming."

He nodded. "Let's get to their ship. Then we can do our thing and double back for these guys."

"Okay."

After two and a half hours, they arrived at the outskirts of the marker. Blake surveyed the views from Ada's drone. The Rogundan heavy corvette had flattened several trees where it landed. Outside it were three Rogundans milling around. Blake lowered his helmet and sniffed the air. "That presence I felt earlier. It's here too. Multiple this time."

"Where?" asked Ada.

"Near the ship, I think."

"It does not seem coincidental that they are here," said Ada. "I am also not detecting any perimeter defenses."

Blake nodded and raised his helmet. "Presence or no presence, that ship is going down, but not before we have time to search through it." He pulled out his FHP-10. "Get your FHP-10 out. We're going to hit those three outside and then rush the ship. Once inside, we can take whatever we run into, and then you can hack into their systems."

Ada nodded as she pulled out her FHP-10 and took aim at a Rogundan.

Blake sighted another one. "Go!"

Ada and Blake fired, hitting two of the three Rogundans. The two Rogundans that were hit fell to the ground.

Ada swung her arm and aimed at the third, who had ducked down and was running toward the ship. She fired, hitting it squarely in the back of the head.

"I love your autoaim," said Blake.

Ada smiled.

"I'll go first," said Blake. He pulled out his blades and activated his chameleon shield. "Come when I say it's clear."

Ada nodded.

Blake crept as close as he could to the ship and then broke into a run toward the ramp of the open doorway. He jumped back when Commander Mozrah emerged, flanked by two Rogundans with heavy weapons pointed forward.

"Blake Brown . . . we've been waiting for you," said Mozrah. "And yes . . . we can see through your shield. Disable it."

Blake narrowed his eyes. Mozrah was giving off the same vibe as Delkis, but the other Rogundans were not. They probably did not know that Mozrah had something in him. Blake peered back. He saw that Ada was coming forward surrounded by four Rogundans, all pointing weapons at her. He sighed as he turned off his chameleon shielding.

"I did not plan on losing these three, and I'm sure you ran into one of our patrols, which means it's probably gone," said Mozrah. He raised a claw and clacked it. "But I have captured you. I guess I won't need to . . . *bug* . . . you about it."

"It sounds a lot better when I say it," said Blake.

Mozrah stared at Blake for a moment and then gestured forward. "Once the other patrols are back, your ship destroyed, your crew captured . . . with maybe one missing for a snack, then we'll head out."

Ada stood next to Blake. "I did not detect them."

"Of course you didn't," said Mozrah. "You think Blake is the only one with chameleon shielding?"

The Rogundans clicked and clacked and made a deep fizzling sound.

Mozrah's antenna flailed around. "Subdue them."

The Rogundans bathed Blake and Ada in stun beams.

Blake tried to resist, but it was too much. As he fell to the ground, his last sight was the boots of the Rogundans coming toward him.

////////////

Sarah sighed as she looked over her workstation console in the command center. It had been about an hour since the others had left. The Rogundan missile had done much more damage than she had originally thought. Thankfully, the *Exceltion* was much tougher than it looked. The missile had left a crater near the engine room, and Luke was busy repairing it. Kane was working on the technical systems, which were experiencing some issues. Seth was across from her and looked like he was taking a nap. Her job was easy relative to Luke's and Kane's, she just had to monitor everything inside and out.

Beep! Beep!

She swallowed hard as she gazed at her console. That was the proximity detector. Although one of the drone launchers was acting up, the other one was working, and she had launched a drone to provide aerial reconnaissance of the area. The interface showed six red dots approaching the ship from the left. Another six a bit farther out were coming from the right. Directly north of them and a bit away were another six red dots. She glanced over at Seth. "We got incoming!"

Seth sat up in his chair. "How many?"

"Eighteen, the closest six approaching from our left side. They'll be here in about ten minutes or so at their current pace."

"Oh, shit," said Seth. He ran his hand over his chin as he studied his console interface. "Damn. We're gonna have to fight those fuckers. I was really hoping Blake and the others woulda wasted them."

"Maybe they got some at the ships," said Sarah. "Mozrah's Rogundan ship was large. It probably had about thirty or forty mercs on it."

Seth sighed. "Yeah." He tapped at his console. "Kane, Luke, come to the command center."

They both acknowledged Seth over the comms.

When they arrived a few minutes later, Seth tossed a hand out. "We got incoming Rogundan patrols, and it looks like we're going to be fighting. Luke, how are the repairs coming?"

"Slow," said Luke. "That damn missile hit one of our fusion reactor containment areas, which automatically stops when damage is detected. The failover to the other reactor didn't go through due to the damage. I can fix it . . . but it's gonna take longer than what I told you before. Not only that, one of our power reserves was hit, and it's draining fast. I need to get the backup offline reserve up and running. I don't know how much longer we have on our current backup reserve, but I wouldn't guess long. It'd be a lot easier to repair without being attacked."

Seth sighed. "I know. Kane, what'd you find?"

Kane nodded. "I did my assessment. Critical systems are up, but the power distribution system is going wild. If Luke can hook up that backup offline reserve, we should have full power again, at least enough to get the fusion reactors going."

"Huh," said Seth. He glanced at Luke. "How long would it take to get the backup offline reserve up?

"Probably a few hours."

"Great. We don't have that time right now," said Seth.

"I should have focused on that instead of trying to repair the immediate damage," said Luke.

Seth shrugged. "I think Blake thought we would have the other ships out before then." He licked his lips. "I guess not. I hope they're doing okay out there."

Sarah's breathing intensified. "So . . . are we going to fight those patrols then? We could direct what remaining power we have to a drone launcher and have it hunt them out."

"I like that idea," said Kane.

Luke shook his head. "That won't work long-range. This atmosphere is hostile to communication. I'm surprised that you were able to stay in communication with the drone we launched earlier, although I'm guessing it's having difficulty if we're just now seeing the Rogundans."

"Well, short-range they could work, but I see your point. We could use the defense robots, although I've never given them a full run before," said Kane.

Sarah gulped. "Okay, so we got defense robots and can use drones if the Rogundans are closer. I guess Luke can guard Kane while he's in the weapons control center. We have four entry points. The platform, which is raised at the moment so that should be okay, and then we have docking hatchways on both sides of the ship and also one near the front. If they're going to come in, it'll be through the hatchways. Even then, they'll need to jump up to it since they sit about fifteen feet off the ground."

Luke sighed. "They're gonna blow the doors up and then grapple in, aren't they?"

Sarah glanced at Seth. "I don't know, but if they do, they'll get a face full of weapons fire."

"Yeah, but then we need to cover all those hatchways, and fight solo against a group. We do have one advantage, though," said Seth. "The patrols are spread out, so they won't come in one big group. Their patterns also show they don't know we're here, at least until they come within a certain radius. That means we're dealing with six at a time. I'd almost say . . . let's lower the docking platform. It'll draw the closest group to one point instead of dealing with potentially three at once, and then we can fight them there with cover. If it gets too hot, then we'll raise it and prepare to fight them on the ship. At least we can weaken them that way. Kane can use his drones, we got the defense robots, and between Sarah and I, we can beat them."

Sarah smiled. "Risky but . . . I think that'll work."

"Good," said Seth. "Let's get suited up. Kane, head to the weapons control center, and then get some defense robots to the docking platform. Keep some on the ship just in case." He raised a finger. "Oh, and when you're controlling the drones, try not to hit us."

"I got you, S-man. We have six robots, so I can send three down to help," said Kane. He grinned big. "Don't worry about the drones, although they might zap you if you're underperforming."

Everyone shared a laugh.

"All right," said Seth as he stood. He looked around. "Let's roll."

Sarah's heartbeat shot up as she went to her living quarter to get her armor. This was the second firefight she would be in, and she was intent on making sure she did better this time. After donning her armor and grabbing her pistols and striker, she met Seth on the docking platform. She saw the three defense robots that Kane was controlling. They looked like stick figures with weapons. As long as they could fire was all that mattered to her.

"You ready for this?" asked Seth as the docking platform lowered.

"Yep," said Sarah, raising her head a bit. She wanted to prove that she could handle herself, and this was a good opportunity.

The docking platform stopped as it hit the ground.

Seth, Sarah, and the defense robots took up positions behind shipping containers they had moved to serve as cover. A drone launched and was immediately shot down.

Sarah focused on the spotty overview of the incoming dots. She jerked her head back as weapons fire erupted near her.

"They're here!" said Seth. He tossed a shrapnel grenade over the cover.

As the grenade flew toward the massing Rogundans, they shot it in the air before it hit them, causing it to explode.

"Shit!" said Seth, diving to the ground.

Another drone launched and shot at the Rogundans.

They retaliated by taking down the drone, then firing on the drone launcher.

"Damn it, they messed up the drone launcher port," said Kane over comms.

"We'll do without!" said Seth.

"They're moving in!" said Sarah. She helped Seth back up.

"Focus fire on the one I'm firing at," said Kane over comms.

The defense robots moved out of cover and began to rain metal down on the incoming Rogundans.

Seth and Sarah peeked out of their respective sides.

Sarah used her striker and focused on the Rogundan whose kinetic shielding was lighting up. With sustained fire, the shielding broke, and the Rogundan went down. She saw that another one went down as Seth and the robots hit it. Her heart jumped when two defense robots went down in a hail of gunfire.

The four remaining Rogundans charged and made it to the shipping containers.

One of them burst forward and knocked away the remaining defense robot's weapon, then smashed the robot.

Seth and Sarah lit the Rogundan up, shredding the shielding and then the Rogundan.

The other three Rogundans went around the shipping container on Seth's side.

Seth fell to the ground and shot up at an angle, weakening one of the Rogundan's shields.

Sarah followed up and fired, finishing off the shield and then the Rogundan's head.

Seth scooted back toward Sarah.

The two remaining Rogundans rushed Sarah and Seth.

Sarah grimaced. It was apparent the Rogundans were trying to capture them alive; otherwise, in their current position, they could have killed her and Seth.

Seth fired point-blank at the left Rogundan, weakening its kinetic shielding.

The Rogundan charged Seth, and together they went tumbling off the docking platform.

The other Rogundan charged forward and grabbed Sarah. It slammed her face-first toward the shipping container. She dropped her striker and extended her hands above her and at an angle and slapped the container while turning her head when she came in contact with the container. The thought that the Rogundan might be interested in her made her eyes flare. She spun to the left, using her left arm to knock away the Rogundan's arm. With a swift kick to its leg, she sent it stumbling back. She rolled, picked up her striker, and opened fire.

The Rogundan's shielding flickered, then dissipated.

Sarah continued firing, turning the Rogundan's head into mush. She turned to see that Seth was getting beat on. Given the weight discrepancy between the Rogundan and Seth, she knew he was in trouble. Hopefully his reinforced suit was holding up. Her adrenaline surged as she hustled over and used her momentum to kick the Rogundan off Seth. She winced as pain shot across her foot. With determination, she opened fire on the Rogundan now that it was clear of Seth.

Seth joined in on the firing, and together, they shredded the Rogundan. His breathing staggered as he lay looking up. "Maybe . . . maybe we should have let them come on board and fought there."

"We survived," said Sarah. "You all right?"

"I think so. Those things are heavy. If we didn't have these suits . . . no way would I be alive right now. I was still recovering from the last ass blasting we got," said Seth. He sighed. "If we survive this, I'll need more recovery time. Just great."

She helped Seth get up and then assisted him back onto the docking platform.

The docking platform began to raise.

Seth sat on the ground with his back against one of the containers. He eyed Sarah. "You did good. Think about it. We just took down *six* . . . let me say that again . . . *six* Rogundan mercs."

They lowered their helmets when the platform was raised.

"Yeah, but we lost three robots and two drones, and also our drone launcher. And we still have twelve more incoming," said Sarah, grimacing.

Seth caught his breath. "One step at a time. Worst case scenario . . . we blow the ship."

"Then let's not die before that time," said Sarah.

Seth took a moment to stand and then grinned at Sarah. "If it comes to that, then I'll be damn proud to do it with you."

Sarah exhaled as she smiled. Despite the situation about to get worse, she could see the resiliency in Seth. Her heartbeat was racing, but she was ecstatic that she and Seth had a good bond. Being a critical part of a team made her feel more alive. The days of an operations officer on the *Arcturus* seemed so far away.

Her mind turned toward the other two Rogundan patrols coming in. If just one was this much effort, she figured two more would take all they had. They were down to three defense robots, and fighting on board would damage the ship more. She briefly remembered Blake saying that there might be fighting on the ship. He turned out to be a soothsayer. She hoped he and Ada were doing okay, and Zane and Kal, for that matter. With a sigh, Sarah followed Seth to the command center.

THIRTEEN

lake harrumphed as he sat on an uncomfortable bench on Commander Mozrah's ship. The room he and Ada were in was small, and he got the feeling that the Rogundans that peeked in from time to time wanted nothing more than to come in and beat them. That would be normal for prisoners taken by a Rogundan crew, but Mozrah was different. Blake wondered where and when Mozrah had been converted. Blake's vampiric senses picked up the sound of weapons fire.

"There's a commotion outside," said Ada.

Blake focused. "I know that sound. It's unique, and belongs to the Covendrin."

"Their presence here would be unusual."

"I agree," said Blake.

After ten minutes, the gunfire ended.

Blake narrowed his eyes as footsteps approached the room. The door slid open, revealing a Covendrin merc. The merc had on the signature gold Covendrin armor with a red band on the right arm, and his helmet was lowered. A silver stripe on his left arm indicated this was an elite merc, a rank given only to a select few within the Covendrin merc society. The helmet down was a sign of trust, since Covendrin rarely lowered their helmet for anyone.

The Covendrin were a humanoid race that stood on average about seven feet tall. They had silver skin with red eyes and possessed superior strength and speed relative to a human. They came from an ice world and were much more resilient than a human.

Blake had always wanted to ask about the scaly back part of the head. They had no hair there, and it was more like a shell.

The merc grinned. "Yuldaris, Covendrin commander of the Sixty-Seventh."

"I'm . . . not sure what's going on here," said Blake.

"Oh, you know. Just intelligence gathering."

"This is a pretty *specific* place to be doing that."

Yuldaris laughed. "I guess it is."

"You wouldn't mind taking these cuffs off, would you?"

"I can, but I want you to listen to what I have to say first."

Blake glanced at Ada, then back at Yuldaris. "All right, it's not like we're going anywhere."

"Good. I'll make this quick. A unit in the Sixty-Seventh went missing. Since they were my responsibility, I searched for them. When I found them, their heads were on spikes, and they were killed by someone called Delkis. As I began to look for him, I discovered that your . . . *unit* . . . had already captured him and turned him over to the Fredorians."

Blake nodded. "We did."

"I tried to find out more about Delkis through the information broker, but . . . I was denied."

Blake drew his head back.

"Exactly. The broker refusing to sell information? How rare is that? The broker doesn't like me for some reason," said Yuldaris.

"That's pretty damn rare. Usually they'll say they couldn't find anything, but to refuse . . . that's odd."

Yuldaris smiled. "With that avenue closed, I decided to follow the only person, well, unit, that did have success . . . which was yours. We used the sun to provide cover for our stealth engines."

"And you ended up here."

"We saw the Rogundan ships land. I had my mercs handle two patrols that were on the way to your ship, and sent some to the other decoy sensor to help out, just in case. Nice play, by the way. I figured you were coming here, so I took a few units and waited, and here we are."

"You coulda just sent me a communication. I would have talked to you, and I have a good relationship with the Covendrin, well, last I checked," said Blake.

"I had to make sure . . . you were you."

Blake licked his fangs. "I am . . ."

"I'm aware of the black slime that was in Delkis. We've had some Covendrin fall to this . . . whatever it is. Unfortunately

A D A I R   H A R T

for the slime, we have detectors for things like that," said Yuldaris. He tilted his wrist toward Blake. It showed a mostly green segmented circle with two blue segments. "That's not red, so you live. It does have two blue ones . . . but that's because you're a Daedrould."

"So you've run into it before?"

Yuldaris grimaced. "Yes . . . but whatever this slime is, it's rare. The blue slime, though . . . is much more prevalent. These slimes discovered that Covendrin are not good hosts. Those that were infected became ill, and we purged those we could not drive the slime out of. Not that it mattered. In the end, the infected died due to our physiology."

"Makes sense," said Blake. "So you were following us . . ."

"Yes. We figured you were going to Hadrassus, so what better way to gain entry?"

"How'd you figure that?"

"We were tipped off, by an informant. The how is not important."

Blake chuckled. "You got it all figured out." He wondered if Joshua was the informant.

Yuldaris raised a finger. "Not completely. I want to join your crew when you go to Hadrassus. If the Fredorians are involved in some type of new biological weapon . . . I want to know."

"I don't think they'll like a Covendrin merc company just waltzing in."

"I meant only I go with you. My units will stay out of range and come if needed."

Blake thought about the options. He had heard the name Yuldaris before when trying to find information on the Kreagan Lawnet about Fredoria becoming a full trade partner twenty years earlier. Yuldaris was at the bombed facility where the Arkaron, a Kreagan holy artifact, was assembled. There were a lot of rumors about his involvement there, but his name was cleared. When Blake had tried to pull up the contract, it had been deleted. Still, Yuldaris's name carried weight in the Covendrin, and having him owe a favor might come in handy. There was the aspect of the secrecy of the mission, but it was obvious that the Covendrin knew of the black slime.

"Thinking hard?" asked Yuldaris.

Blake grinned, baring his fangs. "All right. You can come with us. Let's consider this . . . a favor."

Yuldaris nodded. "A favor it will be." He stepped into the room and took off the handcuffs. "So what now?"

"Ada is going to hack into the ship's systems and see what we can find. Mozrah . . . has the sign of the black slime in him."

Yuldaris grinned. "Had."

Blake dipped his head. "It left him?"

"Let's just say . . . the slime doesn't like fire, well, heat, in general, and apparently neither does the host."

Blake nodded. "I can't say I'm broken up about either loss. All right. Once we have the information, we were going to blow the ship."

"I figured. We can fly back to your ship in my shuttle when you're ready."

Blake raised his helmet and then extended his hand. "Sounds good. I guess then this is a temporary welcome to the Fredorian Presidential Guard, Earthborn Unit."

Yuldaris smiled. "Or a temporary welcome to the Sixty-Seventh."

Blake shook his head, then headed back to the command center with Yuldaris.

////////

Seth studied his workstation console. It had been about four hours, but his eyes were glued to his screen. The other red dots that had been farther away had gone off in a different direction, but were circling back. His heartbeat ramped up when six more dots appeared behind the original six dots to the north. On the right, there was an additional four. He closed his eyes for a moment and then turned toward Sarah and Luke. "You seeing it too?"

"Yep. Looks like we now got twelve to the north and ten on the right," said Sarah. "Should we . . . take off maybe?"

"And leave Blake and the others here? No way," said Seth.

Luke tossed a hand out. "We could always come back for them. With the ship taken, and us dead, I don't think we'd help the situation."

Seth sighed.

"Well, guess we're down to six to the north, and four on the right," said Luke.

Seth spun around and checked his console. He was able to verify Luke's observation. "What the hell . . ."

"They should be coming within visual range," said Sarah. She flicked her fingers across her console.

The command center wraparound screen lit up showing a 360-degree view.

The group hustled over to the left side.

Sarah drew her head back. "It looks like . . . Covendrin mercs, and they're carrying Zane and Kal on stretchers."

Seth's stomach dropped. Zane and Kal were motionless, but the ship's sensors indicated they were just unconscious. Covendrin mercs always made Seth's skin crawl. Professional killers from a society that encouraged it. They were even more ruthless than the Rogundans, and the Covendrin presence seemed out of place.

The Covendrin mercs paused outside the ship and then lowered Zane and Kal to the ground.

"They're trying to contact us," said Sarah. She swallowed hard. "Do we respond?"

"May as well," said Seth. He took his seat and then tapped at his console. "This is Seth Williams. Who are you?"

"I am Zurinch, Covendrin First Unit leader of the Sixty-Seventh. On order of Yuldaris, our commander, we assisted Zane and Kal. Unfortunately, a ship blew up on them."

"A ship . . . blew up on them?" asked Seth.

"Yes," said Zurinch. After a pause, he said, "You should be receiving a video feed of our arrival there."

Seth focused on a window that popped up on the wraparound screen. He could see the video had Luke's and Sarah's full attention as well.

The video began playing.

The Covendrin mercs walked up to the burned ship. Zane was just outside the ship, and Kal looked like he had been thrown much farther away. The mercs moved into action, dragging Zane away from the ship as two other mercs went to get Kal. Zane and Kal were loaded onto hovering slabs, and then the video ended.

Seth tapped at his console. "That coulda been doctored . . ."

"You can get them or not. Our orders were to assist them if they need help and, if they were incapacitated, to bring them to the *Exceltion*. We stabilized them for now," said Zurinch. "You can talk to Blake and Ada when they return with Yuldaris if you want."

"Okay . . . well . . . where are the Rogundans?"

"Dead, of course. They faced a Covendrin unit," said Zurinch, raising his head a bit.

"Of course, what was I thinking," said Seth, grinning at Sarah and Luke. "We need a moment to discuss among ourselves."

"Take all the time you need. We'll set up in case more Rogundans come."

Seth watched as Zurinch barked orders and pointed around. The mercs moved into positions facing away from the *Exceltion*.

"So . . . we're getting Zane and Kal, right?" asked Sarah.

"Yeah. I was just thinking how we're gonna do that."

Doc's head appeared on the wraparound screen. "Perhaps I can be of assistance. I can get them. If my body is destroyed, I can make a new one."

"That could work. We'll need to cover the docking platform, just in case they try to sneak on board."

"A safety precaution is always advisable. You may or may not know, but I am quite capable of defending myself in my robot form if need be."

"Really?" asked Luke.

"Of course. My wireframe can carry weapons and conceal them due to my hologram."

"Interesting," said Seth. "All right, let's do that." He pressed a button on his console. "Kane, you get all that?"

"Yep. I'll have the three remaining defense robots go with him," said Kane over the comms.

Seth nodded. "All right. Doc and Kane, get Zane and Kal. Luke and Sarah, follow me and prepare for a fight if necessary."

Luke and Sarah acknowledged Seth.

After five minutes, Seth, Sarah, and Luke were in the cargo bay just outside the docking platform, with weapons drawn. Doc was in his stick robot and hologram form, while three defense robots stood next to him. Seth nodded at Doc. "You ready?"

"Yes."

Doc and the robots moved onto the docking platform.

Seth interacted with the docking platform console.

The platform lowered, and Doc and the robots headed out to the slabs.

Seth licked his lips. "Man, I hate this nervous shit."

"Relax," said Luke. "Worst case, we raise the platform and take down a merc or two if they try to board."

Seth shook his head. "I don't think you've ever fought a Covendrin merc. I fought a rogue one, and let me tell you . . . they're not to be fucked with."

Luke pointed at several panels on the walls. "We should really think about adding wall turrets that can pop out. While they won't take down extremely heavy armor, they'll absolutely shred kinetic shielding."

"We coulda used that earlier. Let's put that on the list of modifications to add," said Seth.

"Great idea," said Sarah, smiling at Luke.

They focused on Doc and the defense robots returning with the slabs. The docking platform raised after they were all on it.

"Their vital signs are good," said Doc. "I gave them something to help speed their recovery. A few hours in my med bay and I'll have them repaired."

"Repaired?" asked Luke, furrowing his eyebrows. "They aren't machines."

Doc paused. "They are organic machines. You, as an organic, repair inorganic machines. I, as an inorganic, repair organic machines."

Luke laughed. "I never really thought of it that way, but I see your point."

Doc nodded and headed off.

Seth sighed. "Well, I guess we wait until Blake, Ada, and Yuldaris come back."

Thirty minutes later in the command center, Sarah perked up. "Looks like we got incoming from the north."

Seth's hands flew over his console. He studied the small shuttle that was inbound.

"I can't get a visual yet," said Sarah.

"Seth, Sarah, can you read me?" asked Blake over comms.

Seth relaxed in his chair as he exhaled. "Yep. What's going on?"

"The Covendrin helped us out. Shit was going bad . . . until they showed up. What's the status on Zane and Kal?"

"They had a ship blow up on them. They're unconscious, but being treated by Doc now," said Seth.

"Oh . . . all right. Well, we'll be at the *Exceltion* shortly. Yuldaris will be traveling with us, and his mercs will be on standby in case they're needed."

"What?"

"I'll go over it in more detail when I get back. For now, the Covendrin are our friends, and you can treat them as such."

"Uhh . . . okay."

Sarah wrinkled her eyebrows. "We're working with the Covendrin now?"

"Yep," said Blake. "I've worked with them in the past, although not this particular company, but this one is well-known."

"Okay. Anything special we need to do?"

"Yeah, lower the docking platform so we can board when this shuttle lands."

Sarah laughed. "I think I can do that."

Seth watched via a window on the wraparound screen as the shuttle landed outside the *Exceltion*. Blake, Ada, and Yuldaris departed from the shuttle along with several mercs.

Yuldaris went to talk with Zurinch, while Blake and Ada headed to the docking platform. Seth glanced at Sarah. "Let's go see what all this is about."

When they arrived at the docking platform, Doc was scanning Blake and Ada.

"We're okay, Doc. Seriously," said Blake.

Ada nodded. "Doc, I have already performed internal scans and sent them to you."

"Okay," said Doc. His holographic form hustled out of the room.

Seth grinned as he slapped hands with Blake. "I see we're making new friends."

"Well, it was fortunate we did. We got captured, but Yuldaris handled it. His mercs also handled the other Rogundan patrols and, from what I've heard, helped Zane and Kal get here," said Blake.

"Yeah," said Seth. "I guess we'll learn more tomorrow in a briefing?"

"Count on it," said Blake.

Sarah wrinkled her eyebrows. "How'd you get captured?"

Ada raised her head a bit. "There were chameleon-shielded Rogundans, and they set up an ambush, one that cost three of their own members."

"Oh," said Sarah. "If Yuldaris wouldn't have come along, would you still be there?"

Blake shrugged. "Maybe. I woulda killed them all eventually, but that would probably take too long. Yuldaris's approach was more efficient."

Seth crooked a thumb at Sarah. "She was a fighting machine when we took on a patrol."

"I guess I was," said Sarah, smiling at Blake. "I used that face-to-the-wall technique you showed me. It worked great."

Blake wagged a finger. "See, I wasn't bullshitting you."

"I never thought you were."

"Still, that's impressive that you and Seth handled six Rogundans. It gives me hope."

Seth laughed. "We also had three defense robots that we'll need to replicate."

"I'm just glad you're safe," said Blake. He glanced around at everyone. "All right, it's been a day. We'll convene tomorrow. I'll send out a communication when to meet. I still need to talk with Yuldaris later tonight and then stop in on Zane and Kal."

Seth nodded as he watched everyone leave. His heart was still racing a bit from the fight earlier, and with the Covendrin around, his skin crawled. The fact that Zane and Kal could have been munched on by some random creature did not escape Seth's thoughts. He grimaced as he touched his side. It was still sore from Lono Hara, and tangling with the Rogundans did not help it much. No matter what he did, he seemed to end up on the wrong side of an ass beating, but at least this time he was able to fight back and win, although at the cost of further injuring himself. He chuckled as he headed to the med bay.

FOURTEEN

Blake eased back into his office chair as he flipped a blood vial in his hands. It was about 9:00 p.m., and he was going over the events of the day. He cursed himself for being captured, and he knew, had he been alone, he woulda killed every Rogundan there. After Freelancing with Seth for two years, he had become accustomed to thinking about who was around him. Had he left to kill the Rogundans, Ada, without chameleon shielding, would have been gunned down. He took a sip from his blood vial. As warm blood oozed down his throat, he closed his eyes and savored the pulsing sensations rippling through him.

Knock! Knock!

His eyes popped open.

Yuldaris poked his head in and narrowed his eyes as he studied Blake.

"Come in," said Blake.

"You wanted to see me?"

"Yeah. I know you're getting settled in, but I wanted to clear some things between us first," said Blake. He motioned at a seat.

Yuldaris sat. "By all means."

"All right. First topic. This is my crew, and I command it."

"Of course. I'm only along as an observer, but one that can fight if need be."

Blake nodded. "Good. I'll introduce you to the rest of the crew tomorrow, but in the meantime, I've forwarded you their basic information."

"No need. I have information on them already."

Blake raised his eyebrows. "Oh . . ."

"There's no cause for concern. If I was to be traveling with this group, I needed to know what to expect. Finding information, as you know, is not difficult if you know where to look."

"Ain't that the truth." Blake exhaled from his nose. "That's settled. Second topic. I know you keep information close to your chest, but if we're going to be working together, we'll be sharing it. I'm willing to make the first gesture by giving you access to information on what we know of the black slime."

"And I'll reciprocate," said Yuldaris. He chuckled. "I understand your hesitation, but I wish to know more about this slime as much as you do. I'm just glad it was you that got Delkis."

"High praise from a Covendrin merc."

Yuldaris shrugged. "You're well-known, and have been . . . neutral . . . with the Covendrin, which is far more than what most can say."

"I've worked with a few . . . and had to kill a few. I guess it all balances out," said Blake.

"It does, and we accept that."

Blake grinned, baring his fangs. "Your culture intrigues me. Ruthless, yet professional. You'd make great vampires."

Yuldaris drew his head back.

"Don't worry. Like the slime, Covendrin blood doesn't sit well with me."

"That's . . . good to hear," said Yuldaris.

Blake chuckled. "Okay, third topic, and this one is more . . . personal."

"All right."

"When you were at the bombed facility on old Kreagus, you were employed by Seeros."

"That's right."

"Every record I've looked up on that situation has been . . . altered, and your involvement is just a high-level statement that you were involved but had no wrongdoing," said Blake.

"That's what it says."

Blake leaned forward in his chair. "Seeros was quite powerful, and with the Covendrin mercs backing him, he still died. I've heard he was strapped to a slab when he was recovered. Well, what was left of him."

Yuldaris sighed. "Yes, he was."

"You . . . not planning on doing that to me, are you?"

"Of course not. That situation . . . was unique. There were," said Yuldaris, grimacing, "powers at play that should . . . *never* exist."

Blake wrinkled his eyebrows. It was the first time he had ever seen a Covendrin exhibit what looked like fear. "Never exist?"

"I dare not say the name, lest it come back and find me. I was given a second chance, and I should have died that day," said Yuldaris. His eyes dulled. "Nothing should have that power."

"So Seeros and you ran into something more powerful, and Seeros paid the price, but you were left alive. I also read that Andia Kiggs and Rakar Ho Jador were there, but like your statement, it's all high level."

"Yes . . . they were there. They know the situation as I do."

Blake eased back into his chair and took a swig from his blood vial. "Whatever that power was that should not exist, it must be very powerful to not only cover up the situation, but keep you from saying its name."

Yuldaris eyed Blake. "Andia and Rakar probably haven't told you its name either."

"You're right," said Blake. "I know of several . . . powers . . . that fit that description, but . . . I was just curious."

"I don't normally speak of the event but . . . I offer it as sign of trust."

"And it's appreciated," said Blake. He gestured his hand out in an arc. "If you need or want to discuss anything with me, I'm always available."

Yuldaris nodded "Anything else?"

"Yeah . . . about those detection devices you got. How accurate are they?"

"They can detect the presence of a slime, but not the color. It's not one hundred percent, but close enough."

Blake nodded. "My assault team could use any spare ones you got."

"It will be done."

"Excellent. I sent out a communication that we'll have a meeting at 11:00 a.m. Earth time. You can check it out on the console in your room, and if you can bring those detectors, even better."

Yuldaris stood. "Very well."

Blake jumped up and extended a hand. "This is going to be interesting."

"I suspect it will," said Yuldaris, shaking Blake's hand. He nodded and then exited the room.

Blake sat back down and went over the discussion in his head. As he began to chew on Yuldaris's words, he noticed Ada peek her head in.

"I waited until you were free. Is this a good time?"

Blake's eyes widened "For my favorite android? Anytime is a good time."

Ada tilted her head as she took a seat. "I don't think anytime is always a good time."

Blake laughed. "Always practical. What's on your neural matrix?"

"I was analyzing our performance at Mozrah's ship. Every simulation I ran showed that the situation would have been improved if I had not been there. The decisions made would have ended up with the Rogundans dead, information retrieved, and their ship destroyed."

Blake shook his head. "And how would I have hacked the Rogundan ship?"

"You could have pulled the data storage for later analysis."

"It doesn't work that way. You're my teammate, and I'm not going to needlessly endanger you for my sake."

Ada's eyes lit up. "Thank you."

"I'll admit, I probably could have wasted all of them with some guerrilla tactics, but I much prefer having you around."

"I see. I calculated that I could have stopped three of them before . . ."

"Before dying," said Blake, eying Ada. "That bothers you, doesn't it?"

Ada grinned. "I've been given a new opportunity, and I'm enjoying it. I realized it could have ended today."

"That's mortality for you," said Blake.

"I have heard you don't fear death."

Blake shrugged. "I'm different. From what my master told me, when someone of my ancient vampire strain dies, we exist in another reality as something different. Make no mistake . . . I'm in no hurry to get there. I like it here."

"Because there's blood and women."

"Those are nice, but more importantly, friends."

Ada smiled.

Blake caught her studying the blood vial. He shook it in front of him. "This seems to interest you."

"I was curious as to how the blood bond has such an impact."

"Think of it as a booster."

"I do, but I saw Sarah on it when she was conscious. She mentioned a burning desire to be with you. I think it was of a sexual nature."

Blake leaned forward. "Oh, she did, did she?"

"Yes. I did not understand why she didn't go to you at that time."

"Well . . . it works both ways, and it was given without consent. It's best not to open that box . . . for now."

"I understand. You don't wish to complicate things."

He pointed a finger at her. "You got it, sister."

Ada tilted her head.

Blake laughed. "Sister in a slang context."

"I see. I will add it to my database. Seth is helping me with it, although there are some unusual terms that have meanings different from what I would expect them to be."

"Like what?"

"Getting down. It does not mean to lower oneself; it means to be in an excited state and express it."

Blake chuckled. "Oh, Ada, how I love talking to you. You make things so much more interesting."

"I try," she said as she stood. "I'll let you get back to drinking your blood, and thank you for taking the time to speak with me."

"Anytime."

"Is a good time," said Ada with a smile as she headed out.

Blake watched Ada leave. The thought did cross his mind that she could have been killed earlier. He still needed to visit Zane and Kal, and the briefing still needed to be prepped for. With a sigh, he leaned his head back and began to think about what had to be done.

//////////

Kal's first sensation after waking up in the med bay was his head throbbing. It took him a moment to gather his senses, and opening his eyes wide into the bright lights was not something he had intended to do. He snapped them shut while grimacing and then slowly opened them, letting them adjust. He took some deep breaths while the rest of his body alerted him that it was sore.

Once his eyes were fully open, he took in the surroundings. Doc was standing off to his left, and to his right, Zane was waking up too. Sounds began to make sense, and Kal could smell again.

"I'm glad to see you're awake now," said Doc.

"Doc . . . how long we been out?" asked Zane as he leaned on his side to face Kal and Doc.

"Approximately five hours. It is now 10:10 p.m. Earth time."

Kal sighed. "Damn, man. We really took a hit. All I remember is that console bleeping at us, then being tossed back from the ship exploding."

"You *were* tossed, and although the explosion would account for some of it, I suspect Zane tossed you."

Kal glanced at Zane.

"Yeah . . . I remember something like that. Kal had grabbed me, and I slingshotted him out of there," said Zane.

"You put yourself at risk," said Doc. "If you were not as resilient, you would have died."

"You saved my life," said Kal.

Zane chuckled, then grimaced. "Let's not go getting all soft on me now."

Kal swallowed hard. Although he knew that he would die one day, and possibly sooner than most due to his line of work, it hit him how close it had been. "I owe you, man."

"You don't owe me shit."

"I do, man. You put me before yourself."

Zane shrugged.

Kal laughed. "You don't take compliments well."

Zane glanced at Doc. "So uhh . . . how exactly did we get here?"

"The Covendrin mercs picked you up," said Doc.

Zane and Kal both drew their heads back and then looked at each other.

"You being serious?" asked Kal.

Doc gestured at the holo area in the room, where a projection played showing the Covendrin mercs assessing, stabilizing, and carrying Zane and Kal away.

"Okay . . . that's kinda random," said Kal. "What were they doing there?"

Everyone's attention focused on the med bay entrance.

"I can answer that," said Blake, grinning and baring his fangs. "Before I do, how they doing, Doc?"

"They are healing well, and suffered a concussion. There was a lot of bruising and some skin issues, but they have been mitigated. They should be back to full strength tomorrow, once the microbots are done with them."

Blake nodded. "Sounds good. Now . . . ," he said, glancing at Zane and Kal, "how are you both feeling?"

"Like shit," said Zane.

"Same," said Kal.

"Well, at least you're awake, and by tomorrow, you both should be all healed up," said Blake.

"I guess," said Zane.

Kal gestured at Zane. "I know he probably wouldn't want me to say this . . . but he tossed me clear of the explosion."

"I know," said Blake. He raised his head a bit. "He put the team before himself."

Zane looked down. "Ahh, man, I wasn't trying to make a point."

Blake grinned. "Not at all. In the heat of the moment, your true nature reveals itself. That's the Zane I've come to know."

"I'm with you there, man," said Kal.

Zane sighed. "I ain't hugging you or nothing, man."

They all shared a laugh.

"Okay, now about these Covendrin . . . ," said Zane.

Blake nodded. "They've been tracking us for a while now. Apparently, those Covendrin mercs that Delkis killed were part of a Covendrin company commanded by Yuldaris. He tracked down Delkis, but we had already retrieved him."

"That's pretty impressive given that there are around twenty units of four to six members each in a Covendrin company. A unit disappears . . . and the commander comes gunning for you with the full fury of the company," said Zane. "That's dedication."

"Huh," said Kal. He wagged a finger. "So then they must have seen we landed here, and then stepped in when they saw the Rogundans were involved."

"Yep. They got you two, and when Ada and I were captured, they stepped in there. They also cleared out some patrols that were headed toward the *Exceltion*."

Zane narrowed his eyes. "Damn, making us look like amateurs."

"Well . . . they were observing remotely while undetected. It's a bit different when you don't know where your enemy is," said Blake. He raised a finger. "Yuldaris will be joining us at Hadrassus, so he'll be on board for this mission. Tomorrow is a briefing where we'll go over everything."

Kal drew his head back. "We got a Covendrin commander going with us?"

Blake nodded.

"That'll be interesting," said Zane. "I assume our previous personal encounters with the Covendrin were factored in?"

"Yeah, Yuldaris says he knows everyone's profiles and interactions. He would definitely be the right person to know, and he said it's not a concern."

Zane exhaled from his nose. "Seems . . . odd."

"I have reason to trust Yuldaris. He'll owe us a favor for this, and you never know when that might come in handy."

"You never want to be the one owing favors, that's for damn sure."

Blake grinned, baring his fangs. "All right, you two rest up. If you want to heal faster, I can bite you."

Kal laughed. "I'm good."

"Yeah, me too," said Zane. He made several back-and-forth slapping motions in the air. "No ass tapping tonight."

They all laughed.

"Okay, heal up," said Blake. He nodded and exited the room.

Kal shook his head as he glanced at Zane. "Some fucked-up shit going on."

"Yeah, but we'll ride through it."

Kal nodded. Although he was unsettled by the presence of Covendrin mercs, he trusted Blake to do what was right. Kal's own history with the Covendrin was murky at best, and he distinctly remembered killing a Covendrin merc on a justice-hunter contract that went bad.

He had also helped a unit that got in over its head when taking on the jungle world of Elixus. It was his sniper shot that decided whether or not the mercs lived or died. He had thought it was odd that they thanked him, and they told him he was neutral to them now. Apparently with the Covendrin, anything done for or against them is stored and a decision is reached that gives an overall rating. Thankfully, being neutral meant he was not being hunted. He could handle himself, he was sure, but long-term, against a whole society, they had numbers he did not.

FIFTEEN

Ada scanned the crew with her internal sensors as they sat in the briefing room. It was 11:00 a.m., and Yuldaris had joined them. Although she could see externally that everyone seemed calm, the faster heartbeats and heightened signs of anxiousness were present, except for Blake and Zane. They were steady and relaxed. She understood that Yuldaris's presence could be intimidating, given that he represented a force that took down the Rogundans. It intrigued her that despite the general feeling she had observed, the external displays were the opposite. Human behavior was confusing to her at times.

A silence filled the room.

Blake grinned and bared his fangs. "Good morning. I wanted to introduce Yuldaris, commander of the Covendrin Sixty-Seventh Company. They were responsible for helping out yesterday when shit hit the fan, and we're thankful for that. For the time being, he will be joining us while we go to Hadrassus." He glanced at Yuldaris. "He understands that I run this operation, and he is here as an observer."

Yuldaris nodded.

"Furthermore, any previous history any of you may have had with the Covendrin was already factored in. Anything you want to add to that, Yuldaris?"

"I do, actually," said Yuldaris, tossing a hand out. "As you may or may not know, we use a global point rating system. An individual's actions can either add or subtract from their score, and based on that, we determine how to approach the individual." He motioned at Zane. "You have the lowest score, but it is still in the neutral band. Everyone else is at the default score, which is true neutral, although Blake is in the favored band. This operation, assuming it succeeds, will add positively to everyone's score."

Zane laughed. "I'm the lowest. Go figure."

Yuldaris eyed Zane. "It's not an issue here. Earthborn start with a higher default score than true neutral."

"Why's that?" asked Sarah.

"As a group, Earthborn tend to be more honorable about their dealings. If a group conducts itself well over a period of time, they tend to get a higher default start score when we encounter new ones. Of course, individuals can always lose or gain points, but that's rare with Earthborn mercs. They are what they say are, usually. In addition to that, Earth will one day enter the Kreagan Star Empire. When it does, we will be friendly with them."

Sarah narrowed her eyes. "Are you friendly with Fredoria?"

"Not as a whole," said Yuldaris.

"Why does Earth get favorable treatment then?"

"Because they'll become a power broker. It's just a matter of time."

Luke tilted his head. "You really think so?"

Yuldaris grinned and pointed at Blake. "He's just one of what Earth calls Daedroulds. There are thousands on Earth, not to mention all the other powerful groups. Not only that, Earth is . . . *protected* . . . by many layers, and even the Kreagans give it an unusual amount of attention as of late. There are also . . . *things* . . . beyond what should be possible that the Covendrin are aware of. Earth is special, and we think we can work with Earth better than Fredoria."

"Oh," said Sarah, drawing her lips flat.

"It's not a knock on you as a Fredorian. You're here, which means you're far beyond what I'd call a typical Fredorian."

She smiled. "I guess so."

"Why do you do this rating system?" asked Ada.

"It's what makes the Covendrin efficient," said Yuldaris. "It's information, and it gives us an advantage. Your FDF has a similar system, except it's most likely hidden."

Ada glanced at Blake.

Blake grinned. "He's right, and the FDF version is nowhere near as complete as what the Covendrin have. Nonetheless, he'll be with us until we complete this mission. Now, we have shared information on the slimes, and the Covendrin have much more on it than we do." He gestured at Yuldaris.

Ada noted in her records that Yuldaris was a natural leader. She observed that the crew seemed to have relaxed some.

Yuldaris tapped at the table console.

A projection shot up from the center of the table, showing a grid with four cells, each containing different-colored slimes.

"These slimes, for lack of a better term, are all related, and the only ones we *know* of. There are probably others. When someone has one in them, we call it being slimed. You've run into Emrakus and Delkis, who were both black-slimed," said Yuldaris. He pointed at the black slime. "As far as we know, it can control any host it inhabits and prevents any memories from being stored. They are exceedingly rare and seem to be the slime consciousness, if that makes sense. We've only seen two, including Mozrah, and now know of two more in Emrakus and Delkis."

"Four down, unknown amount to go," said Kal.

Yuldaris nodded and then pointed at the blue slime. "The blue slime can inhabit a body and prevent memories as well, but it doesn't actively control the host on its own. The host is only controlled when a black-slimed being is nearby and wants to control it."

"Like a proxy," said Kane.

"Exactly. So they could blue slime a lot of people, and the only time they would be controlled is if a black-slimed came near and wanted control."

"What distance are we talking about?" asked Sarah.

Yuldaris raised his finger. "A good question. Our tests show it to be about roughly one and a half of one of your Earth miles."

Seth shook his head. "Damn, that's crazy."

"Yes, it is." Yuldaris pointed at the green slime. "This one is different. It can inhabit a host but can't control it. However, if a black-slimed is near, it can access all the host's senses without the host's knowledge."

"Remote viewing," said Blake.

"Yep. In one of our tests, we had a black-slimed in one room and a green-slimed in another. We questioned the green-slimed and received our answers from the black-slimed."

Luke gulped. "This sliming is some nasty shit."

"It gets worse," said Yuldaris. He pointed at the red slime. "This one causes massive mutations. We discovered it's based on whatever species it inhabits. It failed with us since our physiology is hostile to the slime, and it doesn't like extreme temperatures, especially on our home world."

"You got any images?" asked Seth.

Yuldaris interacted with the table console.

Ada examined the red-slimed creatures that appeared. Most looked like a larger version of the species she had in her database. What seemed common among them all was brown coloring and large welt-like structures on the back. Hardened plates covered the forearms, and sharp claws and a twisted face finished it off.

"Wow . . . those are disgusting," said Sarah.

The projection changed back to the slimes.

"We suspect that Hadrassus is dabbling in red slime," said Yuldaris. He pointed at the black slime. "One of these probably exists at Hadrassus with blue-slimed and green-slimed helping out. The black slime is a quick study. I dread to think what it could do with the operation at Hadrassus. Although my initial thought was that Fredoria was creating something new, based on the FDF presence at Hadrassus, I'm beginning to think this is something different, and not produced by Fredoria."

"Most likely," said Blake. "If it was produced by Fredoria, I would know. Well . . . at least I think I would."

Ada tilted her head. "I would expect that there would be more green-slimed than blue-slimed."

"That's . . . correct," said Yuldaris. "How'd you come to that conclusion?"

Ada ran a simulation in her head. "If the black-slimed moved out of control range from a blue-slimed often enough, then the blue-slimed host and those around them might figure something was wrong. That could complicate things. The green-slimed could be everywhere without that issue."

Yuldaris grinned. "That was our thinking too. Impressive."

"Thank you," said Ada with a smile.

"Does this alter our current plan?" asked Zane.

Blake shook his head. "We'll still visit Administrator Zoldan and then head to the northern hub first. There are key departments and personnel there that we can question, thanks to Captain Rusch's data. Our team will be assigned who to contact and where. Ada will also attempt to gather as much information as possible from their data center. Once we do all that, we get the hell out of there. Any black-slimed at Hadrassus probably know we're coming, so I expect a trap."

"They know we're coming and why?" asked Yuldaris.

Blake licked his fangs for a moment. "They do. When we were on the *Storetz*, I was informed that Hadrassus would be preparing for our arrival."

"Hmm, all right. I'll gear up then, expecting a fight."

"We all will," said Blake. "Zane has his juggernaut suit, so if things start popping off, whoever is on the receiving end will get punished."

Zane pulled his lips to the right as he nodded.

"We won't be able to communicate with you, so you're on your own down there," said Kane, gesturing at Yuldaris.

"I see," said Yuldaris.

"We'll be able to communicate between our group inside, though," said Blake. "If anyone really needs to reach us, they have a control center topside that can be accessed. I'm not expecting that'll need to happen, though."

"There could be more Rogundans arriving," said Kane.

"Maybe, but we're there on business, in an FDF-controlled facility. Rogundan or not, whoever is going in there will either respect that or have to deal with the FDF. I doubt the FDF likes *any* Rogundan near Hadrassus."

Kane shrugged. "A'ight. I'll keep the *Exceltion*'s weapon systems ready to go. It still needs some work, but that's something I can mess with while y'all are down in the slime pit."

The group chuckled.

"A very fitting name," said Yuldaris, nodding at Kane. "I've given Sarah and Seth the CID for Zurinch, First Unit leader of the Sixty-Seventh Company. He is, for all intents and purposes, my second in command. If my company is needed for anything topside, contact him. He's on standby, and his standing order is to assist the *Exceltion* as needed."

"That does make me feel a little better," said Sarah.

"If Rogundans or whoever decide to interfere, then *death* be unto them," said Yuldaris, raising his head a bit.

A silence fell across the room.

Ada noted the increased heartbeats. Although she suspected they were okay in general with Yuldaris, he instilled some fear. Perhaps due to being Covendrin or being a commander. As expected, Blake and Zane showed no signs of anxiety.

"I'm with you there," said Blake. "All right, we land in about an hour. Get geared up, handle any personal business you need to, and I would suggest a light lunch. Pack any food and drink you think you might need. I'm not sure I'd trust whatever Hadrassus provides. Ada, make sure that all the suits have the proper update on the layout and the information."

"I will do so," said Ada.

"Before everyone goes, I brought a slime-detection device for each of you per Blake's request," said Yuldaris. "It can't differentiate between the slimes, but it can detect if someone or something is slimed." He reached down and slid the devices across the table to everyone.

"Works for me," said Zane, grabbing a device and looking it over. After everyone had grabbed theirs, they began to head out.

Ada watched as the group dispersed, leaving just her and Blake in the room.

"You ready for all this?" asked Blake.

"I am."

Blake narrowed his eyes. "Can androids feel fear?"

"Not like a human would know it. We only fear losing our mortality. However, emotions are emulated and can be shut off if needed."

"Must be nice."

Ada tilted her head. "It can be."

"Good. Let's see what's in store for us at Hadrassus."

///////////

Blake studied the group that had exited the *Exceltion* with him. Zane had on his juggernaut suit and stood imposing over everyone else. Yuldaris wore his golden armor with the signature red band on the right arm. A small arsenal was tucked away all over his armor, but it was the large assault weapon on his back that showed he meant business. Ada and Kal chose lighter suits. Kal had all his gadgets and devices strapped on, while Ada had her large backpack.

Blake grinned that all he wore was a heavier suit than Kal or Ada, but nowhere near Yuldaris or Zane. It was a trade-off between speed and power. Based on his previous experience with the suit, he had no qualms about its weight.

It had been about an hour since the meeting, and they were ready to meet Administrator Cadris Zoldan.

Blake tapped at his forearm. "Comm check. Everyone hear this?" he asked over the group communication channel.

Everyone acknowledged they did.

"Good. We can lower our helmets once we're inside. If you need to talk, do it discreetly, or if you really need to be private, just raise your helmet and do it," said Blake.

The group nodded.

"Let's move out," said Blake. He surveyed the spaceport as they crossed it. The environment was harsh, barren, and rocky, and the large topside entrance to Hadrassus stood before them. Several ships were near the *Exceltion*, some much larger. He narrowed his eyes as he recognized one of them to be Rogundan.

"Is that what I think it is?" asked Kal, pointing at the Rogundan ship.

"Yep. At least we know they're here. Shouldn't bother us, and if they do, well, they'll get their business handled."

Yuldaris laughed. "Earthborn slang always amuses me."

"Get used to it," said Kal. "We sling it left and right."

"It amuses me as well, but I'm getting used to it," said Ada.

Blake motioned forward. "Looks like enforcers are guarding the entrance."

"No surprise there," said Yuldaris.

They approached the entrance.

Blake showed the two Fredorians his forearm screen, and they motioned for the group to enter into a small room.

Once inside, the room sealed and the group was bathed in lights. They exited the room once it unsealed.

Blake studied the large, spotless room as they entered it. The shiny metallic floor and white walls stood out, but the four large glass cylinders in the back caught his attention. He knew them to be elevator units. To the sides of them were what looked like stairwell entrances. In front of them was an arced desk with two men in brown FDF cloth uniforms. On each end of the desk was an enforcer in full gear. Blake lowered his helmet and sniffed. Sterile. Just how Fredorians liked it. He motioned ahead. "I guess we check in there."

The group arrived in front of the desk.

Blake could sense that the men had been slimed, although he was not sure what color it was. He activated his forearm screen and showed it to the man on the left.

"Presidential guard, Earthborn Unit," said the man.

"That's us."

"Your arrival was expected," said the man. He pointed at Yuldaris. "He was not on the list."

"He joined our group after we were attacked by Rogundans on the way here," said Blake. He glanced at the guards, then back at the man. "The Covendrin helped us kill the Rogundans. Funny thing that Rogundans are allowed to roam free and attack others, don't you think?"

The man gulped. "Oh. I see. Okay . . . I've registered him with your group. Administrator Zoldan would like to speak with you."

"We planned on it."

The man shrugged and tapped at a console in front of him. After a moment, he said, "You've been tagged with the appropriate access. Per the rules here, no weapons are allowed."

"I don't believe so," said Ada. "Per the protocol for this station, in section four A, subsection three B, it states that visiting groups of a certain clearance can carry weapons. We have that clearance."

The man checked his console. "Huh. I guess you *can* carry weapons based on your clearance."

"You done hassling us?" asked Blake.

The man smirked. "I just have to be sure with Earthborn."

"Uh-huh," said Blake. He moved to go around the desk toward the elevators, but the enforcer did not move out of the way. Blake growled. "You don't want me to move you."

The enforcer harrumphed and then stepped to the side.

As the group filed past, Zane shook his head while glancing at the enforcer. "What a bitch."

The enforcer narrowed his eyes.

"C'mon," said Blake. "Forget those assholes."

The group reached the glass elevator on the far left. Once inside, it began to descend.

"Is it always like this between Earthborn and Fredorians?" asked Yuldaris.

"Yeah," said Kal.

Yuldaris shook his head. "I've heard of it, but never really saw it before. It doesn't make sense. You're all human."

"They just want something to make them feel superior," said Zane.

"Is this a human thing or a Fredorian thing?"

"Sadly, both," said Blake.

Yuldaris nodded.

After fifteen minutes, the elevator came to a stop, and the group stepped off.

An enforcer greeted them. He motioned forward. "Administrator Zoldan is awaiting you in his office. Please follow me."

The group complied.

As they walked, Blake took stock of the surroundings. Like the large room above, the hallways were immaculate. He noticed that brightly colored text hung just off the metallic paneled walls, identifying rooms as they passed by. The various rooms were sealed, although he did get to see into some via a glass-like panel that was interspersed throughout. The high-tech aesthetic was in full effect.

After thirty minutes, they reached Administrator Zoldan's office.

The enforcer tapped at a console.

The office door slid open, and the group entered the room.

The glass-paneled wall opposite the group stood out to Blake. It had structural supports equidistant from each other. A wraparound desk sat in the middle of the room, and the side walls were covered in various floating displays that hovered just off the wall. In front of the desk was a long couch, with two separate chairs on the sides.

Blake observed the man with his back to them. His hands were clasped behind him, and he wore a dark-gray crisp trench-coat-like uniform. A silver strap with blue highlights wrapped around the midsection. Given that it was Administrator Zoldan's office, Blake figured that was him. He could also sense that Zoldan had been slimed.

"It's beautiful, isn't it?" asked Zoldan.

The group assembled before the desk.

Blake glanced at the others, then tried to peer out the window. He saw that Zoldan's office seemed to sit above a floor that was packed with workstations, consoles, and people moving around with purpose. "What's beautiful?"

Zoldan moved his hands out to each side. "The brains of Hadrassus. It's amazing to think that all these organic and inorganic components come together for the greater good."

"What greater good?" asked Blake.

Zoldan pivoted around and smiled. "Fredoria's, of course. I'm Administrator Cadris Zoldan, as I'm sure you're all aware."

The group acknowledged Zoldan.

Zoldan took a seat and then tapped at his wraparound console. "Please, have a seat."

Blake and the others complied.

"Now . . . this is quite a surprise. The presidential guard . . . Earthborn Unit. A new unit, from what I hear. The *Storetz* informed me of your arrival, and it got me curious as to *why* such a unit would want to come here, especially one that's . . . suited for a fight."

"It's confidential," said Blake.

Zoldan nodded. "Perhaps, but Hadrassus's operations are under my control. You can surely understand my hesitation when a unit I know very little about, in battle gear, decides to drop in and . . . visit."

"I understand your concern," said Blake. "We should be in and out fairly quickly."

"I see. I received your itinerary of the departments and personnel you want to investigate," said Zoldan. He tapped at his console, causing a holographic screen to appear on his desk, showing the agenda. "Is it accurate?"

Blake studied it for a moment. "Research and development, storage, containment, and the testing areas. Yep, all there."

"That's a lot to cover," said Zoldan. He narrowed his eyes at Yuldaris. "I was unaware that the presidential guard was hiring Covendrin."

Blake grinned, baring his fangs. "He's a new member, and he helped us waste some Rogundan scumbags that tried to take us out on the way here. Well, to be exact, all the Rogundans died, including a very . . . *unusual* . . . captain. I still think it's odd that roaming bands of hostile Rogundans are allowed to fly around the Zolidack system. They even have a ship near ours outside."

Zoldan's lips turned down for a moment, and then he smiled. "They have their uses."

"And that would be what?" asked Blake.

"Confidential. That works both ways."

Blake shrugged. "We're just going to look around and ask some questions, and then we'll be out of your hair."

"Of course. The appropriate departments and personnel have already been notified of your arrival and are expected to cooperate . . . like we do with *any* government intrusion."

"It's appreciated," said Blake.

Zoldan grinned. "We're on the same side, you know."

"Yeah, maybe," said Blake. "Your corporation was on the other side a while back."

Zoldan's grin disappeared. "That was under different leadership. We adapted, and changed. Change is good, don't you think?"

"It can be, but changing for the sake of change is not always a good thing."

"You're wiser than you appear," said Zoldan. "Well, I don't want to take away from your time here. I just wanted to meet who would be in my facility."

"Of course," said Blake as he stood.

The others stood with him.

"We appreciate the meeting."

Zoldan touched his fingertips in front of him and smiled. "Anytime."

SIXTEEN

T wenty minutes after leaving the meeting, Blake eyed the transportation system the group had entered. They were on a large platform, and he could see that there were two sunken transportation lanes with rails on the bottom. On the sides were some type of locking mechanism. As he understood it, underneath the platform they were on was another layer meant to haul cargo, whereas the current level was for passengers.

He studied the heavily armored rectangular-shaped transportation units that sat in the transportation lanes. The units were long, and the glass-like windows he saw looked like they could close up at a moment's notice. He thought that was an odd design choice if the goal was just to move people.

"This place is like a maze, even with the layout up in my HUD," said Kal.

Ada pointed at a nearby transportation unit. "It's logically designed to move both people and cargo."

"I guess."

Yuldaris looked around. "I noticed on our way here that people were moving out of our way. Even now, the platform is empty. That seems unusual."

Blake gestured forward. "Raise helmets, and we can discuss in the transportation unit."

The group complied and then boarded the unit and took a seat as the doors sealed behind them.

"I noticed that as well," said Blake over the group comms.

"These transportation units look like they're meant for battle," said Zane, looking out the glass window as the unit began to move.

"The trip to the northern hub is only five miles, so we should be there shortly," said Ada.

Blake nodded. "Then we can split up from there. Ada and I will hit the data operations and management department. Zane, Kal, you two will go to the microbot technology department. Yuldaris will get the genetic engineering department."

"Sounds good," said Kal. He gestured at Yuldaris. "So about these detectors . . . mine was going wild around Zoldan and that guy upstairs. What colors you think those people were?"

"The Fredorian we met at the entrance was most likely green-slimed," said Yuldaris. "Zoldan . . . I'm not sure. He could be either blue or black. Given that he runs Hadrassus, black-slimed makes more sense. I did notice he was not happy on learning about Mozrah's death. I hope to learn more about the slimes on this mission so we can enhance our detectors."

Kal nodded. "If you do, hook a brother up."

"For what reason?"

A silence spread over the comms.

Zane laughed. "He meant if you enhance them, he would like one, not that you should actually put a hook through someone."

"Oh . . . I see," said Yuldaris. "I figured it was Earthborn slang, but I didn't see an entry for that in my database. I'll add it, and of course, I will . . . *hook* . . . everyone up."

"Sweet," said Kal.

After ten minutes, the unit slowed then stopped. The doors unsealed, and the group exited the unit.

Blake noted that the platform they were on was similar to the one they had just come from. Ahead was a large arched hallway, and to the sides, displays hovered just off the side walls. "All right. This is a decently sized area. You know where to go, and who to ask for. Meet back here in two hours."

The group acknowledged Blake, then dispersed.

Blake glanced at Ada. "You ready?"

"I'm ready," said Ada.

"Good, let's roll out."

They entered the arched hallway and navigated the maze of hallways before reaching the data operations and management department.

Blake noted that everything seemed easy to find due to the text displays that hovered a few inches out from the walls. He found that he could interact with the walls, probably a virtual intelligence. According to the detailed layout from Captain Rusch's data, this is where most of the database servers were housed. The goal was to access them. He motioned off in the distance. "Let's find this Director Asula Mizira and see what we're up against."

Ada nodded and followed Blake.

They arrived at a hub with a large pillar in the middle. Slanted consoles hung off the side, with screens higher up on the pillar, showing various bits of information. Doorways to individual offices were spaced out evenly around the room's edge, and a large hallway opposite them led off into the distance.

Ada pointed at one of the doorways. "She would be there."

Blake nodded, and they headed over. When they arrived, Blake studied the semitransparent wall in front of them. Looking around, he was not sure of its purpose. He knocked on it.

A display of a middle-aged fair-skinned woman appeared. She had jet-black hair and wore a device over her left eye. "You must be Blake Brown. And she must be Ada."

"And you must be Director Asula Mizira," said Blake.

The wall slid up.

Blake examined the office as they stepped in. It was high-tech, and Asula sat in a chair behind a desk loaded with holographic displays. Screens blanketed the other three walls, giving a view of various department sections that changed every few seconds. He sensed that she was not slimed, and his detector verified it.

Asula gestured at the two seats in front of her.

They took them.

Asula eased back into her chair. "So I'm supposed to answer your questions per Administrator Zoldan."

"That's the plan," said Blake.

She sighed. "I get the feeling this is some type of political hit job."

"Politics has nothing to do with it," said Blake. "We're just looking into a disturbing development, and now we're here."

"And what would this development be? There's nothing disturbing going on here. Our corporation has already paid the price, and everything is clean now. I suspect . . . this is just the Fredorian government, *once again*, harassing us."

Blake shook his head. "Not at all, and I can't really speak about the development. What I can do . . . is ask you to give Ada a list of everything you're working on. Summary level. That would be a good start."

Asula narrowed her eyes. "Great. And *why* did you bring an android in here? They're dangerous. Maybe you're fucking her."

"Whoa, whoa, whoa," said Blake, tossing a hand out. "There's no need for that."

"It's okay," said Ada.

Asula smiled as she accessed her desk interface. "Okay . . . *Earthborn*. You have your access."

Ada tilted her head. "I'm connected. Downloading summary information."

"You got an attitude," said Blake, pointing at Asula.

Asula shrugged. "The Fredorian government must be really scraping the bottom of the barrel to send you here."

"You know I'm a Daedrould, right?"

"And . . ."

Blake grinned and bared his fangs. "Look into our abilities sometime, and be thankful I'm holding back."

Asula raised her eyebrows. "Is that . . . a threat?"

"Not at all. It's a promise if you keep antagonizing me."

She harrumphed.

"Summary information has been downloaded," said Ada.

"Good," said Blake. He stood. "We're going to the data centers next."

Asula smiled. "You'll get the same courtesy you got here. Fredorian-government types aren't welcome here, especially when it's Earthborn masquerading as them."

"The FDF is a joint sponsor of this facility," said Ada.

"Those idiots reside topside. They don't come down here where the real action is."

Blake circled a finger. "Are all directors bitches like you?"

"We're Fredorians. *True* . . . Fredorians. When those of . . . lesser abilities . . . question us, of course we're not going to like it."

"You wear your hate well," said Blake. He motioned for Ada to leave. As they began to head out, he turned back toward Asula. "You may see me again."

"Great. Let me know when you want me to waste more time."

Blake shook his head as they left.

Heading toward the data center, Ada glanced at Blake. "She was quite rude."

"Yeah, she was. I'm used to it . . . but you don't need that shit tossed in your face."

"She believed we were . . . sleeping . . . together. Does this bother you?"

Blake laughed. "Not at all. Let them think whatever they want. However, if they ask how I was, just say I was great."

Ada tilted her head. "I will do so."

"I was kidding," said Blake, chuckling. He motioned forward. "C'mon."

They crossed through a large circular room. Ahead of them, the words "Hadrassus Data Operations Center" hovered above a large arched doorway.

Blake noted the two enforcers standing outside it. He nodded at them as he passed them. Once inside, they followed the internal map on their HUD until they arrived at a room that had glass walls with an open entrance. Inside were rows of large cabinets anchored in place by pillars from the ceiling. He scanned around and located a mobile workstation hooked up to one of the cabinets. "Let's check that out."

As they approached the workstation, a thin, red-haired, bearded, pale man in a two-piece blue suit ran up to them. "Hold on! Who are you and what are you doing?"

Blake showed his credentials to the man. "We're authorized to be here."

The man studied Blake's forearm screen. "Presidential guard, Earthborn Unit." He smirked as he tapped a cabinet.

"What are you planning on doing? You know these are pretty tough if you plan to shoot at them."

Blake narrowed his eyes.

"I plan to access the workstation," said Ada.

The man eyed Ada. "Ahh . . . an android. That makes sense."

"What, you don't think I could access these systems if I wanted to?" asked Blake.

The man shook his head. "You don't exactly have a . . . smart look about you. We'll keep an eye on you. The both of you."

"You do that," said Blake.

The man harrumphed and took off.

"He was unusual," said Ada.

"Data-center types. Comes with the territory," said Blake.

When they reached the workstation, Ada located an input port and extended her hand.

"Good luck in there," said Blake. He looked around. "I'll cover you, and . . . shoot . . . the place up if something attempts to stop us."

Ada paused. "I hope we don't have to shoot the place up or down."

Blake grinned as he watched her connect.

/////////

Ada scanned her surrounding environment. She assumed her familiar orb form in the Hadrassus data-center system. A quick scan revealed that the layout here was different from the *Exceltion*'s systems. The virtual representations of systems were free-floating bright-blue clouds with green electric tendrils connecting them to a thick multicolored pipe.

She noted that one cloud was orange and stood out from the others. The surrounding environment was pitch-black except for the lights of the clouds and pipe. She could see that there was a lot of data, and it would take a while. The time dilation factor would give her an advantage, though, since time moved faster inside the system.

A trio of orange cubes approached her.

She scanned and identified them as end points of a security system.

The cubes washed a beam over her. One of the cubes spoke. "Registered. Ada. Presidential guard, Earthborn Unit." They then flew away.

She was thankful that her registration held; otherwise she would have had to enact her own countermeasures. When she got to the first cloud, she attached to its surface, then eased through. Her first goal was to study the structure and layout, since every system she went into was usually different. The environment changed to a brightly lit one, where orbs of various colors connected to each other with tendrils of light. Given the amount of orbs, she understood that her form had shrunk when it crossed over. She flew up to an orb and connected to it.

The environment changed again, and she was now inside one of the orbs. It had a grid of cubes embedded on flat sheets that were stacked one on top of each other. Openings allowed movement between the sheets. She cruised along, emitting a scan over each cube as she went. Inside each cube was a set of data points. Given the number of cubes and sheets and the pace at which she could scan and analyze, she calculated that it would take a very long time to find anything of consequence. She pulled out of the orb and then the cloud and back into the pitch-black environment lit by the clouds.

The orange cloud sparkling in the distance was her next destination.

She flew toward it. As she neared the cloud, she detected the husks of other visitors. There were also orange pyramid objects floating around outside the cloud. She determined they were most likely responsible for whatever happened to the husks, so she scanned one and then enacted her mimic countermeasure to assume a similar form.

Several of the pyramid objects scanned her but did not react.

She attached to the orange cloud and then eased into it.

The environment changed to a large circular room with a massive cylinder in the middle. The room had glass walls on a part of it, exposing an orange slime moving around in a dark fluid. She had never seen anything like this in a digital environment before. Looking down, she realized she appeared in her humanoid form, which was unusual. The place was busy, with many different types of aliens walking around. A man in a red robe and hood approached her. "Welcome. Do not be afraid."

"I'm not," said Ada. "Where am I?"

"You are in the Zolidack Saskarin repository."

"I . . . don't understand. What's a Saskarin?"

The man lowered his hood, revealing a face with no eyes. In their place was a band that circled his head. "The Saskarins are everywhere. When the Saskarins are in control, this is where you go. Don't worry, you won't remember your time here. Relax and enjoy yourself."

"I will. Thank you," said Ada. Her hunch was that Saskarin was the species name of the black slime.

The man nodded and then went away.

She began to walk through the large room. Around her were many smaller rooms, and she tried to analyze all the aliens she was seeing.

A Fredorian man walked up to her. "Hey."

She studied the man for a moment. "Hey."

"Interesting place, huh?"

"I'm unsure if I would characterize it as interesting."

The man chuckled. "I'm Toris Gilldan."

"Ada."

"Good to meet you. I was scared when I first came here, but . . . I'm getting used to it now."

"How did you get in here?"

Toris eyed Ada. "Same way you did. Blue slime enters the body, and when a Saskarin takes control, our consciousness comes here, or rather, to the nearest repository. In my case, I work in the testing hub."

"Of course."

"Funny thing is . . . I don't ever remember the blue slime, but that's what I've gathered since I've been here. I bet you don't remember either."

She decided to use misdirection. "I don't. One moment I was preparing to sleep, the next I was here."

Toris laughed. "Yeah, about the same for me. We won't remember any of this, but when we're here, we remember the last time we were here. I guess . . . this is now a part of our life. One interesting thing is that even if our physical body dies, we'll still exist here. So . . . immortality, I guess. Out there, I have a bad leg. Although I've had some work on it, it still hurts from time to time. They said they could replace it, but . . . I'd rather stay fully myself, you know? In here . . . there's no pain at all."

Ada nodded. "I see. That's very interesting." She looked around. "Do you mind showing me this place?"

"Not at all," said Toris with a grin. His eyes roamed her body. "Maybe later we can . . . acquaint ourselves better."

She tilted her head. "You wish to engage in procreation activities."

Toris's eyes widened. "Well . . . I wouldn't put it quite like that." He wagged a finger. "You know . . . your speech is odd. Kinda reminds me of an android's but . . . they can't come here, at least I don't think they can." He shrugged. "C'mon, I'll show you around."

She followed Toris as he pointed out the various rooms, structures, and people. Every object, location, and item she scanned was put into her internal memory. There were aliens present that she did not have a record on. It was apparent that the Saskarins had been busy. She kept one part of her focused on Toris as he led her around. He was talkative, and she gave minimal responses. The majority of her focus was attempting to catalog everything.

Toris stopped.

She focused on him. "Is everything all right?"

"Yeah . . . but you seem distant. Are *you* all right?"

"I am, but this is my first time here. I'm coming to grips with . . . something possessing me."

Toris nodded. "Oh . . . yeah . . . I guess I've been here so long I forget that it can be jarring to those who are new."

"Where would I learn more about these Saskarins and the other slimes?"

"Oh, c'mon," said Toris.

She hustled after Toris as he entered a small room. Vials of various slimes were held along the wall like a spice rack. What surprised her was the sheer quantity of slime colors. She pointed at some. "Do they all have different purposes?"

A man similar to the one she had seen when she first arrived approached her. He lowered his hood. "Yes, they do. Are you interested in a specific one?"

"I'm interested in learning about them all."

Toris laughed and glanced at the man. "She's a first timer. Got the jitters."

"I see. That's not uncommon," said the man. He motioned over to one of the rows of vials. "The most important one is the black one. They're the Saskarins, beings from another reality. They are a superior form of life, and we are but flesh vessels waiting to be filled with their embrace. Since you're here, you most likely came in through a Saskarin or a blue slime, although there are other slimes that can do that as well, depending on species. Blue usually covers most, though."

She pointed at the orange slime. "Is that one responsible for integrating the Saskarins with inorganic material, like a data-center server?"

The man narrowed his eyes. "It is . . . How'd you know to pick that one . . . specifically?"

"I noticed the orange slime in the large room before I came here. I was just curious."

The man paused for a moment, and then the group focused on a floating octahedral crystal that flew into the room. The man pointed at Ada. "I don't think she belongs here. She can see the orange slime."

The crystal scanned her and then said in a deep, monotone voice with a digital rasp, "Hadrassus has been compromised. Shutdown protocol in effect." It shot out a tendril of light toward Ada.

The environment changed back to the data center when Ada was hit by the tendril.

Blake caught her as she stumbled back.

She moved her head around rapidly, assessing the environment. Red lights flashed around her, and an alarm was blaring.

"Are you all right?" asked Blake.

She gathered her senses and then stood. "Yes. There is a virtual environment of some sort in there. I ran into an orange cloud where slimed consciousnesses go. They detected that I should not be in there, then said Hadrassus had been compromised and that they were going to shut it down. I have it all recorded. The most important aspect I learned was that the black slimes are from another reality and they call themselves the Saskarins."

"Saskarins, huh? Interesting. All right. We can check the video feed later," said Blake. He shook a finger at her. "In there for five minutes and all hell breaks loose."

"I apologize."

He grinned. "I was teasing you. Anyways, this shutdown doesn't sound good. For now, we need to regroup."

Ada nodded. In the virtual environment, it was illuminating to truly be treated as an equal when no one knew she was an android. She could see the allure for an organic of living in a place without pain or fear, even beyond physical death. For an android, that meant moving their matrix into a system that could support it. She ran a quick self-diagnostic and verified that there were no external agents in her system. It was now time to deal with the shutdown.

//////////

Zane eyed everyone as he and Kal passed them. His detector showed that roughly half of the people had been slimed. Some had a distant look in their eyes and were overly friendly. Others were jittery, scattering when he passed them. His skin crawled to think that they did not know that they could be possessed. He was glad his helmet was up so that he could view people without them seeing his face.

"Man . . . this is some next-level invasion-of-the-body-snatcher shit going on here," said Kal over their personal comms.

"Yeah," said Zane. "Half of them probably don't even know there's something going on."

Kal nodded as they continued on.

After a brisk fifteen-minute walk, they reached the micro-bot technology department.

Zane studied the bright text hovering over the arched doorway. Inside was a bustling open area that had hallways leading off to various locations. He checked the internal map on his HUD, then said, "Director Hulios Guerra's office is nearby. Let's check it out."

They spent another five minutes navigating the hallways and arrived outside Hulios's office.

Zane lowered his helmet and then peeked his head in the open doorway.

A man behind the desk looked up at them. "Can I help you?"

Zane noted that the man had not been slimed. He motioned at Kal to lower his helmet, which he did.

"I'm Zane Gibbons, and he's Kal Modan. We're with the presidential guard, Earthborn Unit. We have some questions to ask."

The man eased back into his chair. "Well then, come on in. I'm Director Hulios Guerra, but I suspect you already knew that."

They took their seats.

"We do now," said Zane.

Hulios nodded. "So . . . what questions can I help you with?"

"All right," said Zane. "What is it you do here exactly?"

Hulios laughed. "Not much of researcher, are you?"

"Huh?" asked Zane.

Kal shook his head. "He's saying that we should have done some research before coming here, because to him, the answer is obvious."

Zane angled his eyebrows. "Oh . . . well . . . the question stands."

"All right," said Hulios. "The purpose of this department is to advance microbot technology for the greater good of Fredoria. In conjunction with the FDF, this facility provides us with the research and testing equipment. That's it at a high level."

Zane nodded. "Have you seen anything . . . out of place lately?"

"And if I did? You think I'd tell you?"

"You're supposed to cooperate," said Kal. "If you don't want to, we'll just note you were not cooperative."

Hulios grinned. "Fine. No, I haven't seen anything weird, other than the odd quirks of individual researchers."

Zane tossed a hand out. "You know a Renee Swerning? The records show she was assigned to this department, even though her previous job had her in genetic engineering."

Hulios accessed his desk surface for a moment. "Yes, she's here, and arrived recently." He tapped at the interface.

The display on the desk surface shot up facing Zane and Kal.

"The green dot is where her work area is."

Zane nodded. "Can you get us a list of the high-level projects you're working on?"

"I can. What's your CID? I assume all information transferred is kept confidential," said Hulios.

"Of course," said Kal.

"Very well. Your CIDs, please," said Hulios.

Zane and Kal showed their forearm displays to Hulios.

Hulios scanned their displays and then tapped at his desk surface. "Done. Anything else?"

Zane eyed Hulios. "You know . . . I'm gonna cut right through the bullshit. We're investigating some bizarre incidents. People not acting like themselves. If it's occurring here . . . and you're not telling us . . . this may be your last chance to do so. Whatever happened to them . . . could happen to you. We don't report to the FDF, or to Administrator Zoldan. If anything, they hate us. So . . . it's up to you. If you're good, we'll leave. If you have something to say . . . now would be a good time."

Hulios ran his hand over his mouth while eying Zane and Kal. After a moment of awkward silence, he accessed his desk interface. One tap later, the door sealed. "This room is secured. Yes, I have seen some . . . odd things. This Renee Swerning, appearing out of nowhere and not even educated in our field, decides to change project details. I went to Administrator Zoldan, and he said to let her do whatever she needs to." He harrumphed. "What's the point of my job if I'm going to be overruled by outsiders I know nothing about? Does that seem strange?"

"About as strange as how she left her former position. She's a target of our inquiry," said Zane.

Hulios breathed a bit easier. "That's good to hear. I went to the FDF as well, and they . . . shrugged, acting like I was crazy or something. That was their official position, and of course, they laughed at me. I'm not even sure why they're here, to be honest."

Kal nodded. "All right, we'll note that. What else have you noticed?"

"Well . . . it seems some people are more distant, and they seem to be forgetful of faces. It's like . . . they're not who they say they are, I guess kinda like what you two are investigating," said Hulios. He chuckled. "This must be confirmation for you that whatever's happening has made it here."

Zane nodded. "Yep. That bizarre behavior is not only occurring here as you've witnessed; it's becoming more widespread. Andia Kiggs formed our unit to investigate things like this, things the FDF won't."

"I hope you figure it out," said Hulios. "I'm not sure how much more I can take here. This place is becoming odd very quick. On top of that, I haven't seen my family group in over six months. They're restricting who can go on vacation and when."

"If we find anything, we'll let you know," said Kal.

Hulios sighed. "All right. What's your next move?"

Zane glanced at his detector, then back at Hulios. "Since you're not affected, I'll tell you. We're gonna talk with Renee Swerning and then go from there. Don't worry, we won't mention this conversation to her. It's confidential."

"Okay," said Hulios. He tapped at his desk interface, and the office door opened. "Good luck."

Zane and Kal nodded and exited the office. They raised their helmets to speak over the personal comms.

"Interesting meeting," said Kal.

"Yeah. The black slime must be trying to take over this facility, but it seems it's not everywhere . . . yet. Let's find this Renee chick," said Zane.

They navigated the hallways until they came to Renee's work area.

Zane noted that like the other subdepartments they had seen, hers had an arched doorway with a text display over it. He motioned forward. "According to this map layout, her work area is not too far."

They arrived after five minutes.

Zane observed that it was an open area with various worktables, holographic projections, and people bustling around in one-piece lab coats. There were sealed-off rooms with displays showing what was inside. He figured those were where the microbots were. He pointed at Renee, who was seated at a worktable, pouring over a holographic screen. "There she is."

They approached her with lowered helmets.

"Got a moment?" asked Zane. He noted that according to his detector, she had been slimed.

Renee swiveled in her chair and looked them over. "I'm busy."

"This will only be a moment. Oh, and Charles Duton says hi."

She paused. "Who?"

"Oh, you know . . . the guy you worked under for five years and were close with prior to coming here," said Zane.

"Oh . . . that Charles. Yeah, I remember him now."

Zane glanced at Kal. "Okay . . . we had a few questions we wanted to ask you."

She narrowed her eyes. "And who are you exactly?"

Zane and Kal showed their credentials via their forearm screens.

"Presidential guard, Earthborn Unit. You're pretty far from Fredoria. What's this about?"

An alarm blared and red lights flashed.

Zane looked around. "What the hell is that?"

"Shutdown protocol," said Renee. "Probably just a drill. If you two don't want to be sealed in here for two hours, you should leave now."

"Oh, great," said Kal. He nodded back. "Let's get out of here." He focused on Renee. "We'll be back."

"Okay," said Renee with a smile.

As they left, they raised their helmets.

"Yeah . . . she's a bit off," said Kal.

"I guess we'll wait this out in the hallways. We can contact Blake when we get there."

"Sounds good," said Kal. "This slime shit makes my skin crawl, man."

"Yeah . . . me too," said Zane. He was not sure what type of slime had Renee, but the difference between Hulios and Renee was clear as day. With a drill test going on, they would be delayed for a few hours. He was eager to get back and question Renee and wondered how much she knew. They would know in a few hours.

SEVENTEEN

Zane looked around the silent, empty hallway. The alarm had faded, and since the discussion with Renee had been cut short, he was eager to get back in and question her. Although he knew she was slimed, he was curious to see how a slimed person interacted more in-depth.

Kal motioned at Zane. "Awfully quiet out here."

"Yeah, I'm checking in with the group," said Zane. He tapped at his helmet. "Blake, me and Kal are outside the microbot technology department. Some type of alarm going off."

"That was Ada's doing," said Blake over the group comms. "She was in the data center, poking around, and came across a . . . virtual environment or something. Apparently the black slimes are from another reality, and they call themselves the Saskarins. We'll make sense of it later. Yuldaris, you there?"

"I'm here," said Yuldaris. "I was able to get some information from the genetic engineering department director. I think I'll now be able to differentiate between slimes when we get out of here."

"We got some information from our director as well," said Zane. "He's noticed some changes and has had some of his projects overruled, ironically by Renee Swerning. We were just beginning to talk to her before this alarm went off."

"Hadrassus is being shut down," said Blake.

Ada interjected. "The protocol says for each division to seal everyone inside their work areas. They'll be retrieved by the FDF later when possible."

Kal shook his head. "Great. So I guess we, what, leave Hadrassus?"

"No. We stick to the plan," said Blake. "For now, meet back in the central room of this hub."

Click. Clack. Click. Clack.

"All right, I think—" said Zane. He tilted his head. "Hold on a moment. You hearing this shit, Kal?"

"Yeah. Sounds like something tapping on metal, sorta."

"Blake, we'll meet up with you after seeing what this is."

"All right," said Blake.

Zane switched to personal comms. He lowered his hellfire thrower and aimed down the hallway. "Whatever it is, it's coming from around the corner."

Kal pulled out his dual pistols and readied them to fire.

Zane scrunched his face at the two-foot-tall creature with digitigrade legs, pointed ears, gray scaled skin, and sharp claws on its hands and feet. "Looks like someone lost their demon-from-hell pet."

Kal laughed.

The creature turned toward them. Its eyes widened as it began to shriek loudly.

"I think it's screaming at you," said Kal.

Zane took a step forward, and the creature scurried off. "All right . . . that's more like it."

The sound of multiple clacks in addition to heavier ones reverberated around the hallway.

"Oh, shit, I think it got its bigger brothers," said Kal.

Zane watched as larger versions of the creature, with heavy chitin-like armor and long blades on their forearms, appeared. It looked like they were geared for battle, and their red eyes just helped that perception. Unlike the smaller creature, these had humanoid legs, and they carried a weapon of some type that reminded him of a bulky assault rifle.

The creatures roared and opened fire while charging forward.

Zane's shielding lit up. "Son of a bitch!" He activated his hellfire thrower. It began to churn out a hailstorm of bullets, shredding the creatures.

The creatures that had dodged out of the way retreated.

Kal shook his head. "Go out in the hallway, Renee says . . . I'm beginning to think that was on purpose."

"Yeah. I—" said Zane, as he stared at the small creature that had reappeared. Arriving behind it was a small army of them. "Ahh, shit." He aimed and fired forward.

Some of the creatures were hit, but others flew around and began to swarm Kal. Others jumped on Zane's armor, slashing at it.

Kal screamed as the creatures took him down.

Zane began pulling off the creatures and crushing them with his heavy gauntlets.

Kal was able to get out from under the creatures. "Get back!"

Zane hustled behind Kal as he tossed out a line mine.

The line mine whirred into action, shredding the creatures. The ones that survived were gunned down from a dual volley from Kal and a burst of fire from Zane.

They took a moment to catch their breath.

"We need to meet up with the others. They're probably running into this shit too. I'll update the group as we go," said Zane.

Kal nodded and followed Zane out.

Zane accessed the group comms. "We got attacked by some creatures. The big ones weren't that bad, but the small ones, they swarmed us. Some even got through Kal's armor."

"We ran into something similar on our end," said Blake. "They discovered they were no match for my dual blades or Ada's raw strength. Yuldaris?"

"I haven't run into anything yet, but sounds like I might. I'm on my way to our rendezvous point," said Yuldaris.

"All right. Everyone, keep in contact if something comes up."

Zane switched back to personal comms. "Damn, I wish I was as fast as Blake."

"Yeah, me too," said Kal, laughing.

"C'mon, let's get the hell out of here."

They continued out of the department and into the main hallways that separated the departments.

Zane checked his internal map. "We're not too far away now." He glanced at Kal, who stood still. Following Kal's gaze, Zane saw a humanoid with yellow skin and black eyes. It wore a suit of black light armor and wielded two glowing blue blades. A semitransparent metallic covering rested over the mouth and chin. Zane knew this creature was meant for speed and agility. He pulled out his mace. "Now what the fuck is this?"

The creature spoke. "You fought well back there, but they were brainless, for the most part. This body, though . . . is not." It smiled.

Zane pointed his mace at the creature. "And who . . . or what . . . are you supposed to be?"

The creature smiled. "Names . . . such importance is given to them by your kind. They're meaningless. However, if it's a name you want, you can call me a Saskarin slicer."

"That's a type, but okay," said Zane. "You're in our way."

The slicer cracked its neck. "Am I now? Why don't you . . . come around me . . . if you can."

Kal shook his head. "This Saskarin shit is using us as combat test dummies."

The slicer tilted its head.

Zane shrugged. "All right, bitch." He put his mace back and lowered his hellfire thrower.

The slicer hit its belt and shimmered out of view.

"Shit, he's got camouflage shielding. Thermal vision!" said Kal.

Zane activated his thermal vision and saw the slicer was almost on them. He knew there would be not enough time for his hellfire thrower to wind up before getting sliced. Letting the hellfire rest, he grabbed his mace and swung out.

The slicer dodged and sliced forward, cutting into Zane's juggernaut suit.

"Son of a bitch!" said Zane. He rushed forward and bear-hugged the slicer.

Kal slid up to the side and pointed both pistols at the slicer's head, then fired.

The slicer went limp as half its head went splattering onto the wall.

"Damn . . . stealth, fast, and that was one ugly-ass creature," said Kal.

"And that was just one . . . Can you imagine a bunch of them?" asked Zane.

Kal exhaled. "Yeah, I don't want to. Let's get the fuck out of here."

They continued on until they arrived at the transportation hub, then activated their group comms. Blake and Ada were already there. Around Blake were three dead slicers.

Zane pointed at the bodies. "Ran into one of those fuckers back there."

Blake nodded. "They tried to hang with me, but they're too slow."

"Too slow . . . man . . . ," said Kal.

Blake laughed. "Believe it."

Kal looked around. "Where's Yuldaris."

"I'm on my way and almost to you. I have a group of creatures following me, so I'm coming in hot," said Yuldaris.

Zane jumped into action and positioned himself in front of the hallway that Yuldaris was coming from. Kal took aim with his dual pistols while Blake pulled out his striker. Ada activated an assault drone and drew her FLP-40.

When Yuldaris burst into the transportation hub past the defensive line the others had formed, a horde of the small creatures with a few larger ones appeared. They went down in a blaze of gunfire. The creatures that survived retreated.

Yuldaris took a moment to catch his breath. "Nasty critters. Their tactics were weak. Rushing headlong into weapons fire . . ."

"Man, you know you do that shit too," said Zane.

Yuldaris eyed Zane, then burst out laughing. "Yeah . . . I guess I do sometimes."

Zane crooked his thumb at the hallway he and Kal had come from. "We ran across one of those slicers, and it talked to us."

"It did?" asked Blake. "Ours didn't say shit. Just jumped on us and then died."

"Yeah . . . it called itself a Saskarin slicer."

Blake glanced around the group. "Well, at least we know about them now. I don't think the slicer itself was a Saskarin, but modified or controlled by the Saskarins somehow."

"It could be," said Yuldaris. He pointed at some of the dead creatures from the hallway he had come from. "I thought these were red-slimed at first but . . . that requires a base host. I've never seen aliens or creatures that looked like that."

"A different type of slime then, maybe one that can be grown," said Ada. "In the virtual environment, I saw a room with many different types of slimes."

Yuldaris nodded. "I'm looking forward to seeing what you found in there."

"Well, right now, we need to get to Administrator Zoldan. I'd like to have a word with him," said Blake.

"How we gonna do that?" asked Kal.

"According to what Ada discovered on the protocol, the administrator goes to a secured command center. Unfortunately for us, that's five miles back to the main hub, then five miles west."

"And the transportation system is down, because of course it is," said Zane with a sigh.

Blake chuckled. "You wanted to try out the juggernaut suit. Consider this a second test run."

"I'm good. Let's find that dickbag."

Ada tilted her head at Kal and then scanned him. "It appears you have not been infected."

Kal exhaled from his mouth. "Good. They got through my light armor, but it's nothing serious."

"Well, at least I won't have to bite you then," said Blake.

Kal laughed. "Yeah . . . I don't need a hard-on about now."

The group laughed.

Blake motioned down the transportation tunnel. "All right, we can walk along the platform all the way back. Ada, launch a surveillance drone. Let's get moving."

As the group walked along the platform toward the central hub, Blake sniffed around. He had lowered his helmet to get a better feel of the environment. The odor had changed dramatically since the shutdown protocol went into effect. Gone was the sterile smell, and in its place was a strong rotting-flesh smell. Given that they had all fought some unusual creatures, that was not out of place. It was the skittering and clawing sounds punctuated by odd cries and growling that had him on alert. Against the backdrop of dim emergency lighting, it created a dark atmosphere. He knew they were not alone in the tunnel.

"Man, you know what's going to happen," said Kal.

Blake tilted his head. "And what's that?"

"I'm gonna die first."

Yuldaris glanced at Kal. "Why do you say that?"

"The black guy always dies first."

Zane and Blake burst out laughing.

"I don't get it," said Yuldaris.

Kal chuckled. "It's a thing from Earth."

"Is that common?"

"Only in fiction."

Yuldaris nodded. "Sounds . . . quite odd. Do you miss Earth?"

"Yeah, I do. Man, ain't nothing like catching football on Sunday with your friends. Out here . . . the sports are weird. Everything is virtual."

"The Covendrin like physical sports as well. I've seen Fredorian virtual sports. They are . . . interesting."

Ada tilted her head. "I'm familiar with Covendrin sports. Which one do you prefer?"

"Battle ball, without a question," said Yuldaris.

"Never heard of it," said Zane.

Blake grinned, baring his fangs. "They run around in heavy armor and knock a bouncy ball around. The goal is to knock the ball into one of the opponents' nets. Violence is encouraged. Think soccer, except far more brutal, and with three teams."

Zane nodded. "Sounds like my type of sport. I'll check it out."

Blake raised a hand. He studied the drone's view in his HUD. A man was racing toward them, and behind him looked to be several tactical squads of some sort. "Ada, put the drone near the man. I want to talk to him while he's running from whatever is chasing him."

Ada nodded. After a moment, she said, "Done."

Blake nodded and focused on the projection that showed the man running. "This is Blake Brown of the presidential guard, Earthborn Unit. Who are you?"

"Lieutenant Gris Doolin!"

"What are you running from?"

"I . . . I don't know!"

Blake narrowed his eyes. "You're approaching our position. If you're not who we think you are . . . we'll gun you down. You do anything to provoke us, same thing. Understood?"

"Oh, great selector, yes!"

Blake motioned at Zane. "Fire up the hellthrower just in case."

Zane complied.

"Ada, send the drone and see what's been following him."

Ada acknowledged Blake.

The group watched as Gris came into view.

Gris slowed and then stopped. He bent over and put his hands on his knees.

Blake did not sense that Gris was slimed and, with both blades out, approached him. "So what are you running from?"

"I . . . I wish I knew."

"How'd you get here?"

Gris took a deep breath as he stood. "I'm corporate security. The shutdown protocol has everyone check in the main hub. I was nearby, so I did with my detail." He paused to catch his breath. "We waited on the enforcers to come down. When they did . . . we were all attacked by . . . I . . . I'm not sure what they were."

"You have a personal visual feed?"

Gris shook his head. "We don't use those down here for security purposes. What happened would be on the network cameras, though."

"All right . . . according to what I'm seeing from the drone ahead, it looks like your security detail and enforcers and . . . ," said Blake, tilting his head, "something else are what's chasing you." Gris's unit was easy to pick out since they had on no armor and just a two-piece suit. The enforcers had on black tactical armor with multiple red lights on their helmets, but the dark-gray lightly armored humanoids caught Blake's attention. They were all behind large morbidly obese, almost-naked humanoids that stood around eight feet tall and were waddling in front of the group. Around their bare waists was a metal belt, which had two extensions that ended with a flat panel attached to them. Blake glanced around. "Anyone seen those things before?"

No one acknowledged Blake.

Gris sighed. "I think . . . they're shielders."

"Could be," said Blake. "Why is your security detail and the FDF chasing you if you were attacked?"

Gris shuddered. "There was a . . . thin . . . tall . . . thing. It kissed them, and then they just followed its orders. I got the hell out of there, and here I am."

Blake glanced at Ada. "What's the nearest side room?"

"Scanning," said Ada. After a moment, she said, "There are four maintenance entrances ahead, two on each side of the tunnel."

"All right, we'll split up there. That'll give us a defensible position, and if anything gets through, we can fall back to the north hub entrance and use it as a kill zone. The goal is to get past whatever's coming and then head to the main hub." He glanced at Gris. "If we get there, can you make it topside?"

Gris nodded vigorously for a moment and then tilted his head. "The presidential guard has Covendrin members?"

Yuldaris raised a finger. "A temporary member."

"Oh," said Gris.

Blake cleared this throat. Based on the drone scan of the entrances, he noted that those on the left side of the tunnel had numbers one and two, and the right side had three and four. One and three were on opposite sides, same with two and four. "Everyone see the four maintenance entrances?"

Everyone acknowledged Blake except Gris.

"All right, here's the plan. Zane, you're at entrance one. Yuldaris and I are at three. Kal, Ada, Gris, you all are at two. Kal can snipe long-range while Ada watches over him. Yuldaris and I will shoot anything that comes into medium-range, and Zane will use a firing arc that mows anything in short-range. Everyone understand?"

Everyone nodded and then followed Blake as he hustled ahead. After a few minutes, everyone was in position.

"All right, let's rock these bitches," said Blake. He knelt with his striker and aimed forward. Yuldaris was a bit behind Blake and exposed more.

The enemy group came within long-range.

Blake watched the drone's view as Kal began to snipe. What surprised Blake was how tough the shielders were. It took three hits to break their shields. While Kal reloaded, the hit shielder would move back and another would take its place. Blake wrinkled his eyebrows when he saw Kal shoot something that attached itself just ahead of and above the enemy group.

"Watch this," said Kal over group comms.

Blake watched as the object extended itself and then began spewing acid on the group below.

Chaos reigned as the enemy group pushed forward out of the acid rain dropping on them.

Blake could see that most of Gris's security detail did not make it through that, but the armor on the others seemed to have held.

"Now their armor should be weakened. Their kinetic shielding wouldn't prevent that acid from getting through," said Kal.

The enemy group moved into medium-range.

"We're up," said Blake. He launched a grenade in front of the shielders.

The grenade exploded, tossing the shielders back.

Yuldaris launched a grenade into the hole that had opened in the enemy ranks.

The blast sent several shielders flying back while some of the enforcers were shredded.

The shielders charged toward Yuldaris and Blake's position. They unleashed a torrent of gunfire that forced Blake and Yuldaris to duck into the maintenance entrance.

Zane took aim as the enemy group entered into short-range. Firing at a forty-five degree angle, he dumped a hailstorm of metal on the shielders. Although their kinetic shielding was stronger than normal, it could not withstand the pure firepower of a hellthrower.

Four shielders went down immediately.

Several enforcers and the dark-gray lightly armored humanoids were able to reach Zane's position. They poured into the entrance and were met by Zane's mace.

"Shit," said Blake. He knew he couldn't fire to help Zane since it would put Zane in danger.

"Cover me," said Yuldaris.

"Wait!" said Blake. He growled as he shot out to cover Yuldaris. Although the enemy group was now close range, they were funneling in on Zane, who seemed to be holding his ground.

Yuldaris used his forearm blade to slash one of the enforcers' necks. He grabbed the body as it went limp and used it as a shield as he crossed over to help Zane.

The enemy group tackled Yuldaris.

Yuldaris landed on his back.

The enforcers pounced on Yuldaris.

"*I . . . ,*" said Yuldaris, headbutting an enforcer that had landed on his waist.

The dark-gray lightly armored humanoids piled on.

"*Am . . . ,*" said Yuldaris, kicking out and hitting a humanoid in the face.

Four shielders had reached Yuldaris and were trying to box him in.

"*Covendrin!*" said Yuldaris, emitting a pulse from his shields, sending the pile flying out in all directions. He stood and headed toward Zane.

The shielders went sliding back.

Blake shot at the ones that tried to get back up.

Yuldaris reached Zane and began to engage in hand-to-hand combat with the dark-gray lightly armored enemies.

Blake sighed. "Kal, I'm gonna go out and handle the pile that just got tossed. Watch my back."

"Got it," said Kal.

Blake pulled out one blade and his FLP-40. He ran into the mass of enemies. As he zoomed around them, he sliced those who came close and sprayed the others with his FLP-40, all the while making sure not to aim in Zane and Yuldaris's general direction. Blake's first goal was to disable the rest of the shielders. There were only four left, and most of the enforcers had been killed. The remaining enemies were the dark-gray lightly armored humanoids.

The humanoids focused on Blake. They pulled out batons that crackled with light-blue arcs.

Blake grimaced. He knew those weapons well. Stun batons. It was apparent that they wanted him alive.

One shielder broke off and headed toward Kal and the others. Another shielder went to attack Yuldaris and Zane. The remaining two encircled Blake, while the humanoids tried to swarm him.

Blake lowered himself and sliced around in a circle while aiming with his FLP-40 at a forty-five-degree angle.

The first wave of humanoids was shredded. The shielders attempted to crush Blake between them.

Blake somersaulted off the nearest shielder, using his FLP-40 to fire down and kill even more humanoids. When he landed, he placed his blade through the shielder's neck, killing it instantly. Using the body as a launching pad, he leaped over the second wave of humanoids, wasting them with his FLP-40. The second shielder suffered the same fate as the first when Blake was done with it. A burst of gunfire from Zane's direction erupted all around Blake.

After a moment, all was silent.

"Hell of a fight," said Yuldaris over group comms, catching his breath.

"Fuck yeah," said Zane. "I'm ready for more!"

Everyone assembled around Blake.

Kal looked at the bodies. "Damn, man, you went wild up in here."

Blake lowered his helmet, then grinned, baring his fangs. "A decent workout. It seems everyone else held their own."

"Yeah, that shielder that came toward me went down quick once I got its shields down."

Ada emitted a beam over the corpses of the shielders and the dark-gray lightly armored humanoids. "These creatures are registering as multiple species."

"What?" asked Blake.

"You mean these things have been genetically altered?" asked Zane.

Ada nodded. "It would appear so."

"But from what?" asked Yuldaris.

Blake wagged a finger. "Good question, and one I think our good friend Zoldan can answer."

"Wow," said Gris. "I can't believe what I just saw."

"Believe it," said Blake. He motioned forward. "C'mon. It's not too far from the main hub. We'll see what we can find there."

The group acknowledged Blake and headed off.

CHAPTER
EIGHTEEN

S eth eased back into his chair in the command area on the *Excelion*. With Blake and his assault crew down in the facility, there was not much to do other than monitor things. It had been several hours, and so far nothing out of the ordinary had happened.

"Umm . . . what's going on with the facility?" asked Sarah. She flicked her finger across her console.

A window appeared showing the top of the facility flashing with red lights.

"That's interesting," said Seth. He wrinkled his eyebrows as he studied his console interface. "And now it looks like there are five Rogundan ships inbound, about thirty minutes out."

"That can't be good."

"Probably isn't. Whatever's going on down there, we need to update Blake," said Seth. He paused for a moment. "Blake said there was a control center topside we could use if we needed to contact him. I'll head in and see if I can reach him."

Sarah nodded.

"Go ahead and fire up the *Exceltion*. Make sure she's ready to jump out of here if need be, and inform the others."

"I'm on it," said Sarah.

Seth grinned. "I'll be right back." He went to his room, got his light-armor suit, and verified his pistols were ready to go. As he exited the *Exceltion*, he updated Sarah, then walked toward Hadrassus's topside entrance. The lack of guards stood out to him immediately. If they were gone, then something took them out or drew their attention elsewhere. He looked around when he arrived at the entrance, then pressed on the doors, but they were sealed. He sighed and headed back. "Sarah, meeting in command center in five."

"Got it," said Sarah.

After Seth got to the command center, he addressed Sarah, Kane, and Luke. "I need to get inside that facility to contact Blake. The doors are sealed, though."

"Maybe we could blow them open," said Luke.

"Maybe," said Seth. He glanced at Kane. "Or . . . it could be hacked . . ."

"I got the tools if we want to try," said Kane. "Only issue is if they have security that wants to shred me, and there's no guarantee that I'll be able to crack their security."

Doc appeared on the front screen. "Perhaps I can be of assistance again."

Seth drew his head back. "How so?"

"I'm an AI, and I can help if need be."

Kane pointed at Doc. "He's got a point."

Seth nodded. "All right. You going in one of the robot bodies?"

"I can, and as long as we remain topside, I can control it remotely," said Doc.

"I like it," said Seth. "Okay. So Kane will be the backup then, and it'll be the three of us. I'm thinking, once inside, every place is going to need to be hacked into, but with Doc and Kane, we should be good."

"Damn right, S-man," said Kane.

"Good," said Seth. He perused his console interface. "I don't know how long we'll need inside, so, Sarah, stealth the ship and then head out."

"Doc won't be able to control the robot body if we head out," said Sarah.

"Oh, shit, that's right," said Seth.

"I'll leave a copy of myself here. I can be in two places at once. When back in range, I'll sync up," said Doc.

Sarah smiled. "Must be nice to be able to do that, but what about the Rogundans if they decide to go in?"

"They'll have to blow the doors open then because we'll seal them after us," said Kane.

Seth wagged a finger at Kane. "Yeah, and by the time they come, we'll hopefully be secured somewhere inside. If we have to fight, we will, but with the amount of Rogundans coming in, easier to just hide somewhere."

"All right," said Sarah.

"When you leave, contact Zurinch. Let him know about the situation."

Sarah nodded.

"Kane, are there any utilities or gadgets we can use to our advantage inside?"

"Yeah. I have some of the mines I gave Kal that we could use. Also could probably use some sensor scramblers if we need to hide."

"Hmm," said Seth, rubbing his chin. "A chameleon shield would be nice, but we saw how effective that was with them. All right, we got the plan, let's roll."

"Aye, aye, captain," said Luke.

Seth eyed Luke, and they shared a laugh.

"I'll go get suited up," said Kane. "Meet you outside in about five."

"I will as well," said Doc. "The meeting part, not the suiting-up part."

Seth chuckled. "Sounds good."

After ten minutes, Seth, Kane, and Doc in holographic robot form stood before the sealed doors.

Kane put a device on the console and then tapped around in the air. "They got some good security here. You'll have your work cut out for you, Doc."

Doc nodded and then paused as he accessed the console remotely via Kane's device.

After a moment, the doors unsealed.

"Fredorians . . . they rely too much on physical security for digital devices," said Doc.

"Lucky for us," said Kane. He slapped at Doc's shoulder, then shook his head when his hand went through the hologram and hit Doc's underlying robot body.

Doc slapped Kane's shoulder.

"Ow. You're supposed to heal me, not hurt me."

"Oh. I'm sorry."

Kane laughed. "I was kidding, man."

"Oh."

"C'mon, let's get inside, seal these doors, and see what we're dealing with," said Seth.

///////////

Kane extended his multiple small screens in front of his head. Perusing them, he could see what Doc did to the security system. "Nice job, Doc. You rerouted the security check into a loop that brute forced its way in. Ingenious, man."

Doc nodded. "Thank you. I'm not as well versed as Ada, but I saw it was possible to inject code into the security check, which seems like a big security flaw."

"Well, to be fair, there usually isn't a disruption device like what we used to get access. Usually get shot before then."

"Of course. Thankfully for us, there are no guards around."

Seth surveyed the environment. "I'm not sure if that's a good or bad thing yet."

Doc tilted his head. "For what reason?"

"Well, it could be that they were killed or, if they were controlled, sent off somewhere that we need to get to," said Seth. He motioned forward. "According to Rusch's map, the control center's not too far from here. Let's hit it up."

They continued on.

The silence outside the muffled alarm made Kane sweat more than normal. His usual response to alarms was to run. That typically meant something bad had happened or was happening. The dim red lighting and absence of anybody added to his sense of dread.

After fifteen minutes, they reached the outer doors of the control center. Two hallway entrances sat on either side.

Kane placed the disruption device on the console and then extended his arm in a flourish toward Doc. "All you."

Doc froze as he accessed the terminal. After a moment, he said, "There is something here preventing me from accessing the door controls. I'll need some time."

Kane connected to the system. "All right, I'll see if I can help." He perused the system to see what Doc was encountering.

"I'ma check the hallways," said Seth.

"A'ight," said Kane. He activated a screen that showed Seth's view, where he was checking each hallway to make sure there was no one there. When he checked the right one, slight movement near the end of the darkened hallway caught Kane's eye. "You see that?"

"Yep, investigating," said Seth.

Kane watched Seth interact with his forearm console to cycle through the various views. The motionless bodies on the ground made Kane's skin crawl.

"Think I found something . . . Gonna check it out," said Seth.

"Need backup?"

"Nah, keep doing what you're doing, and get that door open. I won't be long, and comms are open."

"A'ight," said Kane. He focused on the system internals and saw that Doc had made good progress. The holdup was a program that seemed to act like an AI, but was not. "Damn, Doc, you're tearing shit up in here."

"Thank you, I think," said Doc.

Kane focused on Seth's view.

Seth had pulled out his pistol and was creeping down the hallway. His thermal scan showed the bodies still had some heat, but they were dead. When he arrived at one of them, he scanned around. The only light was the dim flashing light from where he had come from.

Kane studied the bodies. Exposed flesh showed the body to have small, red, circular marks of some type. One of the bodies was missing an arm. "What the fuck happened to those guys?"

"Not sure, but they're enforcers. They got wasted by something," said Seth.

"Maybe you interrupted it."

Seth laughed. "Yeah, ri—" He aimed forward as he heard movement ahead of him. "We're not alone up here."

"I can head over in a sec."

"No, just get that damn door open. I got this," said Seth.

Kane focused on the six glistening specks that sat about eight feet off the ground. They looked like eyes. He swallowed hard when he realized it was a face staring intently. "Oh, shit, it's a creature of some type! Get out of there!"

Seth backpedaled and pulled out his other pistol.

The creature surged from the darkness.

Kane noted that the creature wore light armor. Its head had tentacles where a mouth and chin should be, and the bulbous head had three eyes on each side. Its massive humanoid body possessed two large arms ending in sharp, elongated claws for fingers. The legs looked like tree stumps made of flesh. Whatever the creature's intent was, Kane figured it was probably what killed the enforcers.

Seth fired and then rushed back to Kane and Doc. "Get ready, it's coming."

Kane lowered his screens and pulled out a pistol, while Doc positioned his arm to shoot.

"Ready, S-man. Whatever this thing is, it's about to get wasted," said Kane.

"How's the door?" asked Seth.

"Doc is still working on it, but we got past the hurdle."

Doc nodded. "I should have it open momentarily. Once inside, I would suggest we close it immediately."

"Yeah, no problem there," said Seth.

The creature burst around the corner.

"Holy fuck!" said Kane. With much more light available, he could see why the enforcers stood no chance. This creature was built to kill. Blood dripped off its mouth tentacles, and its claws looked like they were coated in gore. The eyes were long and angled along the sides of the head.

Seth raised both pistols and fired.

The bullets hit the creature's kinetic shielding.

"Shit, it's shielded," said Seth. "Burst its shielding down!"

The creature charged them.

Kane and Doc unloaded on the creature.

Its shielding began to flicker, but not before it had reached Seth and knocked him away.

Doc ran up and grabbed each of the creature's arms. "The door is opening. Get inside!"

Seth shook his head and jumped to his feet. As he ran toward the door, he fired at the creature, hitting it several times in the head.

It roared as it stumbled back. Its head trembled and then the body went limp.

Everyone paused to see if the creature was dead.

The sound of bullets hitting the ground echoed out as they fell from the creature's head.

"What the fuck!" said Kane. "It's got healing or something!"

"Let's go," said Seth. He hustled to the door and motioned inward.

Kane barreled through the doors.

The creature jumped up, roared, and rushed to the door.

Doc stood in its way and grabbed the creature's arms again. "Go! I'll hold it here."

"Doc! You'll die!" said Kane.

"Only this temporary body. Remember, I'm still on the *Exceltion*."

"C'mon, man!" said Kane.

"Go. You know that I can't come unless this creature comes as well," said Doc. "I do have a self-destruct. You need to be sealed in before I can use it."

Kane's stomach churned. Doc was right, but Kane felt like he was abandoning Doc. Kane sighed as he stepped in.

The doors began to close.

Doc swiveled his head toward them. "Good luck."

The doors slid shut.

A loud explosion echoed out beyond the door.

Seth put a hand on his forehead and then slammed the wall with his open palm. "Shit!"

Kane ran a hand over his mouth and chin. "You weren't kidding about wild missions, S-man."

Seth normalized his breathing while scowling at the door.

"C'mon, we still need to contact Blake," said Kane.

"You're right," said Seth, licking his lips. He shook his head. "At least we can show Doc our video feeds."

"Works for me," said Kane.

They headed down the small hallway and entered an empty control center.

Kane surveyed the multiple rows of workstations and seating. On the front wall was a massive screen that was shut off.

Seth gestured at one of the consoles. "You gonna be able to get this going?"

"Yeah, but nowhere near as fast as Doc. If he hadn't come along . . . we'd still be out there right now."

Seth sighed. "All right. You do that, I'ma check out the rest of this section."

Kane nodded.

CHAPTER
NINETEEN

Seth headed out through a doorway that was down a bit and to the right of the doorway they had come through. He entered a smaller room with several tables in the middle. Replicators sat off on the walls, and like the other areas he had seen, it had a muffled alarm and dim red flashing lights. On one of the tables was a layout of snacks and drinks, almost like they had been abandoned mid break. Looking around, he could make out that there were doorways all around the room. Probably offices of some type. He walked by each one while tapping at their door console.

One of the doors slid open. Three men and a woman stepped out with weapons raised.

Seth dropped to the ground as they fired. He aimed and hit the lead man.

The man crumpled.

Kane came running to the room entrance with his side pistol drawn.

Seth looked around and then stood. The remaining three people were standing still, and they had dropped their weapons.

"What the hell's going on?" asked Kane.

Seth shrugged. "I'm not sure. These people burst out of the room and fired. I killed one of them, and now . . . this."

The men and woman began to shake violently, and then they exhaled loudly.

One of the men looked around with a confused look. "What . . . what's going on? And . . . who are you?"

Seth waved a finger between himself and Kane. "I'm Seth Williams, and that's Kane Walsh. We're with the presidential guard, Earthborn Unit. We're doing an investigation here, but the facility went into shutdown. Why were you shooting at me?"

"Huh?" asked the woman. "We didn't shoot at you."

Seth gestured at the man he had shot. "Actually, you all did. I killed the one on the ground; otherwise I wouldn't be here talking to you."

The woman gasped as she looked down.

One of the men stepped forward. "You killed the facility operations director!"

"Yeah, because he tried to kill me, all of you did. You don't remember?"

The man squinted and rubbed his temples. "No . . . and I have a massive headache. I'm Nathan Hedris, assistant facility operations director."

"Welcome to the real world, Nathan," said Kane. He wagged a finger at Seth. "They've been slimed, at least that's what the detector shows. Maybe they're blue-slimed, and the guy who you killed was black-slimed."

Seth shook his head. "That might be true, but no black slime slithered away, at least as far as I know. Maybe it's a different type of slime or something."

"Slime . . . what are you talking about?" asked Nathan, who had stepped forward.

Seth sighed. "Not important. Kane, did you contact Blake?"

"Yeah, he's waiting on you on the main screen in the other room."

"All right, let's go."

"What about us?" asked the woman.

Seth shrugged. "I dunno . . . I guess just hang here with us until we sort all this out."

Everyone assembled in the main control room.

The screen showed Blake, Zane, Yuldaris, Kal, and Ada standing in another control room.

"Seth! What are you doing up there?" asked Blake.

Seth chuckled. "Well, we saw the facility go wild with flashing lights, and then we picked up Rogundan ships inbound."

"How many?"

"About five, and they're large. If they land here, you're looking at maybe one hundred and fifty Rogundan mercs entering the facility."

"Where's the *Exceltion*?"

"I had Sarah stealth it and launch. She's gonna contact the Covendrin and go from there."

Blake sighed.

"How's it going down there?" asked Seth.

"Like shit. We found some interesting stuff . . . but seems a few . . . things . . . got loose down here. They didn't know they were fucking with Earthborn, though." He gestured at Yuldaris. "And Covendrin."

Zane laughed.

"All right," said Seth. "I just didn't want you to be caught off guard. I guess we'll hole up here, although . . . if those Rogundans land, Kane and I may be joining you down there."

Blake nodded. "Sounds good, and appreciate the heads-up." He narrowed his eyes as he looked at the people Seth had run into in the other room. "Who are they?"

"I think . . . they were being controlled. They tried to kill me, but I killed one of them, and now they have no idea what's going on."

"You should kill them just to be safe," said Yuldaris.

The woman's eyes widened.

Blake grinned, baring his fangs. "They're more useful alive. Find out what you can, and if all goes well, we'll be joining you topside soon. We have a meeting with Administrator Zoldan. He just doesn't know it yet."

Kane did a two-finger salute. "Good luck, man."

Seth raised a finger. "Oh, before I forget, we had Doc come with us as a clone in a robot body. He sacrificed it when we were attacked by some . . . creature out in the hallways. Apparently the creature killed the enforcers up here."

"Interesting," said Blake. "I guess we could show Doc video feeds to get him up to speed if we get out of here."

"That's my thought too . . . and no if . . . when ," said Seth.

"Of course, my abductee brother. All right. Good luck," said Blake.

The screen went dark.

////////

Sarah exhaled as she studied the console interface before her. She hoped Seth and Kane would be okay. Since they had entered Hadrassus, she had not been able to contact them. To her left was Luke, who was also engrossed in his console interface. She focused on the blips approaching the planet. Although the Rogundans were still a bit out, she did not think the facility going into shutdown and the Rogundans' arrival was a coincidence.

Luke chuckled.

She glanced over at him.

Luke looked back at her. "It's crazy to think we worked together on creating the *Exceltion* . . . and now here we are flying her in the face of danger."

Sarah smiled. "Yeah. It *is* a little crazy. I'm just glad that it was you that Seth chose to be the engineer. Trustworthy, loyal, and hardworking. He couldn't have gotten anyone better."

He coughed and then took a deep breath. His eyebrows furrowed as he looked away. "Right."

She noted Luke's unusual reaction. The expectation was that Luke would laugh or smile and make a joke, not the serious look on his face. "I need to contact Zurinch. See what we can come up with."

He nodded.

She verified that the *Exceltion* had cleared orbit. Although their stealth was engaged, she knew that the two Rogundan ships in low orbit would be able to detect them. After looking up Zurinch's CID, she tapped at her console.

Zurinch appeared on the main screen in a large window.

"How is everything?" asked Zurinch.

"Not sure yet. Blake and the others are in the facility, and it went into shutdown. Luke and I took off with the *Exceltion* since it seems we have Rogundan ships inbound, and we didn't want to be there when they arrived."

Zurinch nodded. "We saw them. It looks like a battle cruiser, a drone carrier, and several other smaller ships. That's a Rogundan quick-response fleet. I've called in our own ships, and they're on their way."

"Okay. Where are you now?"

"We're three ships at the moment and near the sun, using its heat signature for cover."

Luke tossed a hand out. "How did the FDF let those Rogundan ships in?"

Zurinch shrugged. "Your guess is as good as mine. I suspect the FDF will intervene once they detect a full Covendrin battle fleet headed in. How they respond . . . will be up to them."

Sarah's console beeped at her. She studied the blip that had broken off from low orbit and was now in pursuit. "Looks like we didn't make a clean break."

"I have an idea," said Zurinch. "I'm sending you our coordinates. Head there, and bring that ship."

"Aye, we're bait," said Luke.

Zurinch grinned. "I hope your ship can last that long."

"She'll hold. We're still damaged from that damn moon, but only one ship should be no problem, even if it outguns us. We move faster at least."

The *Exceltion* shuddered.

"And it looks like that Rogundan ship hit us with short-range lasers," said Luke. He grinned. "Not a problem with reflective armor, but it can be if it gets hit too many times, or by more powerful weapons. We need to get out of range and enact evasive maneuvers."

Sarah nodded as she tapped at her interface. "Evasive maneuvers activated." She glanced up at Zurinch. "We'll be at your coordinates in about twenty minutes. What's going to happen when we get there?"

"The Rogundan ship will find itself outmatched," said Zurinch.

"What if those other ships come this way?" she asked.

"They'd have to find us first. If they did come, we would just need to hold them until our fleet arrives. Let's see what they do when the first Rogundan ship is destroyed."

"Okay," said Sarah.

The screen went blank.

Sarah eased back into her chair. The *Exceltion*'s small, quick adjustments as it flew had an effect on the lasers trying to hit it. She could see the lasers adjusting but knew that they had a mechanical aspect that moved them on the Rogundan ship, one that was not able to keep up with the fast shifts of the *Exceltion*.

After twenty minutes, they reached Zurinch's coordinates. She contacted Zurinch. "We're here."

"Good. They should already be having trouble trying to find you," said Zurinch.

Sarah verified Zurinch's claim by noting that the Rogundan ship had stopped firing and was performing a standard search pattern.

"Our turn," said Zurinch. "Fire on our mark."

She nodded and watched as three blips appeared on her localized map.

"Now!" said Zurinch.

The *Exceltion* and Covendrin ships focus fired energy beams on the Rogundan ship.

The Rogundan ship initially took the hit, but with multiple beams hitting the same point, they were able to defeat the reflective armor, causing the Rogundan ship to explode.

"Yeah!" said Luke.

Sarah smiled. "One down, many, many more to go."

"It appears we've drawn the attention of the other ships. They're headed our way," said Zurinch. "The other one in low orbit is moving down to the planet."

"Ahh shit," said Luke.

"No need to worry," said Zurinch. "Our fleet will be here by the time those Rogundan ships arrive. They've probably detected them en route already."

"Then we should go hit that remaining ship. If it lands, it's a sitting duck," said Luke.

Sarah wrinkled her eyebrows. "A what?"

Luke laughed. "A target with no protection."

"Ohh . . . Earthborn slang thing."

"Yeah, these translators are weird sometimes," said Luke.

Sarah focused on Zurinch. "See any issues with us going to hit that other ship?"

Zurinch shook his head. "That Rogundan fleet is going to focus on us. If it comes after you, just condense space jump out."

"A good plan," said Sarah. She smiled at Zurinch. "Thanks for the help."

Zurinch nodded, and the screen went blank.

Sarah sighed as she glanced at Luke. "If you would have told me we'd be working with the Covendrin when I first joined, I would have laughed. But not anymore. They're nothing like what the FDF said they were."

Luke shrugged. "That's the FDF for ya. They like to control the narrative."

She nodded and interacted with her console. "Headed back to Hadrassus."

After thirty minutes, they arrived in low orbit around Markus II.

She scanned her console interface. "Looks like the Rogundan ship's landed, and the others are headed toward Zurinch's position."

"Aye, that's a good thing about the other ships. The one that landed has probably already unloaded," said Luke.

"Okay, taking the *Exceltion* down. Hitting the Rogundan ship with a missile could cause collateral damage, but we can strafe it with the flak cannons and laser turrets."

Luke grinned. "That's what I'm thinking too."

The *Exceltion* angled itself and then flew toward Hadrassus.

When the *Exceltion* neared Hadrassus, Sarah ran a scan of the spaceport. "Looks like the other Rogundan ship is still there. I tried to raise Seth and Kane, but got nothing. I'm also not detecting their CIDs on either ship. I guess we can assume they're still safe inside."

Luke wrinkled his eyebrows. "Yeah . . . I guess if the Rogundans had captured them and brought them out, we should have been able to reach them." He angled his eyebrows. "I've locked on both ships."

Sarah nodded. She navigated the *Exceltion* to hover some distance above the two Rogundan ships. "Fire!"

The *Exceltion* shot down a hail of flak accompanied by laser strikes.

The two Rogundan ships caught fire, and one of them exploded.

"That's that, and a lot less messy than a missile," said Luke.

Sarah smiled. "Yes, it is. Let's land and wait. If Seth and Kane come out, they'll be able to reach us. If that fleet comes here, we'll jump out."

"Works for me," said Luke, easing back into his chair.

B lake studied the data center they were in. After the tunnel fight, it had taken them around twenty minutes to reach the main hub, where Ada was able to detect Seth trying to contact them. The relative peace and calm was only punctuated by the hum of the data-server fans. It was a nice change of pace, and Blake could feel himself beginning to relax.

"Seth is contacting us again," said Ada.

"Already?" asked Blake. "Patch him through."

Ada motioned at a nearby screen on the wall, where Seth appeared.

"I bet you're glad to see me again," said Seth.

"Always. What's up?"

"Those Rogundan ships I told you about? I'm guessing at least one landed. The others seem to be headed toward the sun."

"I'm guessing the one that landed is not here to quote regulation to us," said Blake.

"Yeah, probably not," said Seth, chuckling.

Blake nodded. "All right, we'll watch for them. Ada is just collecting information; then we'll head out to find Zoldan."

"Cool. I would wish you luck, but . . . you're Blake Brown."

Blake grinned, baring his fangs, while raising a finger. "Never forget that."

The screen went dark.

"All right, so it seems we got incoming," said Blake. He glanced at Gris. "I'd suggest you don't take the stairs."

Gris sighed. "There's some secure areas I can head to."

Ada tilted her head. "There are five in this area. One is on the way to the transportation system that leads to storage, where Zoldan's beacon says he is."

Gris's eyes widened. "You're . . . going after him? With all this going on?"

"Yep," said Blake.

Gris exhaled from his mouth.

Zane gestured at Gris. "So you're corporate security. Why would FDF security be needed here?"

Gris shrugged. "I don't know. Most think they're here to spy. I mean . . . all the FDF does is provide protection from mercs and make sure we're not raided by other corporations. Our security group had a handle on things . . . or so I thought."

"Well, those enforcers seem to have been taken down pretty quick."

"So was my group," said Gris, grimacing. "I don't think there's any security units left, outside your group, of course."

"We're here for another purpose," said Blake. He eyed Gris. "What do you know about the research here?"

"Not much. We stayed out of the way of the researchers. They didn't . . . care for us much."

Kal chuckled. "Probably thought you were just a tad bit too low on the totem pole to talk with."

"I'm not sure what a totem pole is, but I understand they probably do consider us lower than them," said Gris. "What I do know is that some researchers began acting unusual, even for being aloof in general."

"That's not unusual for researchers," said Yuldaris. "Have you noticed anything else odd, like smells, assignments, or the like?"

Gris paused for a moment. "Yeah . . . actually, there's been a strong odor every now and then. We had some complaints about it, but when we went to talk to those who mentioned it, they didn't seem to remember placing the complaint. I guess, looking back, that is kinda odd."

"There may be a reason for that," said Ada. "According to this system, there are additional rooms in each of the research centers. They're all connected to another room near the transportation platform at the north hub's entrance. It seems there were containers there, ones meant to store organic material."

Blake eyed Ada. "Organic material like those fat boys with shields that ran at us. So if the shutdown protocol kicks in, they get released."

"That would explain how we ran into those things so fast," said Zane, raising a finger.

"Are there any additional rooms like that here in the main hub?" asked Kal.

Ada nodded. "Yes, but they are empty."

Blake grinned. "Yeah, they took out Gris's crew and the enforcers, then ran into us. I didn't see that tall, thin creature that Gris said kissed everyone. Maybe it got out of Dodge after seeing what we did to its boys. Anyways, I suspect the storage area is going to be a bit harder."

"We'll handle that shit," said Zane.

Gris gulped. "You guys are crazy."

"Earthborn, actually, but I guess the same thing," said Zane. He pointed at Yuldaris and then Ada. "Well, he's Covendrin, and she's an android."

Gris sighed. "I guess."

Blake nodded. "All right. Let's get you to your secured area. Most of the researchers are locked up already, I'm guessing so they don't get damaged when those creatures clean out the place, or try to." He glanced at Ada. "You got everything you need?"

"I do," said Ada.

"We move," said Blake.

After twenty minutes of light conversation, they reached the secured area.

Ada interacted with the door console.

The sealed door slid back.

"I'll be okay in there," said Gris. "It has replicators and other support rooms. It's meant to self-sustain, although

I'm not sure for how long." He swallowed hard. "Thank you for helping me."

Blake grinned, baring his fangs. "Just remember to tell whoever asks that it was the presidential guard that helped you."

"I can do that," said Gris, nodding. He entered the room and faced the group.

Ada accessed the console, and the door slid shut.

Blake exhaled. "All right, to the transportation system. Ada, is there no way to get those damn transportation units running?"

"They are not under control from here, and each transportation line has its own separate system. The shutdown protocol disables the systems physically, from what I scanned."

"Great. They even built this place so nothing can get out . . . unless they want it to. Probably didn't blow the place in case they wanted to get *something* out," said Blake.

"Something that we'll find out more about," said Yuldaris.

As they headed out, Blake focused on Ada. "So what exactly did you see when you were in the servers?"

"I'm not sure," said Ada. "The regular environment I'm used to changed into something similar to a virtual environment. It would seem that when the Saskarin has control of someone, the host's displaced consciousness appears there, and they have no recollection of being there once they leave. However, upon returning, they do remember being there."

"That's some freaky shit," said Kal.

"Another aspect I noticed was that while I was in the regular data-server environment, there was an orange cloud of some type around the special server."

"Ahh, man, you mean there's an orange slime now too?" asked Zane.

"According to my scans, there are dozens of different types of slimes. I don't know what all their purposes are."

Blake snorted. "Well, we know black, blue, green, and red, and now I guess orange. I bet the orange is what allows the slime to interact with technological systems."

"You think this creature is from some type of slime environment?" asked Yuldaris.

Blake shrugged. "It's from another reality, so it might just well be. It could also be that they're in one form in their reality and a slime in ours."

"Interesting possibilities."

Blake nodded.

Twenty minutes later, the group reached the transportation system.

Blake studied the dim red lighting that still flashed. The sound was gone, but he could almost hear a drum beat every time the light flashed. He lowered his helmet and sniffed the air. There was an odd odor he could single out, but given where they were, maybe it was not too odd. He raised his hand, causing the group to pause. "If these transportation lines are anything like the last one, we can expect a fight. Not only that, but we'll probably have Rogundans up our ass on the return trip."

"Let 'em come," said Zane. He tapped his hellthrower. "I got something for 'em."

Blake slapped Zane's chest. "Hopefully we can save it for when we get to storage. Ada, launch a surveillance drone, and let's roll."

Zane's heartbeat accelerated as he took in the dark confines of the tunnel. There were many nights in Fredorian prison where it felt like the walls were closing in on him. Although he thought he was not claustrophobic in general, it was times like those that made him reconsider. The tunnel was not helping that.

Blake turned his head to peer back at Zane. "Everything all right? Your heartbeat just shot up."

"I'm good, man. Dark tunnel, underground, enclosed space . . . just sorta reminds me of prison is all."

Kal shook his head. "Damn, man, now you got me feeling that."

"Just focus on what's ahead, and you'll be good," said Blake. He stopped and raised a hand. "There's something ahead."

Zane scanned forward, rotating between different views. "I don't see shit, and the drone doesn't either."

"I don't see anything either," said Kal, studying ahead.

Yuldaris bobbed his head as he stared intently down the tunnel. "Same here."

Ada tilted her head. "I don't see anything, but I do hear something."

"There are five of whatever's coming," said Blake. He lowered his helmet and sniffed the air. "They have a formaldehyde scent, and they're moving fast. Humanoid. Some are on the walls."

Zane marveled at Blake's ability to know what was around him. It was no wonder he was as efficient as he was when he was a ranger. Getting the drop on someone you could detect before they even got close would be a great ability to have. Zane was glad Blake could do that, or at least someone in the group. It upgraded their survival chances greatly.

Kal narrowed his eyes. "I can shoot a motion-detecting acid mine ahead of us. If there is something coming, it'll trigger."

"Do it," said Blake.

Kal loaded an acid mine into his sniper rifle and took aim. After a moment, he fired, shooting the mine to the top of the tunnel far ahead of the group. "Done. Now we wait."

"Excellent," said Blake. He grinned, baring his fangs. "The Trickster and his bag of tricks."

"Damn right," said Kal.

Yuldaris eyed Kal. "That's an ingenious use of an acid mine. Where'd you get it?"

"Kane hooked me up. I got several other types too."

Yuldaris nodded. "Perhaps you can . . . hook . . . a brother up."

Kal laughed.

Blake raised a hand and then pointed forward. "Mines activated."

Zane watched as five kinetic shields lit up from the acid interacting with them. Although whatever was coming had chameleon shielding, the acid disrupted it. Two were running on the arched walls near the ceiling, one on the center part of the ceiling, and two others on the ground on each side of the transportation platform. "Damn, you were right. They're running on the fucking walls."

"Hit 'em, Kal," said Blake.

"My pleasure," said Kal. He took aim and fired at the one on the ceiling on the left side.

Zane watched as the drone picked up what was inside the kinetic shielding. The one that Kal dropped had fallen to the ground. The creature inside the shielding had a squid-like head, with tentacles where a mouth and chin would be. It wore black light armor with a metallic harness around its chest. Its sharp claws on its hand stood in contrast to the trunk-like feet with tentacles. "What the hell are they?"

"Not sure, but they're in medium-range now and detectable. Yuldaris, let's light 'em up," said Blake.

Blake pulled out his striker while Yuldaris steadied his assault weapon. They opened fire on the creature on the right-side ceiling.

The creature fell to the ground.

Ada tilted her head. "The drone is showing the left one that was dropped getting back up."

"Ahh shit, they got a high regeneration factor then," said Blake.

"No worries. I'll shred the shit out of them once they're in close range," said Zane. He watched as the creature on the left side of the platform was taken down by cross fire from Blake and Yuldaris. When the remaining two creatures came into close range, Zane unloaded his hellthrower on the one on the center part of the ceiling.

The creature fell to the ground.

The last creature reached the group and jumped at Blake, who evaded the move.

Ada stepped forward, reached through the creature's shielding, and then grabbed it by the neck.

The creature slashed out at Ada, scratching her face and arms. It jerked its head up as two energy blades went through its chest.

Ada tossed the creature to the ground.

Blake studied Ada. "You all right?"

Ada nodded. "I'm immune to the effect that Sarah fell to."

Zane watched as the creature writhed on the ground. "Damn, that thing is still alive." He looked down the tunnel. "The others are still alive, although laid out."

Blake slashed the creature's head off.

It stopped moving.

"That's one way of dealing with it. I'm gonna get the others," said Blake. He bounded up ahead.

The group caught up to Blake after he had finished severing the other four creatures' heads.

Zane kicked at one with his meaty boots. "What are these things? I can see they're slimed."

"I've never seen this species before," said Yuldaris.

"Ada, anything in your database?" asked Blake.

Ada shook her head. "This is either an undiscovered species or . . . a new one."

"That's just what we need," said Kal. "A new and crazy species built for slashing people up while in chameleon shielding."

"I'll get a blood sample," said Ada, setting down her backpack. She pulled out a vial and then proceeded to collect a sample. After she had her sample, she slid her backpack on.

Zane could see that Ada was looking down to avoid showing her face. The creature had sliced her left side, exposing the fleshy parts, but also the circuitry underneath. Although he did not think Ada was vain, he suspected she did not want to appear more android than she already did.

Blake eyed Ada. "You sure you're going to be all right with those cuts? They look deep." He extended a hand toward her face.

Ada looked away. "It's okay."

Zane grinned. "I like that look."

Ada smiled at Zane.

"All right," said Blake. "The storage area entrance isn't too far away."

After twenty minutes without interruption, they arrived at the storage area entrance.

Zane noted that unlike the other section, this one was closed shut, with the only entrance being where the transportation rails went in. Even that aspect was sealed off.

Blake pointed at a side console. "Ada, all you."

Ada headed over and connected to the side console. She found the access port, and then extended her hand, letting the tendrils from her fingers connect. After a moment, she said, "The doors are manually sealed from inside. The connection to it from the consoles has been severed."

Blake sighed. "Great."

"We could always blow the door," said Zane.

"I'm not sure we'd want to be in this tunnel for that," said Blake. He wagged a finger at Ada. "You said that there was a room built into each hub that housed those creatures and went across the hub, but all came from a room near the entrance. It wasn't on the maps, but we know it was there. Spread out and do a deep scan. I'm betting those creatures that attacked us came from those."

The group spread out to check the tunnel sides.

After several minutes, Kal raised a hand. "Over here!" The group assembled around Kal. He pointed at the ground. "Whatever those creatures were, they left footprints crossing from the probably sterile environment they were in to this dusty-ass tunnel."

"Low-tech, but it works," said Blake. He knocked on various parts of the wall. "Here. Zane."

Zane grinned. He stood in front of the door and, using his meaty metallic gauntlet, pounded it in. He lowered his hellthrower and entered the dimly lit room. Unlike the tunnels, there was no flashing red light, but a green one along the ceiling. The room was fairly large, and along the walls were cylindrical capsules with blue liquid in them.

"The hell is this?" asked Kal.

Blake walked up to one of the windows that had something floating in it. He pointed at the creature with wires connecting it to something outside the window. "Looks like some type of incubation chamber. Our squid boys probably came from here. Ada, get what you can, and then let's head to the control center for this hub. I'm guessing that's not where Zoldan is, but maybe we can get more information on what we're facing."

Ada complied.

After surveying the room a bit more, the group headed toward the entrance area.

"According to the layout Ada got from that console, the nearest entry into this hub leads to the other side of the sealed entrance door. Be ready for anything," said Blake.

Zane nodded. It struck him as odd that they had found the room with little trouble. It could be that the Saskarins or Zoldan had not anticipated it, but Zane had a feeling they were meant to go through this route. He knew the whole visit was a trap, and he couldn't shake the feeling that they were walking into the final piece. Trap or not, he would go out with guns blazing if it came to that.

TWENTY-ONE

Seth relaxed into the chair in the command center. It had been relatively quiet, and Kane had been perusing around in the systems. Nathan and the others had retreated to the room that the facility operations director had been killed in. Seth's face turned red when he thought of how the black slime ruthlessly used bodies like they were shells to be discarded.

"Damn, man, these systems are whack," said Kane.

"What'd you find?" asked Seth.

Kane shook his head. "Remember how something held Doc up earlier? I think I know why now."

Seth motioned at Kane to continue.

"There's a server up here that's disconnected from the ones underground. It has an . . . odd . . . configuration to it. Physically, it's larger than the other servers, and it has a shit ton more power going to it. On top of that, most of the system diagnostics are missing. It's a dark server, but get this," said Kane. He tapped at the console interface he was tied into.

The front screen changed to show a black container filled with orange slime and a server sitting inside.

"What the hell is that?" asked Seth.

Kane shrugged. "Got me, S-man. I can't connect to it, route to it, or really do anything other than detect that it's there. The fact that Doc was able to get in and get around it is impressive."

"You don't think the slime can interact with . . . computer systems, do you?"

"If I had to guess, I think it can," said Kane. He laughed. "Man, that's some crazy shit. It can control organic *and* inorganic."

They turned their attention to Nathan entering the room.

Seth pointed at the screen. "You ever seen this before?"

Nathan shook his head. "I haven't. What am I looking at?"

"One of your servers."

"Is that the slime thing you mentioned before?"

"One aspect of it," said Seth.

Nathan took a seat next to Seth. "So you're saying . . . there was a slime in us, or something. And now there's slime in our servers?"

"That's our working theory," said Seth.

Nathan gulped. "We checked the time . . . It seems we've jumped forward about ten days. I don't have any recollection of what I did during that time."

"And that's another aspect of the slime," said Kane. "You're damn lucky S-man didn't shoot your ass up."

"S-man?"

Seth laughed. "That's what Kane calls me."

"Oh."

Seth studied Nathan. "Do you work for the Dorostatic Initiatives Corporation or the FDF?"

"The Dorostatic Initiatives Corporation. I'd never work for the FDF."

"Why's that?" asked Seth. He tossed a hand out. "Not that I care for the FDF either."

Nathan shrugged. "They're power hungry. I'm not saying our company is innocent in that regard, but . . . we don't go around forcing others to do our bidding either."

Kane wrinkled his eyebrows. "You're talking about the FDF at Hadrassus."

"Yeah," said Nathan. "This was supposed to be our first effort at cleaning up our image. The goal was to supply quality-of-life enhancements through genetic engineering, microbots, and other research and development, and all of it would be legal and go through the proper channels. The FDF swoops in, starts acting shady, and they tell us to report any findings to them." He tossed his hands out to the side. "What could we do? We're not a security company with soldiers. We appealed it, but were rejected." He grimaced. "And now I find out my coworker is dead, the presidential guard is involved, some slime thing is running amok in Hadrassus, and I can't remember the last ten days."

Seth eyed Nathan. "You may still be under the slime's influence for all we know."

"How can you tell?"

"We can't, other than that you've been slimed," said Seth.

Nathan sighed. "So what happens now?"

"We sit tight. Our crew is below, and yes, we know that coming here was probably a trap."

"Why would this . . . slime thing . . . want to trap the presidential guard?"

"Because we're damn efficient," said Kane. "It knows we're getting closer to finding out what it really is, and what it's doing."

"But to shut down our facility?"

Kane took a hit off his vaping stick. "Man, think about it. All the researchers are secure in their areas, and our crew is not, well, except for me and Seth. If an accident, say . . . creatures breaking containment, were to claim our lives, it could all be cleaned up afterward with a plausible explanation. Unfortunately for the slime, it underestimated Blake Brown." Kane looked at one of his mini screens. He motioned in the air.

The front screen changed to show the spaceport outside.

"Not to mention, we now have Rogundan mercs about to enter the facility. The final cleanup."

Nathan swallowed hard. "I *hate* Rogundans."

"What do you know about their involvement in all of this?" asked Seth.

"They just delivered cargo. I didn't know what was in the shipping containers, and I didn't ask."

"Yet you were slimed somehow. I suspect that was due to your role."

Nathan looked away for a moment. "I can't believe . . . I tried to kill you. I'm not a fighter."

Seth shrugged. "It's in the past. If you're not being controlled now, you probably still could be."

"How . . . how do I . . . we . . . get this slime thing out?"

"I don't know, but hopefully we'll find out if our group is successful here."

Nathan studied the front screen. "You think the Rogundans are going to storm this command center?"

"Bet on it. They'll at least try," said Seth. He stood up and pointed to the back. "You and the others will need to be sealed into one of the rooms back there."

Nathan's eyes widened. "Why?"

"Because if the Rogundans have a black-slimed host, then they can control you."

Nathan exhaled from his mouth. "I . . . I don't want to be controlled again. Besides, if that's true, what if there was one nearby already?"

Seth motioned at Kane. "He's had a bead on you since you entered the room."

Kane tapped the pistol on his thigh that was pointed at Nathan.

Nathan recoiled. "All right, all right. We'll go. There's no need for that."

"I hope not," said Seth. He escorted Nathan to the back. After five minutes, he returned. "Now what to do about these Rogundans . . ."

"I've tapped into the security systems, but all they have are drones. They won't do shit against that level of kinetic shielding," said Kane.

Seth pointed at the main screen that showed inside the main entrance. "Looks like they're here . . . but they're running from something. Can you switch to wide angle on the spaceport view."

Kane complied.

The screen showed the burning husks of two Rogundan ships. Next to it was the *Exceltion*, with laser and flak cannons pointed toward the topside entrance.

"Damn, I love Sarah," said Seth. "We can head back, assuming the Rogundans are coming down."

Kane grimaced. "I don't think all of them are."

Seth studied the window on the main screen that showed the area outside the sealed command center doors.

A lead Rogundan had stopped and was pointing at the doors. Three Rogundans split off and headed toward the doors while the rest of the Rogundans followed the lead away.

"So we just have three to deal with," said Seth.

"We can do this, S-man. When they open the door, we burst their shields, and then we waste 'em," said Kane.

Seth licked his lips. "Maybe, assuming we can burst their shields in time."

"Ahh, man, two FLP-40s close range? Not much can survive that. We also have our FHP-10s. So we can at least waste one or two with that."

"All right, let's do it, and hope that's the only three we have to deal with."

They headed to the sealed door and pulled out their weapons.

Seth took a deep breath as he aimed both his FLP-40 and his FHP-10 forward. Kane was in a similar position and ready to go. The Rogundans were probably not expecting to be gunned down, but if they had a black slime, then all bets were off. He tapped at the door console to open it, then reassumed his stance.

The door slid open.

Seth and Kane unloaded a hail of gunfire. The FLP-40s shredded the first Rogundan's shielding, and then its head. The other two fell back, but one went down with a precision head shot from Kane's FHP-10. They stepped forward and, with both FHP-10s, put a large hole in the surprised third Rogundan.

Seth waved forward. "Nice job, man. Let's get the fuck out of here."

"No argument here," said Kane.

As they hustled out, Seth hoped there were no more between them and the *Exceltion*. A quick check on his detector showed that the Rogundans were not slimed. If they had been, he suspected it would be he and Kane that would be lying on the ground. Seth admired Kane's bravado. Even if it was due to a lack of fighting experience, it eased the mood. Now it was time to hit the *Exceltion* and relax a bit, although Blake still being below bothered Seth. He knew better than to try to go down and help, though. Being a liability in that environment would be a problem. He focused on the hallway ahead of him as he and Kane rushed forward.

Kal studied the robust control center that was a part of the command area. What he did not expect was what he saw when looking out through the large transparent windows at the front of the room. He could see that the control center sat at the base along the wall of a massive cylindrical structure. There were many levels above the ground floor, each level with a walkway and a ramp between them. Small cylindrical capsules with holographic displays on the side, similar to the one they saw earlier in the side rooms, were spread out evenly on each level.

Looking straight ahead, he could see an arched tunnel covered in a semitransparent material leading to the other side of the cylindrical structure. He noted that there were also lifts positioned as pillars spread around the area. The place made his skin crawl.

"Holy shit," said Zane. "This place is huge." He pointed at one of the small cylindrical capsules on a level above them on the other side of the structure. "Let me guess, more of our squid boys."

Ada connected to the row of workstations that sat before the windows. After a moment, she said, "Not quite. It seems each container holds a different specimen. I'm seeing a wide variety of statistics in relation to each one."

"So storage is where they store their genetic engineering experiments," said Blake.

"That would be my conclusion," said Ada. "I assumed storage was for supplies and equipment."

"That may be how the slime views organics," said Blake.

Ada tilted her head. "I can see that logic."

Yuldaris focused where Zane was pointing. "If what we've encountered so far is a sample, and they have this many experiments, then I would think they're trying to build a super soldier of some type."

"Yeah," said Blake. "One that's easy to control, moves fast, is strong, can regenerate quickly, and doesn't require a lot of maintenance."

"If they have a lot of variations, it would make counter-measures difficult to implement," said Yuldaris.

Zane snorted. "Variation or not, they'll all eat it when a hellthrower is aimed at them."

Yuldaris raised a finger. "*If* you see them coming."

"Speaking of that, we still have the Rogundans on their way," said Blake. "I don't know where they are, but it won't take them long to find us, especially if they're in contact with any slimed. Ada, the storage area on the map doesn't show this massive cylindrical structure."

"It does not. I have downloaded the local layout from this workstation and transmitted it to each of you just now. There seems to be a large room past this structure. It's where Zoldan is."

Kal shook his head. "He's waiting for us!" Although he knew this was initially a trap, it had not gone the way he thought the Saskarins wanted it to go. Despite that, the current situation seemed like it was designed.

"It seems I can't access the door to that room, although it's currently open," said Ada.

Zane smirked. "I've seen this play before. Watch it seal shut once we're in there."

Blake glanced at Ada. "Find anything else of value in that system?"

"I have actually," said Ada. She pointed at a screen near the back of the room.

The screen lit up showing various slimes with detailed information on them.

"Now *that* is useful," said Yuldaris. "Along with what we already have, we could make our detectors *much* more precise with this information."

Blake raised a finger. "And maybe even find a way to remove the slime characteristics."

"Yes, that would be ideal."

Blake studied the screen. "So I see the black and blue slimes, we know about those. The red one too. Check out the orange one."

"It says it allows for interaction with technology. That confirms our hunch," said Ada. "By extension, even androids could be slimed."

"That's messed up," said Kal. He motioned at the yellow slime. "Check that one out. It looks like it's used to grow an organism." A chill went up his spine as he viewed the slime images. It boggled his mind as to what their ultimate purpose was.

"Yes, and it would appear that they take various attributes of different species and guide the specimen's evolution," said Ada.

Zane shook his head. "These damn slimes. The reality they come from must be messed up."

"On Earth, they would be called Outsiders, and I've seen some Outsider realities. I have a lot of experience with that."

Zane sighed. He eyed the purple slime on the screen. "Am I reading that right that the purpose of that slime is to allow other slimes to exist naturally without a host, even in space?"

Blake nodded. "Seems that way. It's a like a . . . creep of some sort. Toss it down somewhere and slime a place, or if in space, it could act as shielding. It also looks like it can consume organic and inorganic material."

"Well, I'm glad we haven't seen that yet," said Zane.

"It must be rare, because I haven't seen it anywhere," said Blake. He glanced at Yuldaris. "Have the Covendrin?"

Yuldaris shook his head. "No records of that. Maybe all this effort is being made to bring that over from where the slime is from. Coating a planet, or even a moon, with this slime would seem to provide a natural habitat for the slimes. If in space, they could hide anywhere undetected for the most part."

"Yeah, that's what I was thinking too," said Blake.

"Your distance metrics on the Saskarins' range of control have been verified, Yuldaris," said Ada.

"It's good to get confirmation on that," said Yuldaris.

"Ada, transfer a copy of everything we've found to Yuldaris."

Ada complied.

Kal grinned. He was glad that Blake was showing some trust to Yuldaris. Having the Covendrin as an ally was a wise move, but hard to pull off. "What? You don't trust the FDF or something?"

"I don't," said Blake. He raised a finger. "But I suspect that if there's going to be research into finding out how to de-slime or detect, going through Fredorian-government channels could get bogged down." He glanced at Yuldaris. "I don't think the Covendrin would have that issue. Of course, it would be appreciated if that knowledge was shared if anything develops."

"We'll share whatever we find with the presidential guard. You'll be our point of contact with Fredoria on this matter," said Yuldaris.

"Excellent," said Blake.

"That assumes we're walking out of here alive," said Zane.

Blake nodded as he looked around. "Ada, how secure is this place?"

"It has double-width sealed doors with shielding."

Blake rubbed his chin. "It would be a good defensive spot if the Rogundans came, since it also seems to be the only entry to the tunnel that leads to that other room."

"I would agree with that assessment. Are we planning on defending here?" asked Ada.

"No, but I'm just marking out places to go if shit heats up."

Ada tilted her head. "I don't want shit to heat up."

Zane and Kal laughed.

Ada smiled.

"Do we have a visual feed of that other room?"

Ada paused for a moment and then said, "No."

Blake sighed. "All right, fire up the surveillance drone. It's time to spring the trap set for us."

TWENTY-TWO

B lake gazed around as they walked through the tunnel that led across the cylindrical structure. The sheer amount of cylindrical capsules was impressive, and he had already seen a sample of what was in a few. It seemed that the Saskarins were mass testing. With a Rogundan supply route of victims, it was an efficient operation. One he knew must be stopped. The surveillance drone had entered the room and showed Zoldan sitting on a chair in the back of the room.

"Man, this place is all screwy," said Kal. "Just imagine all the people that came here. Stuck in a pod, wired up, and then experimented on."

"They would need to be alive for all that too," said Zane.

Yuldaris shook his head. "It's sad, but hopefully we'll put an end to this."

"I don't understand why they didn't use simulations. That would be more efficient than this," said Ada.

Blake chuckled. "Life can be . . . random, at times. Mutations can sometimes be beneficial, and those are hard to model."

Ada nodded.

They reached the other end of the cylindrical structure and entered a hallway.

Blake noted that unlike the rest of the facility, there were no flashing lights. The hallway was brightly lit, with stainless metallic walls and flooring. The ceiling had a light that ran down the middle. The lack of any features on the walls stood out. He lowered his helmet and sniffed the air. Sterile. Up to Fredorian standards at least.

The group arrived at the entrance to a large, featureless room.

"Everyone be ready. Although it only shows Zoldan by himself back there, I suspect he's not alone," said Blake.

Zane lowered his hellthrower. "I'm ready to light 'em up."

Blake slapped Zane's chest. "Make sure your shield is ready. Let's go."

They entered the large room and, after a cautious walk, reached Zoldan sitting on a throne after a few minutes.

"Welcome," said Zoldan.

"You must be a Saskarin," said Blake. He raised his striker and fired, but the bullets hit a shielding that was in front of Zoldan and spanned the width of the room.

Zoldan smiled. "No, but I can understand your confusion." He waved his hand at the shielding. "Your profile suggests you would try to take me out, so the shielding was necessary."

The door to the room closed shut.

Kal shook two fists down. "Knew it!"

Zoldan focused on Kal. "You don't think it would be that easy, do you?"

"Well . . . yeah . . . I was kinda hoping so."

Zoldan laughed. "Earthborn . . . you make me laugh, something I didn't know existed until I came here."

The panels on the sides of the room slid up.

Eight-to-ten-foot-tall bulky humanoids entered. They wielded massive chain guns and wore heavy armor. Next to them were several smaller humanoids, similar to the ones they saw in the first tunnel. The squid-like ones also appeared in large numbers. Looking around, Blake could see they were encircled. He raised a finger. "So this is your game? Put us in a cross fire?"

Zoldan pointed at Blake. "I need you alive. The others . . . ," he said, waving a hand dismissively in the air, "are expendable. Preconfigured husks with low intelligence."

"Fuck you," said Zane.

"I'll be doing the fucking," said Zoldan.

"What's your end game?" asked Yuldaris. "This all seems pointless."

Zoldan smiled. "Pointless . . . no. You see only pieces, but that ends here today."

"We took out two Saskarins on Zakara Prime," said Kal. "We can do it again."

Zoldan scowled. "You killed my siblings, and for that, you will pay."

"So you're related," said Blake.

"Not me, personally," said Zoldan. A panel slid open behind him.

Blake studied the lightly armored eight-foot humanoid male that stepped out. His fair skin rippled with abnormally proportioned muscles, and stretch marks covered his skin. His legs were massive relative to the rest of his body, and a dark cape hung on his back. Bone structures surrounded his face and covered his forearms.

The humanoid stood by Zoldan. "I'm Corinigan, as it is known in your tongue. Zoldan is but another controllable vessel."

"So Zoldan is blue-slimed, and *you're* the Saskarin," said Blake.

Corinigan smiled. "Very perceptive, but not that it matters. You're going to be another vessel for me, one with access to the unique energy in you. I'm looking forward to studying you."

"Yeah, sounds great. Since we're going to die . . . mind answering a few questions?"

Corinigan laughed. "Why not?"

"You call yourself the Saskarins. I suspect . . . you're from another reality and that each Saskarin, while an individual, is connected to the others in some manner."

"Yes, yes, and yes. Your . . . reality is so full of life, different life. Our reality is dying a slow death. We don't plan to stay there, but your reality . . . is endless, and more importantly, young."

"So you want to escape here. You could have just asked for help."

Corinigan laughed. "Why? Every species we've encountered is weak, holding on to husks with limited intelligence. We are superior, on a level incomprehensible to your feeble minds."

Blake shook his head. "Yeah, I've heard that before. You're just another wannabe Outsider race who thinks they're special."

"Enough!" said Corinigan, stepping forward. The shielding dissipated. "Time to claim my prize."

Blake pulled out an energy blade and held it against his neck. "So you know . . . I have a life-monitoring device in my neck. It's tied to some explosives set at critical points. If I die, Hadrassus goes boom and you lose your chance to have me."

Zane, Kal, Ada, and Yuldaris gazed at Blake.

Blake hoped everyone would believe his bluff. If not, it could get ugly fast. He just had to sell it and hope the rest of his group understood what he was doing.

Corinigan's face scrunched up. "Why would you do that?"

Blake grinned, baring his fangs. "Insurance."

Corinigan eyed Blake. "You would put your friends at risk? That doesn't seem believable."

"When it comes to a deluded Outsider that's taking over bodies and has a facility dedicated to creating super soldiers? Worth the risk every damn time," said Blake.

"Then what was your intention in coming here?" asked Corinigan.

"Information, of course. I *was* an intelligence agent. And . . . an offer."

Corinigan scanned the others for a moment. "What do you want?"

Blake nodded back at Zane and the others. "They leave this room, and I'll give myself willingly."

Corinigan smiled. "There's no guarantee that they'll live outside this room."

"We know about the Rogundans, and if I'm slimed, they'll have two fronts, but I *believe* in my crew. Even if you keep me back, they'll still handle their business. At least they'll have a chance."

"Blake, what the fuck are you doing?" asked Zane.

Blake turned his head slightly. "You have the information you need. Get out alive."

"This is not logical," said Ada.

"The trade-off is worth it. Tell Seth . . . I'm sorry. And Yuldaris . . . if the presidential guard falls apart . . ."

Yuldaris furrowed his eyebrows. "There will be other opportunities available. Your sacrifice will be honored."

Kal shook his head. "Are we seriously discussing this?"

"Go . . . and survive," said Blake.

The group looked at each other.

"Go!"

Zane shook his head as he turned to leave. "This is fucked up, man."

Blake turned enough to see them clear the room and head back to the command center. He knew they could handle the Rogundans and get to the *Excelion*. He turned as he focused on Corinigan. "I'd like to have one last drink of blood. A . . . final wish."

Corinigan nodded.

Blake grabbed two concentrated blood vials from his belt with his free hand. He put one on each fang and drank deeply, then put his blade back on his back. With both hands to his sides, he grinned and bared his fangs. "Let's get this sliming shit over with."

The group around Blake rushed in and held him.

Corinigan stood in front of Blake and hovered near his face.

"Ahh, man, you're not gonna kiss me, are you?" asked Blake.

Corinigan smiled. "No . . . there are more efficient ways to be . . . slimed . . . as you call it." He opened his mouth. A black slime formed and extended out toward Blake's face.

Blake closed his eyes as he braced for the slime. He could feel it touching his face and then entering his nose, ears, and mouth.

Everything went black.

////////////

Inside Blake's mind, Corinigan appeared on a desolate wasteland of jagged black crystallized structures, with pools of a bubbling red liquid spread out. Other vats of black liquid held aliens who moaned and screamed in pain.

Standing to his sides a bit away were mutated humanoids of varying shapes and sizes. Their features were exaggerated.

Ahead of him, atop a throne made of skulls and bones, sat a nine-foot male humanoid with dark-red skin, black armor, and bone spikes jutting up out of his shoulder. A cape fluttered around on his back. His face had four glowing silver eyes, a large mouth with razor-sharp teeth, and a black metal headband that meshed into a red crown. He had four massive arms, with each hand ending in pointed claws.

"What have we here," said the humanoid in a deep, grizzled voice. He stood, causing the group around Corinigan to step back.

"What . . . what is this place?" asked Corinigan.

The group around him jeered.

"You stand in the domain of the Daedrould prince Druulkahn the Destroyer."

"I don't understand."

Druulkahn smiled, showing off his multiple rows of sharp teeth. "You must have been trying to possess one of my vessels while they were in blood lust." He raised a finger in the air. "Which one . . . ahh . . . Blake Brown. One of my favorites. It's so rare he lets me in. Even *rarer* that he let something else in. By extension, this environment has humanoid forms, from your perspective."

The humanoids around Corinigan cried out in pleasure.

"This is not how it's supposed to work," said Corinigan. He tried to move but was held in place.

Druulkahn began to walk in a jerky manner toward Corinigan. "You're clueless." He stopped and tilted back his head. With a deep sniff and closed eyes, he flicked out a forked tongue. "Mmm. You're not from Blake's realm, but from another." He raised a finger, as if tasting the air. "And you have the ability to possess others. That could be very useful." He lowered his head and gazed at Corinigan. "Yes . . . very useful."

"Stay away from me!"

"Saskarin . . . an interesting concept. And your realm . . . another to conquer. If it has even a shred of Daedrould energy . . . then I'll find it," said Druulkahn. He stood in front of Corinigan. "Now, let me see what has fallen into my domain." He ran a clawed finger across Corinigan's trembling face, leaving a trail of blood. "Yes . . . you will do." He slapped Corinigan.

Corinigan exhaled sharply.

"I wonder . . . if I consume you, will I gain entry to your realm?" said Druulkahn. He grabbed Corinigan's hand and held it up. "Let's find out." He chomped off one of Corinigan's fingers.

Corinigan cried out.

"Ahh, the fear. The pain. I can feel it."

The crowd cheered.

"Where's Blake!" said Corinigan.

Druulkahn drew his head back while his black eyes narrowed. "Blake Brown. One of my more powerful vessels. He has a bad tendency of avoiding me. His body is mine for the moment, and his mind is," he said, circling a clawed finger in the air, "trapped. Don't worry . . . he can see what's going on here through you."

"We had a deal."

Druulkahn paused for a moment. "A deal." He burst out laughing along with the group around him. "Your deal is *meaningless* to me. The deal I have with Blake, though, is not." He shook a finger at Corinigan. "You think that's why he fears invoking me?"

"His body is mine!"

"No . . . and it will never be. However . . . your mind . . . is available."

Corinigan's eyes widened.

Druulkahn swept his finger across Corinigan's neck.

Blood gushed everywhere.

Corinigan went limp as he went unconscious.

A moment later, the wound had healed, and Corinigan was conscious again.

"What . . . what was that?" asked Corinigan.

"Death, of course," said Druulkahn. "One of many to come. Death will not be your savior here." Druulkahn placed both hands on Corinigan's head. "Now . . . let's see what we can see."

After a few minutes, another being similar to Corinigan popped up.

The being struggled as bone vines lurched from the ground and held tight.

"What . . . Corinigan! What is this?" asked the being.

"Force me out! He's trying to possess us!" said Corinigan.

Another being popped up and was similarly entangled.

"Do it now! Force me out!"

The other beings focused, and after a moment, all the Saskarins disappeared.

Zane's eyes were glued to a screen in the control center that showed what was going on in the room with Zoldan and Blake. Seeing the Saskarin enter Blake was a gut punch that Zane had not anticipated. He knew Blake was bluffing about the bomb and did what was best for the team, although it was hard to fathom what the plan was. Downing two blood vials probably put Blake into blood lust, although Zane did not understand the effects or what happened when that occurred.

Although the group was to head back to the *Exceltion*, it was a unanimous decision to wait to see how everything played out. The control room was defensible, and the Rogundans would have to file in from a choke point. It had been about five minutes, and everyone had agreed to leave if Blake were truly compromised.

"Look!" said Kal.

Zane's head bobbed around as he tried to make out what was happening. The Saskarin slid out of Blake's nose and mouth. It snaked its way over to Corinigan's body and reentered it after slithering up to it. "Uhh . . . what just happened?"

"No idea, but look at Blake's eyes. They're red," said Kal.

Yuldaris glanced at Ada. "Is there a significance to the color of Blake's eyes?"

"Unknown. They are usually light blue."

They watched as Blake got to his knees.

Corinigan pointed at Blake. "You went back on your deal."

Blake stood and circled his head. He tipped his head up and uttered a low growl. "Blake's not here at the moment. Mmm. I'm back. All these blood sacks, just waiting for me."

"Druulkahn! Kill him! Kill him now!" said Corinigan, jumping back.

The controlled group began to move toward Blake.

In a flash, Blake had pulled both dual blades out and leaped over one of the large humanoids wielding a chain gun. He stabbed it in the head. Then, using the body as cover, he lifted up the chain gun and fired, melting a swath in a 180-degree arc. Once out of ammo, Blake leaped over the body he had used and zoomed between the remaining humanoids. He danced around, decapitating some and gutting others. Some had parts of their body sliced off.

Corinigan had grabbed a weapon and aimed at Blake.

Blake appeared next to a startled Corinigan and, in a deep guttural voice, said, "I'm not done with you yet." He knocked the weapon out of Corinigan's hand and then body slammed him into the wall. "Stay." Blake jumped back into the fight and decapitated a trembling Zoldan and then targeted one of the other large humanoids. Its shielding had protected it in the first attack from the other large humanoid's chain gun. Blake got behind it and sliced off its chain gun arm, then hit it in the back, sending it careening into the others like a bowling ball. As it went flying through the others, he jumped on its back and sliced anything that came close.

After another minute, all was silent except for the excited breathing from Corinigan.

Blake walked toward him. "Now . . . in this reality . . . there is truly no place to hide."

"No!" said Corinigan. He leaped forward and tried to run around Blake.

Blake grabbed him and then tossed him back into the wall. "I need to ingest you, and that body needs to go." He sliced outward with both blades, decapitating Corinigan.

The Saskarin slithered out of Corinigan's nose and moved to a corner of the room.

As Blake headed over to it, he stopped and trembled. "No! This is *my* body now! Stop fighting me!" He painstakingly grabbed his FHP-10. "You called me! Me!" He aimed at the Saskarin. "Don't kill it! It's mine!" He fired, evaporating the Saskarin. "No!" said Blake as he crumpled to the ground. He shook his head while growling and then calmly stood, looking back toward the tunnel leading to the control center. "That's right. It's *my* body now!"

"Oh, shit, what the fuck just happened?" asked Kal.

"I dunno, but Blake's headed this way, and he just trashed a room of those suckers," said Zane.

"He's in blood lust," said Ada. "It's a dangerous state for him to be in."

Yuldaris readied his assault weapon. "Be ready, and let's hope that . . . whatever . . . Blake is now, it is the one we left in the room."

"Damn it," said Kal. He pulled out both pistols. "This shit is crazy."

Ada and Zane aimed their weapons at the tunnel entrance.

Zane furrowed his eyebrows. Although he had heard of blood lust, it was not anything like what he saw occur in the other room. Corinigan calling Blake Druulkahn also made no sense, unless the translator was not working. Not knowing if Blake was going to try to fight or not made

Zane sweat. He knew how powerful Blake was. "Ada, can you close the door to that room?"

Ada nodded. "I can now that the Saskarin is gone, but for what reason?"

"Maybe his bloodlust will wear off or something. His eyes are still red."

Kal gestured at Zane. "Yeah, I'm with him."

Ada glanced at Yuldaris.

"It couldn't hurt," said Yuldaris.

Ada paused for a moment.

Zane watched the door shut. He shook his head as he saw Blake run at the door and attack it. "Yeah . . . I'm thinking that was a good idea."

After twenty minutes, Blake had settled down and looked up at the camera. "I'm in control now. You can let me out."

"What do you think?" asked Zane, glancing at the others.

Yuldaris motioned at the screen. "Look. He's moving slower, and his eyes are blue again."

"Yeah, but there's a slight tinge of red to them, but nothing like before. I say open it," said Kal.

Zane pointed at Kal. "I agree. Yuldaris? Ada?"

Yuldaris nodded.

Ada paused for a moment, and the door to the room Blake was in opened.

"Get ready for anything," said Zane, aiming at the control room tunnel entrance.

The others prepared themselves.

After a moment, Blake zoomed into the control center. He surveyed the group and then grinned, baring his fangs. "Well, I'm glad to see you too."

Kal gulped. "Blake . . . is that . . . *you* you?"

"Yeah, it is, and yes, I was in blood lust, but I'm coming down. I need to burn the rest of it off."

"What happened in there?" asked Zane.

Blake exhaled from his nose. "Wait here for twenty minutes, then head to the main hub. I'll be there, waiting, and I'll explain everything. For now . . . I need to hunt, and kill, and since you're still here, that means there are Rogundans out there."

The group stood to the side, with weapons still pointed.

Blake nodded and then burst out of the room in a flash.

Zane sighed. "Damn . . . . He said twenty minutes . . . I want to see that room while we wait."

"I would as well," said Yuldaris.

The others agreed and headed toward the room where Corinigan and Blake had fought.

When they got there, Zane's eyes widened. It was a blood-bath. There was gore of varying colors everywhere. He could barely recognize any of the humanoids he had seen before.

"Holy shit," said Kal.

Yuldaris shook his head. "This would explain the Hostar incident. We had a contract to take out a scumbag, but when we got there, it looked like . . . this. We learned it was Blake Brown, solo, that took out over thirty Grozadian mercs. By himself. I didn't believe it, but . . . I'm beginning to."

Ada headed to the back of the room. She extended her hand and scanned around. "I have located Corinigan."

The group assembled around her.

Zane studied the dead eyes of Corinigan. The Saskarin had messed with something it should not have.

"Man, I'm gonna be sick," said Kal.

Yuldaris looked around. "Not much to see here, but I'd like to get one of our research crews in here to get samples of everything, before the FDF come and close everything down."

Zane nodded back the way they had come. "Well, by the time we get to Blake, it will have been twenty minutes. I'd say we move out."

Yuldaris nodded.

They exited the room and then the storage hub.

As they walked along the transportation line back to the main hub, Zane spotted a few Rogundans on the ground. He pointed at them. "Looks like Blake hit 'em." When they were closer, he could see that the Rogundans had been sliced to shreds. One looked like half its face was bitten off.

Kal shook his head. "Man, I don't know if I'm more afraid of Blake or the Saskarins."

"Judging by what we've seen, I'd say Blake," said Yuldaris.

They continued to walk.

Zane studied each group of Rogundans as he walked past them. Blake had hit them hard, and probably by surprise, judging by the way the bodies were laid out. It was like a tornado had gone through the area. Some of the Rogundans had missing limbs, others had holes in their heads, and others didn't even have heads.

They reached the entrance to the main hub. Blake sat against the wall with one leg out and one knee bended. He grinned, blood dripping from his lips.

The group approached cautiously.

"Blake . . . ," said Zane.

"It's all right. The bloodlust has passed," said Blake.

The group lowered their weapons and assembled around Blake.

"So . . . what exactly happens when you go into blood lust? We saw the Saskarin enter you, then come back out," said Yuldaris.

Blake nodded. "Well, as you know, I'm a Daedrould. That means I have an exotic energy known as Daedrould energy coursing through me. When I go into full blood lust, my mind retreats and my body is controlled by the domain that filters Daedrould energy into the universe. At least that's what my master taught me. The domain is controlled by the Daedrould prince Druulkahn the Destroyer. When my eyes are red, he's in control, and I'm in full blood lust. Usually when I go into blood lust, it's partial, so I can still control my body. Unfortunately for Corinigan, he got me in full blood lust."

Kal shook a finger. "Corinigan said Druulkahn after he left your body."

"Yes . . . and for good reason," said Blake. "I saw the interaction between them in my mind. *Fear* would not be a strong enough word to describe Corinigan's reaction to being there. Druulkahn toyed with Corinigan. When Corinigan left me, I was still in full blood lust. That meant Druulkahn controlled my body still. He took advantage of the situation."

Zane shook his head. "Man . . . you went on a tear back there. Wasn't much left to look at."

Blake sighed. "As expected. Unfortunately . . . Druulkahn doesn't respect life here. He sees everything as potential blood donors. He would kill all of you and Seth in a heartbeat."

"How do you control it?" asked Yuldaris.

Blake tapped at the side of his neck. "I have a device in my neck that releases a compound that takes me out of blood lust. It takes about twenty minutes or so from detection of bloodlust to kick in."

"And if that failed?" asked Ada.

"Then I would go on an unending crusade to kill everything and everyone."

Zane raised his eyebrows as he glanced at Kal. "That sounds like a curse to me."

Blake ran his tongue over his fangs. "In time . . . I will be a lord, assuming I survive that long. An ancient vampire lord can prevent a prince from controlling the body yet still reap the rewards of being in blood lust. It's the best of both worlds."

"And how long does it take to become a lord?" asked Kal.

"Thousands of years and lots of practice of controlled blood lust," said Blake. "There are only four lords, and my master, Lord Noskov, is one of them."

Ada smiled. "You have a few years left to go then."

Blake grinned. "Yes, I do. More to the point . . . I killed Corinigan, and now we know the Saskarins are individuals that are linked together by some connection to their dimension, not unlike how Daedrould energy works in me. We need to get topside, contact the others, and then go from there. The FDF will most likely be coming."

"Your plan was bold," said Yuldaris.

"Well, I didn't tell you all because if you were to be slimed . . . it would give me away. I apologize for the deception."

"Whatever, man, it worked," said Kal.

The others nodded in agreement.

"I'd like to get some crews down here to get as much data and samples as we can. I suspect . . . the FDF is going to torch this place," said Yuldaris.

Blake nodded. "We'll need to do the same. There are still a lot of blue- and green-slimed people here. With no Saskarin around to control them, as far as we know, that's going to be interesting to deal with, on top of what to do with all these specimens." He hopped up and looked around at the group. "Let's get topside and see what we're dealing with."

TWENTY-THREE

B lake stood outside the *Exceltion*, taking in the view. It was not much, but standing outside after being underground for so long was a breath of fresh air, even if the air was not fit for humans. He could still feel the aftereffects of Druulkahn's control. Ada, Zane, Kal, and Kane were in Hadrassus, collecting as much information as they could and getting blood samples. Blake was going to join them, but figured he should be up top for when the FDF arrived. His helmet picked up the sound of footsteps. He knew it was Yuldaris.

Yuldaris stood next to Blake. "This has been an enlightening mission."

Blake glanced over at Yuldaris. "Yes, it has. Your boys coming down?"

"They are, and they took care of the other Rogundan ships. I'm not sure what will happen when the FDF come, though."

"I would probably have your crew on the way out when they get here. I can hold them for at least that long," said Blake.

Yuldaris nodded. "It's appreciated. Zurinch also wanted me to relay that Sarah did exceptionally well in coordinating against the Rogundans."

"That's good to hear. It seems we all had our part in this."

Yuldaris narrowed his eyes. "Something's bothering you."

Blake sighed. "We know of the Saskarins now, and I realize just how deep it goes. This was one facility of many. The others may be further along than this one . . ."

"Meaning we may see a super soldier sooner than later," said Yuldaris. He stared out into the bleak environment. "I'll make sure the Covendrin know what to look out for."

"I do appreciate you sharing any developments you get from this research. I have a bad feeling that this will get bogged down in politics on Fredoria."

"Such is the way of Fredoria. On one hand, perhaps it's good that things move slowly. That forces a certain stability to hold. On the other hand, not being able to respond to immediate threats sounds like an issue."

"Yeah, and I'm no politician. Still . . . I'll report what I found and await my next mission."

Yuldaris grinned. "I suspect we'll cross paths again. Who knows, maybe we meet at the end of this Saskarin threat."

"You never know," said Blake.

"We'll stay in contact. It's probably best we use an intermediary for that. I'll arrange something with the information broker, assuming I can set that up."

Blake nodded. "I'm not sure how well your involvement will go over, but then again, I'm Earthborn, so they know the unexpected is not uncommon."

"That's what I like about you. You should be proud of your group. They performed worthy of a Covendrin unit."

"More high praise coming from a Covendrin commander. Careful, that shit could go to my head."

Yuldaris chuckled. "I should get going. Zurinch is about to land, and I need to update him in person."

Blake extended a hand.

Yuldaris eyed it for a moment, and then shook it.

"Until then."

Yuldaris nodded. "Until then." He headed off to another part of the space port.

Blake exhaled from his nose. There was a lot to go through, and he needed to make sure that this knowledge did not go too far. There was still the issue of faking information for the FDF that would need to be done, and there was also the briefing when he got back. He was unsure how Andia and Rakar would feel about Yuldaris and the Covendrin being involved, but their help had been more than welcome. He heard another set of footsteps approach him.

"You all right, man?" asked Seth, standing next to Blake.

Blake looked out. "Yeah. It got a bit rough down there."

"I heard. You went into full blood lust. Druulkahn."

"Yeah . . . and it was hard to retake control of my body this time. I . . . took in more concentrated blood than I normally do."

"I thought it was supposed to get easier as you got older," said Seth.

"I haven't been practicing dipping into bloodlust like I would be on Earth. Maybe I should start," said Blake.

"You think your inhibitor is messing up or something?"

"Nah, it did what it was supposed to. Otherwise I would still be in bloodlust and probably gunning for everyone in Hadrassus," said Blake. He glanced at Seth. "I heard you had to do some fighting yourself."

"Yeah, and I didn't get my ass kicked," said Seth, laughing.

"I appreciate you giving me a heads-up. We would have been blindsided down there."

"Yeah . . . but we have to give Doc props. He bought us time to get into the command center."

Blake cast a sidelong glance at Seth. "Speaking of AIs, Ada found some weird environment in the servers. One where someone's consciousness went if they got slimed. Apparently there's an orange slime that facilitates it. She learned a lot about them. I expect unpacking it all is going to take a while. She did suffer some gashes from a creature, though."

"She'll heal. I'm just glad she's okay," said Seth.

"I bet you are. Be kinda hard to get with her otherwise."

Seth laughed. "Ahh, man, quit clowning."

"You know I'm right," said Blake with a grin.

Seth smiled while hitting Blake's arm with the back of his hand. "Yeah." He cleared his throat. "About your bloodlust . . . I know you didn't want to advertise it, but I think that cat's out of the bag. I still have my vial that would shut you down in case of that, but . . . do you think the rest of the crew should have it too?"

"I dunno. Maybe Ada could also have it, and I'll just make sure I'm within distance of either of you."

Seth nodded. "That could work." He looked up and out. "So the FDF is on its way then."

"Yep. Thankfully, we have a supporter in Captain Rusch. I contacted him and had to . . . bend a few facts, but he has the gist of what's going on. He wasn't happy about the Covendrin presence, but . . . the destruction of the Rogundans seemed to give him some relief."

"What do you think the FDF is going to do with Hadrassus?"

Blake shrugged. "I'd guess that they probably try to keep it as silent as possible. There are a lot of researchers with knowledge of operations down there, so I'd expect a lot of questioning. From us, they'll get a high-level summary with misleading information via Luke. The Covendrin won't give them anything, but Yuldaris and I will keep in contact via information drops through the broker."

"Sounds like a plan," said Seth. He wrinkled his eyebrows. "What do you think the Saskarins' purpose is? General conquest or something?"

"A misguided attempt at survival, but who knows if that's the truth. I do know they fear me now, but that's a given."

"I know, I know, because you're Blake Brown."

Blake raised a finger. "Well, in this case, because I'm also the Daedrould prince Druulkahn the Destroyer at times."

"Crazy shit," said Seth. "Makes me wonder what's next."

"Yeah. Now that we know more, and will hopefully soon have a way of detecting them, we'll be a step ahead."

"If we do get that detection shit going, it should be on every FDF ship."

They looked at each other, and then laughed.

"Sounded good, didn't it?" asked Seth.

Blake nodded. "We'll learn in time just how deep this shit goes. Anyways, prep the *Exceltion* to make one more stop before heading back to Fredoria."

"Where to?"

"Jirwana III."

////////

Blake surveyed the dusty side street he walked on in the small district on the outskirts of Goolash, capital city of Jirwana III. Next to him were Ada and Zane. Although it was midday Earth time, Jirwana III had a different cycle, and it seemed like morning to Blake.

The few Jirwanians he had seen scattered out of the way as the group passed. He had been to a Jirwanian colony before, and although they had a humanoid form, they were about half the size of a human and had oversized heads. They were quick talkers and often used hand gestures in an animated fashion since it was a part of their language.

"This is an interesting place," said Ada, looking around. She glanced at Blake. "Have you been here before?"

Blake shook his head. "Not here specifically, but the Jirwanians are not unknown to me." He glanced at Zane. "You all right, man?"

"I will be once this is done," said Zane.

Blake nodded, and they continued on.

After an hour of navigating the back alleys and hidden streets of Goolash, they arrived at a building with bright neon lights over it.

"You sure this is the place," said Blake, glancing at Ada.

Ada nodded. "Assuming the information Zane gave was correct, this is the place."

"It is," said Zane.

"All right. I don't know what to expect here, but follow my lead," said Blake. He slapped Zane's chest. "I know it's gonna take a bit to hold back, but . . . we'll get Tillian. You have my word. You with me?"

Zane exhaled. "I'm with you."

Blake could hear Zane's heartbeat accelerate. Although storming the place and gunning down Mortikki Sans and any mercs was probably Zane's preferred approach, Blake decided to go another way. "All right, in we go." He approached the two Jirwanian men outside the building. Their odor, rapid fluttering of eyes, and increased heartbeat signified to Blake they were scared. He motioned off to the side. "If I were you two, I would get lost. The Duar Gwan, who I contacted prior to our arrival, no longer protects Mortikki Sans. We're here to collect." Blake showed them his forearm screen.

The Jirwanians' eyes widened, and then they scrambled away.

"Easy enough," said Blake. He pushed open the door. The interior reminded him of a saloon he used to visit in the nineteenth century, except this one was a bit more advanced-looking. Stairs on the sides went up to a second level, with various hallways leading off. In the middle of the room was a set of lounges, couches, and love seats. The dim lighting, smoke-filled air, strong odors, and unusual music gave it a lively ambiance. In the back was a counter, and behind it a set of matter replicators.

They headed toward the counter.

When they got there, Blake flagged down the Jirwanian female behind the counter.

She eyed them. "What's your pleasure?"

Blake looked around behind him, then back at her. "Looking for Tillian Walz. We know she's here."

The woman ran her finger across a console, then shook her head. "Not seeing that name."

"Visual then. Show us a list of your . . . employees," said Blake.

She tapped at the console, causing a screen to raise.

The screen showed a grid of faces.

Blake grimaced as he looked at them. Half of them were kids who probably had no idea how they got there.

Zane pointed at one of the images. "That's her."

The woman leaned forward and studied where Zane was pointing. She then went back to her screen. After a moment, she said, "That's Red Cream. She just started a session."

Zane's breathing intensified. "Her name is Tillian Walz."

Blake leaned forward and licked his fangs. "Go get her. Now. And I'd suggest you be very . . . very . . . quick about it."

The woman's eyes widened as she looked at Blake.

"Go!" said Blake.

The woman took off.

Blake faced Zane. "Hold it together for a bit longer." He looked around. "Security. What do you see?"

Zane exhaled and looked around. "Four mercs, two cameras. Low-end security, but one of the mercs is probably high level. There may be other mercs spread throughout."

"So nothing we can't take."

Zane nodded.

Ada motioned to the stairwell on the right. "Look."

Blake focused on the woman and a tepid Tillian walking down the stairs. Tillian was looking down and had a frown on her red-skinned face. She wore black lingerie and a collar around her neck.

"Son of a bitch!" said Zane, bursting forward.

The girl looked up. Her lips quivered. "Zane?"

Zane's face scrunched up as he knelt on a knee and put his arms out. They both trembled as they hugged.

Blake gestured at the woman. "Go get Mortikki Sans, then get the hell out of here."

The woman nodded her head vigorously and took off.

"Are you okay?" asked Zane, wiping a tear off Tillian's face.

Tillian frowned as she shook her head. A river of tears flowed down her face.

Zane pulled her in and hugged her tight.

Tillian's breathing went haphazard.

Zane eased her back and motioned at Blake and Ada. "This is Blake Brown and Ada. They're my friends, and we're taking you out of here."

Blake nodded while Ada extended a hand.

"Take Ada's hand. She'll help you out of here. I'll be out . . . shortly after. Okay?"

Tillian grabbed Ada's hand and nodded at Zane. She looked up at Ada, who smiled at her.

"Let's go outside," said Ada.

After a moment, Ada and Tillian had left the building.

Mortikki Sans entered the room with the woman who had fetched him and four mercs behind him. "What is the meaning of this?"

Blake sized up the Trag mercs. One was larger than the other three. Blake pulled out one of his blades and pointed at the woman and then motioned off to the side. "Get out of here."

The woman scrambled out the front door.

Blake swung his blade and pointed it toward Mortikki. "Mortikki Sans, I take it. The *meaning* of this is that Zane 'Wild Dog' Gibbons would like to have a word with you. However . . . ," said Blake, pointing his blade at the mercs in sequence, "your merc friends each have a choice to make. Stay . . . and I'll kill you. I just killed over sixty aliens yesterday. Leave . . . and I'll . . . *forget* . . . I saw you. To help your decision, know that the Duar Gwan have revoked Mortikki's ownership of this facility." He showed his forearm screen with his free hand.

The mercs studied the screen, and the three smaller ones dropped their weapons and left.

Mortikki smiled as he turned his head halfway to the side. "You were saying?"

The large merc smirked at Blake and then walked past him, bumping into his shoulder.

"Where are you going?" asked Mortikki with wide eyes.

"You're not worth dying for," said the large merc before exiting through the front door.

Blake grinned, baring his fangs. "Left by Trags . . . That's gotta hurt." He put his blade back and then slapped Zane's chest. "All yours, big man. I'll be outside with Ada and Tillian."

Zane's nostrils flared as he nodded.

Blake headed out and closed the doors behind him.

Tillian jumped when she heard shouting inside. "Is Zane going to hurt Mortikki?"

"Yeah . . . and I don't think you'll hear from Mortikki ever again," said Blake. He narrowed his eyes as the smell of blood washed over his nose. Whatever Zane was doing in there, it was generating copious amounts of blood.

Ada placed her hands over Tillian's ears when the anguished cries of Mortikki swept through the air.

Jirwanians scattered from the immediate area around them.

Blake could hear Zane's laborious breathing and various thuds. Taking a peek inside, Blake saw parts of Mortikki tossed around the room. Blood coated everything, and it took everything in Blake to calm himself. He closed the door and nodded at Ada. "Head to the ship."

"Is Zane coming?" asked Tillian.

Blake knelt and placed a hand on Tillian's shoulder. "He sure is, but we have some things to clean up here. Ada will take you to Zane's room on my ship. Okay?"

Tillian pursed her lips and nodded.

Blake dipped his head and then stood. He watched them take off. After they were out of sight, he slipped into the building and closed the door. He pulled a small spray bottle from one of his suit's pouches. "I brought this to get the blood off you."

Zane licked his lips. "It's done."

"I know . . . and I wanted to make sure you were cleaned up before seeing Tillian."

Zane grabbed the bottle and sprayed over his armor. The blood slid off. He handed the bottle to Blake to do the back side.

Once the blood was off, Blake handed Zane a towel for his face.

Zane washed over his face and then stared at Blake. "Thank you for this. It . . . means a lot."

"Ahh, man, you don't need to get all mushy on me."

"I'm serious. Not many would give a shit about me, but you did. You could have told me to fuck off when I pulled that dumb shit on Lono Hara, but you didn't," said Zane. His eyes reddened. "And now you helped me get Tillian. That shit *means* something to me."

They slapped hands while staring at each other.

"I got you, brother," said Blake. "Now, head back to the ship. There's a little girl who's excited to see you. Since this place is closed down, I need to wait here for the Jirwanian authorities to help the others out here."

Zane smiled. "All right, man." He slapped Blake on the arm and then headed out.

TWENTY-FOUR

Luke sighed as he looked around the bleak room known as an FDF safe house. He was not looking forward to seeing FDF Special Agent Crimson Horoll again. A grin crept onto Luke's face as he thought about the doctored data that Ada had produced. He was amazed at her thoroughness. Even so, it still made him sweat to think that outside a few, no one knew his double-agent role. Although he had been given a second chance, the thought that he had already done as much as he had sickened him.

The door to the room opened.

Crimson came in and took a seat. He rifled around the devices on the table. "It's all here?"

"Yes," said Luke.

Crimson pulled out a tablet-like object and plugged one of the devices into it. "Let's see what we have."

"I don't need to be here for this," said Luke, standing to leave.

Crimson pointed a finger at Luke. "Sit your ass down!"

Luke sighed and sat back down.

Crimson ran a finger around on his tablet. "I'm not seeing much from Lono Hara."

"What were you expecting to see?"

"There was an incident there."

Luke shrugged. "I don't remember an incident. We stopped in so Blake could visit some old friends. The others took advantage of the local culture."

Crimson eyed Luke. "And you don't recall any run-ins with the local FDF there?"

"Nope," said Luke. He tilted his head. "Should there have been? Were they planning on trying to stop us or something?"

Crimson eased back into his chair and licked his lips. "None of your business."

"But you want me to keep bringing you all of our business."

Crimson slammed a hand on the table. "You're the traitor here, not me. You do what I *tell* you to do."

"Whatever."

Crimson scowled as he looked through more of the video footage. "So on Hadrassus, you just sat outside in the spaceport, and nothing unusual was found."

Luke nodded.

"No slain Rogundans, bloodstained rooms, or Covendrin presence?"

Luke wagged a finger. "There were some Covendrin ships there, and Rogundan ones too. There are no personal video feeds of the others since I can't get those."

"Did you even try?"

"With two AIs who monitor everything in detail? Are you crazy? Plus Ada implemented a new security protocol. I can try, but if I'm caught, they'll come for you, and I think . . . Blake Brown would probably kill you."

Crimson snorted. "Like he could." He perused the tablet a bit more. "According to this, you didn't find anything of value, other than that there may be more than one type of slime. Sounds like a failed mission to me."

Luke shrugged. "I'm just the engineer."

"And where are all the briefings?"

"Blake doesn't do them anymore. Now he just informs who he needs and goes from there."

Crimson narrowed his eyes. "Why the change?"

"How would I know? It's not like I talk to him a lot. I just keep the *Exceltion* happy. You know, my job."

Crimson leaned forward. "And your job is to keep me informed on the internal details of your missions. Don't *ever* forget that, or there'll be consequences."

"Yeah, you don't need to keep reminding me. If that ever . . . changes for the worse, all bets are off."

"You Earthborn . . . are so irritating. Making threats when you are in no position to do so. That's exactly what I'd expect out of Earthborn."

Luke stood and pointed at Crimson. "I'll get your data for each mission, but don't pretend that these drop-offs are anything more than that. I have no desire to talk to a Fredorian traitor."

Crimson jumped up with a red face. "You better watch what you say!"

"Or what? I have to explain to Blake why I got into a fight between missions? You want that sort of heat on you? Are you *sure* you want that? What do you think Blake will do if he ever finds out?"

Crimson exhaled from his nose and pulled down his shirt, which had crept up when he had jumped. "Fine. Get the fuck out of here, traitor."

Luke smirked and then exited the room.

/////////

Seth sat on the bed in his ambassadorial suite on Fredoria. It was the most luxurious room he had ever had the pleasure of staying in. Having it as their between-mission spot was okay with him. He kicked off his boots and lay on the bed, putting both hands behind his head.

The memory of starting out with Blake and freelancing two years ago seemed so far way. Seth's sides still hurt from the beating, but they had another mission under their belts. He had met Tillian, and Zane and Kal had taken her out to show her New Dakota, the Fredorian city they were in, and her new home. Seth was not sure where the others were, but he knew there was a briefing tomorrow morning.

A knock rang out from the front door.

His eyes furrowed. Maybe it was Kane. Seth had enjoyed working with Kane. "Who is it?"

"Ada."

He slid to the edge of the bed and then stood. "Come in."

Ada entered the room. "I hope I'm not bothering you."

"Not at all. I'm just chilling, you know."

"I didn't know."

Seth chuckled as he gestured at a chair. "You can chill with me. Have a seat."

Ada complied.

He sat next to her and kicked out his legs. "So I see your face is healed up."

She tilted her head. "Yes. Doc is quite proficient at what he does."

"Yeah, he is. I had to laugh, though . . . We showed him the footage from when he sacrificed his clone, and he was all modest about it," said Seth. He clenched his jaw. "If it had been his only version, we woulda lost Doc. That would have sucked."

"I would agree, and my motive for coming here is along that thought line."

Seth pulled his legs in and sat up straight. "Oh?"

"Are you aware of pleasure programming?"

"I've heard about it. The G1s I've been with said it was hardwired into them, and they could flip it on and off at a moment's notice. Couple that with a desire to be around organics . . . and well . . . you know."

"I do know. With the second generation, ours is at the software level. Although we can turn it off and on, it requires more effort."

Seth nodded. "All right." He pursed his lips and bobbed his head around. "That's good to know."

She looked around for a moment, and then focused on him. "I have chosen you to be my pleasure programming partner if you're interested."

His eyes widened. "Really?"

"If you're not interested, I understand," she said, looking down.

He extended his hand and raised her chin up. "I'm interested."

She smiled.

"I didn't know you were choosing someone. What brought all this on?"

Her smile disappeared. "I don't think of my mortality often. There was good reason to do so on our last mission. Given the probability of everyone surviving any given mission, it's important for me to . . . experience . . . what I can in the limited downtime I have."

"I hear ya. That's just life, though. Seize the day, so they say," he said with a smile.

"Also . . . you treat me as a person, and not a machine. You're kind to me, and I feel . . . better . . . when I'm around you. Safer. I enjoy our time together, and the thought of not having you in my existence causes me pain."

He leaned in and placed a hand on her cheek. After a deep kiss, he pulled back and cleared his throat. "Was there . . . anyone else . . . interested . . . ?"

"Others have expressed their interest nonverbally, unless I was misunderstanding the percentage of time they spent observing my body. Kal seems to spend an unusual amount of time focused on my back end. Zane seems to prefer my breasts."

"I could see that," said Seth. "So . . . how does this work?"

"I will bind your profile to my programming. This will configure me to accept pleasure, but only from you."

His eyes narrowed. "Bind my profile?"

"Without the bind, I have no sensation from my erogenous areas. The bind allows me to experience it."

He drew his head back a bit. "Ahh. I didn't have to bind with the G1s from before."

"G1s don't require binding. In that regard, they are more robust than G2s," she said.

"All right," he said. "So I guess this makes you my girlfriend."

She nodded and froze. After a moment, she said, "I have bound you to my pleasure programming." She moved in close to him and caressed his shoulder. "We can begin whenever you wish."

"Begin with . . ."

"Whatever you want to do."

He chuckled. "Now?"

"If you want."

"You don't need to ask me twice," said Seth. He gulped. "Is this the first time you've activated your pleasure programming?"

Ada looked away for a moment. "Yes."

He reached out and grabbed her hand. "So you've never had an orgasm?"

She shook her head.

He smiled. "Then I'm honored to be your first partner."

They both stood.

"I have many positions and techniques stored in my memory," she said.

Seth led her to the bed. He moved in close and kissed her while placing his hands on her waist. His heartbeat accelerated as a wave of excitement rippled through him. As he moved to kissing her neck, he unzipped her formfitting pants. With a little effort, he gently pulled them down along with her panties. He stood and smiled as he looked into her eyes. "Sit."

She sat on the bed, facing him.

"You just relax," he said. He knelt in front of her and placed his hands on top of her bare thighs. After gently pushing her legs apart, he moved one of her hands to the back of his head. He looked up at her and said, "This is about you."

Ada's eyes lit up.

/////////

Blake exhaled as he studied everyone entering the debriefing room. Andia and Rakar were already there, as well as

Luke, Kane, Kal, and Sarah. Seth and Ada were late, which was unusual given that it was 1:00 p.m. Earth time. After a few more minutes, they entered with big smiles on their faces. Blake knew that look well. He burst out laughing.

Everyone focused on Blake.

He grinned, baring his fangs. "Well . . . I'm glad we could all make it."

Seth shook his head as he and Ada took their seats.

"All right, there's a lot to cover," said Blake. He cleared his throat and then interacted with his forearm console.

The screen behind him lit up.

He raised five fingers. "We made five stops on this mission. The first was to Skorith, then to Lono Hara, then to the *Storetz*, then a detour to a moon, and then to Hadrassus."

"Detour?" asked Rakar.

"I'll get to that. I know you've seen the high-level summary, so I'll go into detail when we get there," said Blake. "Our first visit was to Skorith to see about those scientists. We met with Director Charles Duton. From that meeting, we split up. Zane and Kal went to find out more about the five scientists' departure, while Ada and I dug up some information from their previous work areas."

Zane smirked. "We got some shit tossed our way, as usual."

"Yes, but you found out the Rogundans were involved and that the group left as a whole, and didn't necessarily worry about packing anything."

Rakar wrinkled his eyebrows. "They just up and left?"

"It would seem that way. From what we learned at Hadrassus, they were being controlled. We have the video, which is in the evidence I submitted to you already."

Rakar nodded.

"After Skorith, we hit Lono Hara. I met up with some Ogeerians who told me that there were different-colored slimes, something we verified when we were at Hadrassus."

Andia tossed her hand out. "I read through your summary on that meeting. It's very interesting. I also have a complaint filed against the Earthborn Unit. The FDF is saying you were involved in an incident of some type."

Blake waved a finger between Seth and Sarah. "Well, they got beat on at a bar."

"The complaint was on one of their units writing an apology communication, smearing . . . feces . . . on their faces, and all of a sudden proclaiming their love for Earthborn. They suspect it was your unit."

Everyone except Andia laughed.

Andia looked around.

Everyone stopped laughing.

"We may have had a run-in with them after they beat Seth and Sarah to within an inch of their lives," said Blake. "Was that beating in their complaint?"

Andia shook her head.

"Then they're being a bit selective. The medical report from Doc is in my brief summary that I sent to you. You can ask the FDF if they know anything about that," said Blake.

"They most likely filed it for process. I doubt they're looking for a serious response. I'll kick it back to them," said Andia.

"All right," said Blake. "After Lono Hara, we visited the *Storetz* to check in with the FDF. I had an . . . interesting meeting with Captain Joshua Rusch. He was not slimed, and although a staunch FDF officer, he's noticed similar things," he said, waving a finger between Andia and Rakar, "to what you both have seen. He gave me an incredibly detailed map of Hadrassus."

Rakar narrowed his eyes. "Joshua . . . I haven't heard that name in a while. He's always been kind of a thorn in the rangers' side, but it seems . . . he trusts you."

Blake nodded. "Turns out I saved one of his friends on a ranger mission. He actually thanked me."

"Impressive," said Rakar.

"After we were cleared, we shipped off to Hadrassus, but ran into some Rogundans," said Blake. He interacted with his forearm console.

The screen showed the encounter.

"We took out one of their ships and then fled to a nearby moon we had marked earlier. We decided to fight them there, on the ground, since we were outgunned and didn't want to leave the system."

"How many were there?" asked Rakar.

"About forty or so," said Blake. "We fired some decoy sensors to make them think we landed elsewhere, and they bought it. Zane and Kal went to one ship, Ada and I got another, and Seth, Sarah, Kane, and Luke held the ship.

There was some fighting. Zane and Kal had a ship blow up on them. Ada and I were captured, and Seth, Sarah, Kane, and Luke had to fight off a patrol. Thankfully, Yuldaris, Covendrin commander of the Sixty-Seventh Company, was there to help out."

Andia and Rakar sat up in their seats.

With wide eyes, Andia asked, "Did you say . . . Yuldaris? It only said a Covendrin commander in your report."

"Yes, it was Yuldaris, and I made it generic in the report in case it gets out. That way he remains anonymous. I'm aware of your . . . history."

"Did he say anything of our . . . history?" asked Rakar, eying Blake.

"Nope. I tried . . . but he wasn't dishing," said Blake. "Nonetheless, he came through big. As it turns out, he had more information on the slimes than we did. I have everything they knew to that point and, in exchange, agreed to let him come with us to Hadrassus as an observer."

Rakar eased back into his chair. "That was . . . unexpected."

Blake shrugged. "Believe it or not, Earthborn are viewed more favorably by the Covendrin. I had a positive rating according to Yuldaris, so he was happy to help. Besides, after their help at that moon, it was welcome."

"Making allies . . . a wise tactical move," said Rakar.

"If it didn't work out, I woulda gutted 'em," said Blake with a grin, "or drank him dry."

Rakar laughed. "I'm sure you would've."

Blake nodded. "Once we left the moon, we hit Hadrassus. Zane, Kal, Ada, Yuldaris, and I went in and met

Administrator Cadris Zoldan, who was slimed, while the others stayed in the ship. We split up once underground. Ada and I went to the data operations and management department, Zane and Kal went to the microbot development department, and Yuldaris went to the genetic engineering department. Here's Ada's experience inside one of their data servers."

The screen showed Ada's feed.

When it ended, Rakar tilted his head. "I didn't know it could look like that inside a server."

"I didn't know it could either," said Ada. "However, we did learn that there are many types of slimes. The black slimes call themselves the Saskarins, and they use these different slimes to interact with this reality. The slime that enabled the data-server experience was orange, which seems to allow the Saskarins to connect to technological systems. Also, inside that area were the displaced consciousnesses of anyone that was slimed."

"How's that possible?" asked Andia.

Blake grinned. "Well, the Saskarins are top dog, and they all maintain some type of link to each other. How they displace consciousnesses to that . . . Saskarin repository, as it's called, is unknown. What we do know is that the Saskarin are rare. Blue slimes are more common, and whenever a Saskarin is around, they can control the blue-slimed hosts. There's also a green slime that allows the Saskarin to see through the green-slimed host's senses, although green-slimed hosts can't be controlled. Confused yet?"

Rakar shook his head. "All these slimes."

Blake nodded. "Ada was ejected, and it caused a shutdown protocol to kick in. Zane and Kal were the first to run into some creatures that were let loose." He showed the video from Zane's perspective.

Rakar's eyes were glued to the screen. "Those are some strange creatures, and that slicer . . . talked."

"Yeah, but he didn't talk for long," said Zane with a smirk.

"Zane and Kal handled their business, and we all met up again. We had to waste some other creatures that followed Yuldaris, but that was no problem. We then headed back to the main hub, but had to fight a few more things," said Blake. He showed the video from his perspective. Sarah's increased heartbeat caught his attention. As the video played, he eyed her.

She glanced at him and then looked away.

After the video ended, Luke shook his head. "That's a lot of fighting."

"Indeed it was, but nothing we couldn't handle," said Blake. "After we got to the main hub, Seth and Kane contacted us from the topside control center to let us know about some incoming Rogundan ships, and Sarah coordinated with the Covendrin. The Rogundan ships were destroyed, and the one that landed was wiped out by Sarah."

"Yeah, but some Rogundans were able to enter Hadrassus," said Sarah.

Seth nodded. "They left three to try to break into the control center, while the rest went down."

Kane cracked a big smile. "Unfortunately for them, they couldn't handle S-man and me."

"That they couldn't," said Blake. "Continuing on. From the main hub, we continued to where Zoldan was, in the storage area. I'm guessing he was blue-slimed, because we met a Saskarin who called himself Corinigan." He played the video from his perspective.

When the video ended, Rakar said, "You . . . sacrificed yourself for the team."

"Well . . . we knew it was a trap. What Corinigan didn't know was that he walked into *my* trap."

The video from Zane's perspective after Corinigan left Blake's body played.

"Holy shit," said Kane.

"We sealed the doors because we knew that Blake was still in bloodlust since his eyes were red, and bad shit happens when he's in that state," said Zane. "When his eyes were blue again, we opened it up. Blake then rushed over to us, like, in a flash, man. I mean literally."

Blake nodded. "I was coming down off of blood lust. I took care of the Rogundans that had found their way in, and all that was left was cleanup."

Andia eased back into her chair. "Quite a bit going on there. It's going to take a while to sift through it all." She furrowed her eyebrows. "Unfortunately, Hadrassus exploded sometime after you left. There were no survivors."

"What?" asked Blake.

Everyone focused on Andia.

Andia sighed. "I'm guessing . . . all those people down in the sealed areas . . . died as well. There's nothing but a crater there now. The worst part is . . . the FDF is saying that they don't know who blew it up, but the last groups to visit it were the presidential guard, Earthborn Unit, and the Covendrin."

Blake tilted his head. "We didn't blow it up . . ."

"I know, and we can prove that you didn't from your video feeds if necessary. However . . . in terms of optics, your name will be tainted by this."

Blake narrowed his eyes. "Sounds like the FDF really did clean up then . . ."

"That's my thought too," said Andia. She grimaced. "The sad part is that since your video feeds aren't fully complete, the FDF will cast some doubt as to what you were doing when the video wasn't active. You can see where I'm going with that."

"That's so much bullshit," said Seth. "The FDF is framing us!"

"Yes, they are," said Rakar. "And the Covendrin."

Blake sighed. "What about everything we found?"

"I'll present it," said Andia. "However . . . now there will be a cloud if it's fabricated or not."

"So the FDF isn't going to do shit with it, just bury it," said Kal. "What a bunch of bitches."

"I can't believe I used to be FDF," said Sarah.

Blake tossed a hand out. "Well, at least the Covendrin are taking it seriously, and they'll move forward. I would suggest . . . we find researchers on our side who can help and send them over. I think Yuldaris would be open to it. I don't think much is going to happen in the Fredorian government."

"Sadly, I think you're right," said Andia. She glanced at Rakar. "We'll need to use back channels on this."

"Yuldaris said I'm the go-between, so if you need me to relay anything, just let me know," said Blake.

Rakar nodded at Andia. "I'll handle it and work with Blake on getting that going."

"Good," said Andia. She glanced around the group. "Another successful mission, but unfortunately, the FDF is covering it up. You deserve some rest, and you continue to impress me. Great work, everyone. Don't let what the FDF is doing get you down. Hadrassus being blown is a horrible thing, but we can only look forward. I'll handle the politics on that. That's my arena."

The group acknowledged Andia.

Andia and Rakar excused themselves and left the room.

Blake could see the deflated looks as everyone else got up to leave. Although it had been a successful mission, all their hard work was being tossed out by the FDF. He clenched his jaw. The thought that the Saskarins had infiltrated the FDF grew stronger in him, and he would work with Rakar and Yuldaris to see what countermeasures they could conduct. Hopefully the outcome would be better on the next mission.

THE END

NOTE FROM
THE AUTHOR

I hope you enjoyed the second book in the Earthborn series! Blake and crew learned more about the growing threat that is plaguing Fredorian space. Zane and Luke both had to deal with personal issues, while Blake grew as a leader, something he thought he would never be. Seth and Ada took their relationship to the next level, and then some!

One of the fun things I enjoy writing in are the small hooks to the Evaran Chronicles. In this book, you got to read about Yuldaris and some information from his perspective about the events in *The Fredorian Destiny*, book 2 of the Evaran Chronicles. There will be more hooks, but they are merely informational and not integral to the plot, though they do shed more light on the shared setting I've built.

If you liked the book, and have the time and inclination, a review would go a long way in helping out this indie author. If you do submit a review, I'll put in a word to Blake and crew should you find yourself being genetically engineered into a Saskarin slicer! Want to be notified about new book releases? If so, you can sign up below.

WWW.ADAIRHART.COM/MAILINGLIST.ASPX

I will only send you email about new book releases, major updates, and the occasional newsletter, usually once a month. I dislike getting spammed too, so I will use this sparingly to keep you in the loop.

ABOUT THE AUTHOR

I have been dreaming about fictional worlds since I was a kid. I devoured anything related to fantasy and science fiction. I developed a setting over the last twenty years and struggled to find a medium I could express it in. Several years ago I discovered I enjoyed writing. It is a passion of mine now, and exploring my setting with it has been an awesome journey.

I work in the information technology field and have my bachelor's and master's degrees in it. It has helped me to shape some of the concepts I write about. I also enjoy keeping up on futurology and science in general.

I live in central Ohio and enjoy walking, reading, gaming, learning, listening to music, and trying to keep up on my never-ending list of TV shows and movies to watch. If you want to contact me, you can do so on my website at

WWW.ADAIRHART.COM

YOU CAN ALSO REACH ME ON

Facebook............................fb.com/AdairHart
Goodreads.....www.goodreads.com/AdairHart
Email..............Adair.Hart.Author@gmail.com

ACKNOWLEDGMENTS

This was a great journey for me, but I wouldn't be here without the help of others. I would like to thank, in no particular order,

My amazing editor, Laura Petrella. Her intuition helps me to stay on course, and I'm glad to have her on yet another book in the Earthborn! She knows the setting well, and I love having her make sure everything is as it should be. To say she is top-notch is putting it mildly. I continue to mature as a writer, and she has had a big impact on that!

My cover artist, Tom Edwards (tomedwardsconcepts@gmail.com), for another great cover. This cover was not as heavily focused on the characters as it was the environment, but it's still awesome art!

My family and friends who helped encourage me along the way.

My proofreader, Alexa, for providing a thorough service and fitting me into her busy schedule!

My formatter and interior designer, Colleen Sheehan (www.ampersandbookinteriors.com/), for putting up with my scheduling shenanigans and being a pro while doing it!

B O O K S

You can see all books in the Earthborn
and the Evaran Chronicles at

WWW.ADAIRHART.COM/SERIES/ALLBOOKS.ASPX

www.ingramcontent.com/pod-product-compliance
Lightning Source LLC
Chambersburg PA
CBHW051324250626
47155CB00007B/2441